Goodbye,
Columbus
and
Five Short Stories

PHILIP ROTH

Goodbye, Columbus

and

Five Short Stories

With a Preface to the

Thirtieth Anniversary Edition

by the Author

HOUGHTON MIFFLIN COMPANY / BOSTON

For information about permission to reproduce selections from
this book, write to Permissions, Houghton Mifflin Company,
2 Park Street, Boston, Massachusetts 02108.

Library of Congress Catalog Card Number: 89-85214
ISBN: 0-395-51850-4

Printed in the United States of America

BTA 10 9 8 7 6 5 4 3

"Goodbye, Columbus," "The Conversion of the Jews," and
"Epstein" appeared in *The Paris Review*. "Defender of the
Faith" appeared originally in *The New Yorker* — copyright ©
1959 by the New Yorker Magazine, Inc. "You Can't Tell a
Man by the Song He Sings" and "Eli, the Fanatic" have ap-
peared in *Commentary* — copyright 1957, 1958 by Philip Roth.

To my mother and father

"The heart is half a prophet."

YIDDISH PROVERB

CONTENTS

Preface to the Thirtieth Anniversary Edition

xi

Goodbye, Columbus

1

The Conversion of the Jews

137

Defender of the Faith

159

Epstein

201

You Can't Tell a Man by
the Song He Sings

231

Eli, the Fanatic

247

PREFACE TO THE
THIRTIETH ANNIVERSARY EDITION

With clarity and with crudeness, and a great deal of exuberance, the embryonic writer who was me wrote these stories in his early twenties, while he was a graduate student at the University of Chicago, a soldier stationed in New Jersey and Washington, D.C., and a novice English instructor back at Chicago following his army discharge. Eisenhower, who was president, the embryonic writer despised, though not nearly as much as he was to despise Eisenhower's Republican successors. His cultural ambitions were formulated in direct opposition to the triumphant, suffocating American philistinism of that time: he despised *Time, Life,* Hollywood, television, the best-seller list, advertising copy, McCarthyism, Rotary Clubs, racial prejudice, and the American booster mentality. Among the writers he was reading when he wrote these stories in the 1950s — and he was reading all the time, all kinds of books, dozens and dozens of them — were David Riesman, Saul Bellow, Bernard Malamud, John Cheever, James Baldwin, Randall Jarrell, Sigmund Freud, Paul Goodman, William Styron, C. Wright Mills, Martin Buber, George Orwell, Suzanne Langer, F. R. Leavis, David Daiches, Edmund Wilson, Alfred Kazin, Ralph Ellison, Erich Fromm, Joseph Conrad,

Dylan Thomas, Sean O'Casey, e. e. cummings — who collectively represented a republic of discourse in which he aspired to be naturalized.

The magazine to whose strategies of cultural attack and techniques of literary assault he felt an immediate affinity was Philip Rahv's intellectually combative *Partisan Review*; he bought back issues of the quarterly in the used bookstores around Hyde Park and read each new issue in its entirety the day it appeared in the U. of C. library. The magazine that educated him to be both unapologetic and critically freewheeling about the class of Jews whose customs and beliefs had shaped his boyhood society, the magazine whose example encouraged him to recognize as the seeds of stories the mundane household dramas of his Jewish New Jersey, was the *Commentary* of the late forties and fifties. Back then *Commentary*, a monthly supported by the American Jewish Committee, was still a publication in which it was considered not a manifestation of unearned assimilationist superiority or of sick Jewish self-hatred but an expression of ineluctably Jewish self-scrutiny to propose a psychosexual critique of the kosher laws, as Isaac Rosenfield managed to do marvelously in his essay "Adam and Eve on Delancey Street," or to reveal, with mournful joy, the raw, hysterical, primitive energies propelling family life in a Brooklyn Jewish neighborhood, as Wallace Markfield did so masterfully in the story "The Country of the Crazy Horse."

Of the stories brought together in his own first book, two had previously appeared in *Commentary* and another in *The New Yorker*, while the rest (including the longest) had been published in the fledgling quarterly *The Paris Review*. The sympathetic young editors at *The Paris Review* were, by and large, from privileged Gentile backgrounds conspicuously unlike those of the Jewish editors encouraging him at *Commentary* (not to mention his own). The fact that magazines embodying such divergent cultural perspectives could sanction his subject matter had an exhilarating effect on the young writer's sense of freedom. In the beginning it simply amazed him that *any* truly literate audience could seriously be interested in his store of tribal secrets, in what he knew, as a child of his neighborhood, about the rites and taboos of his clan — about their aversions, their aspirations, their fears of deviance and defection, their underlying embarrassments and their ideas of success.

He certainly hadn't imagined, while reading the best of English prose and poetry at college only a few years earlier, that literature of the kind T. S. Eliot praised could be rooted in anything close to him. What did the tiresome tension between parents and children in lower-middle-class Jewish Newark — arguments about *shiksas* and shrimp cocktail, about going to synagogue and being good — have to do with Shakespeare and the stoicism of Seneca, or, for that matter, with all the abundance of the unimaginable life to come? Who among the mothers and fathers on his street could speak as fluently as the high school principal, Mr. Herzberg, let alone like Alexander Pope? He saw himself entering into a world of intellectual consequence precisely by moving beyond the unsubtle locutions and coarse simplifications of the families still living where he'd grown up, a tiny provincial enclosure where there was no longer room for the likes of him.

And perhaps if he'd become something other than a

writer, that kind of predictable leave-taking would have been a natural-enough route to maturity. His particular skills, however, inclined him to reimagine as a species of folk fiction — as unguarded short stories, spontaneously told, that somehow stretched over the bones of the folktale a skin of satiric social comedy — what not that long before has been the undifferentiated everydayness of Jewish life along the route of Newark's Number 14 Clinton Place bus. In this way, without knowing it, he proceeded to make identical the acts of departure and return and to perpetuate those contradictory yearnings that can perplex the emotions of an ambitious embryo — the desire to repudiate and the desire to cling, a sense of allegiance and the need to rebel, the alluring dream of escaping into the challenging unknown and the counterdream of holding fast to the familiar. Altogether unwittingly, he had activated the ambivalence that was to stimulate his imagination for years to come and establish the grounds for that necessary struggle from which his — no, my — fiction would spring.

PHILIP ROTH
June 1989

GOODBYE,

COLUMBUS

THE FIRST TIME I saw Brenda she asked me to hold her glasses. Then she stepped out to the edge of the diving board and looked foggily into the pool; it could have been drained, myopic Brenda would never have known it. She dove beautifully, and a moment later she was swimming back to the side of the pool, her head of short-clipped auburn hair held up, straight ahead of her, as though it were a rose on a long stem. She glided to the edge and then was beside me. "Thank you," she said, her eyes watery though not from the water. She extended a hand for her glasses but did not put them on until she turned and headed away. I watched her move off. Her hands suddenly appeared behind her. She caught the bottom of her suit between thumb and index finger and flicked what flesh had been showing back where it belonged. My blood jumped.

That night, before dinner, I called her.

"Who are you calling?" my Aunt Gladys asked.

"Some girl I met today."

"Doris introduced you?"

"Doris wouldn't introduce me to the guy who drains the pool, Aunt Gladys."

"Don't criticize all the time. A cousin's a cousin. How did you meet her?"

"I didn't really meet her. I saw her."

"Who is she?"

"Her last name is Patimkin."

"Patimkin I don't know," Aunt Gladys said, as if she knew anybody who belonged to the Green Lane Country Club. "You're going to call her you don't know her?"

"Yes," I explained. "I'll introduce myself."

"Casanova," she said, and went back to preparing my uncle's dinner. None of us ate together: my Aunt Gladys ate at five o'clock, my cousin Susan at five-thirty, me at six, and my uncle at six-thirty. There is nothing to explain this beyond the fact that my aunt is crazy.

"Where's the suburban phone book?" I asked after pulling out all the books tucked under the telephone table.

"What?"

"The suburban phone book. I want to call Short Hills."

"That skinny book? What, I gotta clutter my house with that, I never use it?"

"Where is it?"

"Under the dresser where the leg came off."

"For God's sake," I said.

"Call information better. You'll go yanking around there, you'll mess up my drawers. Don't bother me, you see your uncle'll be home soon. I haven't even fed *you* yet."

"Aunt Gladys, suppose tonight we all eat together. It's hot, it'll be easier for you."

"Sure, I should serve four different meals at once. You eat pot roast, Susan with the cottage cheese, Max has steak. Friday night is his steak night, I wouldn't deny him. And I'm having a little cold chicken. I should jump up and down twenty different times? What am I, a work-horse?"

"Why don't we all have steak, or cold chicken —"

"Twenty years I'm running a house. Go call your girl friend."

But when I called, Brenda Patimkin wasn't home. She's having dinner at the club, a woman's voice told me. Will she be home after (my voice was two octaves higher than a choirboy's)? I don't know, the voice said, she may go driving golf balls. Who is this? I mumbled some words — nobody she wouldn't know I'll call back no message thank you sorry to bother . . . I hung up somewhere along in there. Then my aunt called me and I steeled myself for dinner.

She pushed the black whirring fan up to *High* and that way it managed to stir the cord that hung from the kitchen light.

"What kind of soda you want? I got ginger ale, plain seltzer, black raspberry, and a bottle cream soda I could open up."

"None, thank you."

"You want water?"

"I don't drink with my meals. Aunt Gladys, I've told you that every day for a year already —"

"Max could drink a whole case with his chopped liver only. He works hard all day. If you worked hard you'd drink more."

At the stove she heaped up a plate with pot roast, gravy, boiled potatoes, and peas and carrots. She put it in front of me and I could feel the heat of the food in my face. Then she cut two pieces of rye bread and put that next to me, on the table.

I forked a potato in half and ate it, while Aunt Gladys, who had seated herself across from me, watched. "You don't want bread," she said, "I wouldn't cut it it should go stale."

"I *want* bread," I said.

"You don't like with seeds, do you?"

I tore a piece of bread in half and ate it.

"How's the meat?" she said.

"Okay. Good."

"You'll fill yourself with potatoes and bread, the meat you'll leave over I'll have to throw it out."

Suddenly she leaped up from the chair. "Salt!" When she returned to the table she plunked a salt shaker down in front of me — pepper wasn't served in her home: she'd heard on Galen Drake that it was not absorbed by the body, and it was disturbing to Aunt Gladys to think that anything she served might pass through a gullet, stomach, and bowel just for the pleasure of the trip.

"You're going to pick the peas out is all? You tell me that, I wouldn't buy with the carrots."

"I love carrots," I said, "I love them." And to prove it, I dumped half of them down my throat and the other half onto my trousers.

"Pig," she said.

Though I am very fond of desserts, especially fruit, I chose not to have any. I wanted, this hot night, to avoid the conversation that revolved around my choosing fresh fruit over canned fruit, or canned fruit over fresh fruit; whichever I preferred, Aunt Gladys always had an abundance of the other jamming her refrigerator like stolen diamonds. "He wants canned peaches, I have a refrigerator full of grapes I have to get rid of . . ." Life was a throwing off for poor

Aunt Gladys, her greatest joys were taking out the garbage, emptying her pantry, and making threadbare bundles for what she still referred to as the Poor Jews in Palestine. I only hope she dies with an empty refrigerator, otherwise she'll ruin eternity for everyone else, what with her Velveeta turning green, and her navel oranges growing fuzzy jackets down below.

My Uncle Max came home and while I dialed Brenda's number once again, I could hear soda bottles being popped open in the kitchen. The voice that answered this time was high, curt, and tired. "Hullo."

I launched into my speech. "Hello-Brenda-Brenda-you-don't-know-me-that-is-you-don't-know-my-name-but-I-held-your-glasses-for-you-this-afternoon-at-the-club ... You-asked-me-to-I'm-not-a-member-my-cousin-Doris-is-Doris-Klugman-I-asked-who-you-were ... ." I breathed, gave her a chance to speak, and then went ahead and answered the silence on the other end. "Doris? She's the one who's always reading *War and Peace*. That's how I know it's the summer, when Doris is reading *War and Peace*." Brenda didn't laugh; right from the start she was a practical girl.

"What's your name?" she said.

"Neil Klugman. I held your glasses at the board, remember?"

She answered me with a question of her own, one, I'm sure, that is an embarrassment to both the homely and the fair. "What do you look like?"

"I'm ... dark."

"Are you a Negro?"

"No," I said.

"What *do* you look like?"

"May I come see you tonight and show you?"

"That's nice," she laughed. "I'm playing tennis to-night."

"I thought you were driving golf balls."

"I drove them already."

"How about after tennis?"

"I'll be sweaty after," Brenda said.

It was not to warn me to clothespin my nose and run in the opposite direction; it was a fact, it apparently didn't bother Brenda, but she wanted it recorded.

"I don't mind," I said, and hoped by my tone to earn a niche somewhere between the squeamish and the grubby. "Can I pick you up?"

She did not answer a minute; I heard her muttering, "Doris Klugman, Doris Klugman..." Then she said, "Yes, Briarpath Hills, eight-fifteen."

"I'll be driving a — " I hung back with the year, "a tan Plymouth. So you'll know me. How will I know you?" I said with a sly, awful laugh.

"I'll be sweating," she said and hung up.

Once I'd driven out of Newark, past Irvington and the packed-in tangle of railroad crossings, switchmen shacks, lumberyards, Dairy Queens, and used-car lots, the night grew cooler. It was, in fact, as though the hundred and eighty feet that the suburbs rose in altitude above Newark brought one closer to heaven, for the sun itself became bigger, lower, and rounder, and soon I was driving past long lawns which seemed to be twirling water on themselves, and past houses where no one sat on stoops, where lights were on but no windows open, for those inside, refusing to share the very texture of life with those of us outside, regulated with a dial the amounts of moisture

that were allowed access to their skin. It was only eight
o'clock, and I did not want to be early, so I drove up and
down the streets whose names were those of eastern colleges, as though the township, years ago, when things were
named, had planned the destinies of the sons of its citi-
zens. I thought of my Aunt Gladys and Uncle Max sharing a Mounds bar in the cindery darkness of their alley, on
beach chairs, each cool breeze sweet to them as the promise of afterlife, and after a while I rolled onto the gravel
roads of the small park where Brenda was playing tennis.
Inside my glove compartment it was as though the map of
The City Streets of Newark had metamorphosed into
crickets, for those mile-long tarry streets did not exist for
me any longer, and the night noises sounded loud as the
blood whacking at my temples.

I parked the car under the black-green canopy of three
oaks, and walked towards the sound of the tennis balls. I
heard an exasperated voice say, "Deuce *again*." It was
Brenda and she sounded as though she was sweating considerably. I crackled slowly up the gravel and heard Brenda
once more. "My ad," and then just as I rounded the path,
catching a cuff full of burrs, I heard, "Game!" Her racket
went spinning up in the air and she caught it neatly as I
came into sight.

"Hello," I called.

"Hello, Neil. One more game," she called. Brenda's
words seemed to infuriate her opponent, a pretty brown-
haired girl, not quite so tall as Brenda, who stopped search-
ing for the ball that had been driven past her, and gave
both Brenda and myself a dirty look. In a moment I
learned the reason why: Brenda was ahead five games to
four, and her cocksureness about there being just one game

remaining aroused enough anger in her opponent for the two of us to share.

As it happened, Brenda finally won, though it took more games than she'd expected. The other girl, whose name sounded like Simp, seemed happy to end it at six all, but Brenda, shifting, running, up on her toes, would not stop, and finally all I could see moving in the darkness were her glasses, a glint of them, the clasp of her belt, her socks, her sneakers, and, on occasion, the ball. The darker it got the more savagely did Brenda rush the net, which seemed curious, for I had noticed that earlier, in the light, she had stayed back, and even when she had had to rush, after smashing back a lob, she didn't look entirely happy about being so close to her opponent's racket. Her passion for winning a point seemed outmatched by an even stronger passion for maintaining her beauty as it was. I suspected that the red print of a tennis ball on her cheek would pain her more than losing all the points in the world. Darkness pushed her in, however, and she stroked harder, and at last Simp seemed to be running on her ankles. When it was all over, Simp refused my offer of a ride home and indicated with a quality of speech borrowed from some old Katherine Hepburn movie that she could manage for herself; apparently her manor lay no further than the nearest briar patch. She did not like me and I her, though I worried it, I'm sure, more than she did.

"Who is *she?*"

"Laura Simpson Stolowitch."

"Why don't you call her Stolo?" I asked.

"Simp is her Bennington name. The ass."

"Is that where you go to school?" I asked.

She was pushing her shirt up against her skin to dry the perspiration. "No. I go to school in Boston."

I disliked her for the answer. Whenever anyone asks me where I went to school I come right out with it: Newark Colleges of Rutgers University. I may say it a bit too ringingly, too fast, too up-in-the-air, but I say it. For an instant Brenda reminded me of the pug-nosed little bastards from Montclair who come down to the library during vacations, and while I stamp out their books, they stand around tugging their elephantine scarves until they hang to their ankles, hinting all the while at "Boston" and "New Haven."

"Boston University?" I asked, looking off at the trees.

"Radcliffe."

We were still standing on the court, bounded on all sides by white lines. Around the bushes back of the court, fireflies were cutting figure eights in the thorny-smelling air and then, as the night suddenly came all the way in, the leaves on the trees shone for an instant, as though they'd just been rained upon. Brenda walked off the court, with me a step behind her. Now I had grown accustomed to the dark, and as she ceased being merely a voice and turned into a sight again, some of my anger at her "Boston" remark floated off and I let myself appreciate her. Her hands did not twitch at her bottom, but the form revealed itself, covered or not, under the closeness of her khaki Bermudas. There were two wet triangles on the back of her tiny-collared white polo shirt, right where her wings would have been if she'd had a pair. She wore, to complete the picture, a tartan belt, white socks, and white tennis sneakers.

As she walked she zipped the cover on her racket.

"Are you anxious to get home?" I said.

"No."

"Let's sit here. It's pleasant."

"Okay."

We sat down on a bank of grass slanted enough for us to lean back without really leaning; from the angle it seemed as though we were preparing to watch some celestial event, the christening of a new star, the inflation to full size of a half-ballooned moon. Brenda zipped and unzipped the cover while she spoke; for the first time she seemed edgy. Her edginess coaxed mine back, and so we were ready now for what, magically, it seemed we might be able to get by without: a meeting.

"What does your cousin Doris look like?" she asked.

"She's dark —"

"Is she — "

"No," I said. "She has freckles and dark hair and she's very tall."

"Where does she go to school?"

"Northampton."

She did not answer and I don't know how much of what I meant she had understood.

"I guess I don't know her," she said after a moment. "Is she a new member?"

"I think so. They moved to Livingston only a couple of years ago."

"Oh."

No new star appeared, at least for the next five minutes.

"Did you remember me from holding your glasses?" I said.

"Now I do," she said. "Do you live in Livingston too?"

"No. Newark."

"We lived in Newark when I was a baby," she offered.

"Would you like to go home?" I was suddenly angry.

"No. Let's walk though."

Brenda kicked a stone and walked a step ahead of me.

"Why is it you rush the net only after dark?" I said.

She turned to me and smiled. "You noticed? Old Simp the Simpleton doesn't."

"Why do you?"

"I don't like to be up too close, unless I'm sure she won't return it."

"Why?"

"My nose."

"What?"

"I'm afraid of my nose. I had it bobbed."

"What?"

"I had my nose fixed."

"What was the matter with it?"

"It was bumpy."

"A lot?"

"No," she said, "I was pretty. Now I'm prettier. My brother's having his fixed in the fall."

"Does he want to be prettier?"

She didn't answer and walked ahead of me again.

"I don't mean to sound facetious. I mean why's he doing it?"

"He *wants* to . . . unless he becomes a gym teacher . . . but he won't," she said. "We all look like my father."

"Is he having his fixed?"

"Why are you so nasty?"

"I'm not. I'm sorry." My next question was prompted by a desire to sound interested and thereby regain civility; it didn't quite come out as I'd expected — I said it too loud. "How much does it cost?"

Brenda waited a moment but then she answered. "A thousand dollars. Unless you go to a butcher."

"Let me see if you got your money's worth."

She turned again; she stood next to a bench and put the racket down on it. "If I let you kiss me would you stop being nasty?"

We had to take about two too many steps to keep the approach from being awkward, but we pursued the impulse and kissed. I felt her hand on the back of my neck and so I tugged her towards me, too violently perhaps, and slid my own hands across the side of her body and around to her back. I felt the wet spots on her shoulder blades, and beneath them, I'm sure of it, a faint fluttering, as though something stirred so deep in her breasts, so far back it could make itself felt through her shirt. It was like the fluttering of wings, tiny wings no bigger than her breasts. The smallness of the wings did not bother me — it would not take an eagle to carry me up those lousy hundred and eighty feet that make summer nights so much cooler in Short Hills than they are in Newark.

She is an angel who will elevate him out of Newark & the good life

2

The next day I held Brenda's glasses for her once again, this time not as momentary servant but as afternoon guest; or perhaps as both, which still was an improvement. She wore a black tank suit and went barefooted, and among the other women, with their Cuban heels and boned-up breasts, their knuckle-sized rings, their straw hats, which resembled immense wicker pizza plates and had been purchased, as I heard one deeply tanned woman rasp, "from the cutest little *shvartze* when we docked at Barbados," Brenda among them was elegantly simple, like a sailor's dream of a Polynesian maiden, albeit one with prescription

sun glasses and the last name of Patimkin. She brought
a little slurp of water with her when she crawled back towards the pool's edge, and at the edge she grabbed up
with her hands and held my ankles, tightly and wet.

"Come in," she said up to me, squinting. "We'll play."

"Your glasses," I said.

"Oh break the goddam things. I hate them."

"Why don't you have your eyes fixed?"

"There you go again."

"I'm sorry," I said. "I'll give them to Doris."

Doris, in the surprise of the summer, had gotten past
Prince Andrey's departure from his wife, and now sat
brooding, not, it turned out, over the lonely fate of poor
Princess Liza, but at the skin which she had lately discovered to be peeling off her shoulders.

"Would you watch Brenda's glasses?" I said.

"Yes." She fluffed little scales of translucent flesh into
the air. "Damn it."

I handed her the glasses.

"Well, for God's sake," she said, "I'm not going to hold
them. Put them down. *I'm* not her slave."

"You're a pain in the ass, you know that, Doris?" Sitting there, she looked a little like Laura Simpson Stolowitch, who was, in fact, walking somewhere off at the far
end of the pool, avoiding Brenda and me because (I liked
to think) of the defeat Brenda had handed her the night
before; or maybe (I didn't like to think) because of the
strangeness of my presence. Regardless, Doris had to
bear the weight of my indictment of both Simp and herself.

"Thank you," she said. "After I invite you up for the
day."

"That was yesterday."

"What about last year?"

"That's right, your mother told you last year too — invite Esther's boy so when he writes his parents they won't complain we don't look after him. Every summer I get my day."

"You should have gone with them. That's not our fault. You're not our charge," and when she said it, I could just tell it was something she'd heard at home, or received in a letter one Monday mail, after she'd returned to Northampton from Stowe, or Dartmouth, or perhaps from that weekend when she'd taken a shower with her boyfriend in Lowell House.

"Tell your father not to worry. Uncle Aaron, the sport. I'll take care of myself," and I ran on back to the pool, ran into a dive, in fact, and came up like a dolphin beside Brenda, whose legs I slid upon with my own.

"How's Doris?" she said.

"Peeling," I said. "She's going to have her skin fixed."

"*Stop* it," she said, and dove down beneath us till I felt her clamping her hands on the soles of my feet. I pulled back and then down too, and then, at the bottom, no more than six inches above the wiggling black lines that divided the pool into lanes for races, we bubbled a kiss into each other's lips. She was smiling there, at *me*, down at the bottom of the swimming pool of the Green Lane Country Club. Way above us, legs shimmied in the water and a pair of fins skimmed greenly by: my cousin Doris could peel away to nothing for all I cared, my Aunt Gladys have twenty feedings every night, my father and mother could roast away their asthma down in the furnace of Arizona, those penniless deserters — I didn't care for anything but

Brenda. I went to pull her towards me just as she started fluttering up; my hand hooked on to the front of her suit and the cloth pulled away from her. Her breasts swam towards me like two pink-nosed fish and she let me hold them. Then, in a moment, it was the sun who kissed us both, and we were out of the water, too pleased with each other to smile. Brenda shook the wetness of her hair onto my face and with the drops that touched me I felt she had made a promise to me about the summer, and, I hoped, beyond.

"Do you want your sun glasses?"

"You're close enough to see," she said. We were under a big blue umbrella, side-by-side on two chaise longues, whose plastic covers sizzled against our suits and flesh; I turned my head to look at Brenda and smelled that pleasant little burning odor in the skin of my shoulders. I turned back up to the sun, as did she, and as we talked, and it grew hotter and brighter, the colors splintered under my closed eyelids.

"This is all very fast," she said.

"Nothing's happened," I said softly.

"No. I guess not. I sort of feel something has."

"In eighteen hours?"

"Yes. I feel . . . pursued," she said after a moment.

"*You* invited *me*, Brenda."

"Why do you always sound a little nasty to me?"

"Did I sound nasty? I don't mean to. Truly."

"You do! *You* invited *me*, Brenda. So what?" she said. "That isn't what I mean anyway."

"I'm sorry."

"Stop apologizing. You're so automatic about it, you don't even mean it."

"Now you're being nasty to me," I said.

"No. Just stating the facts. Let's not argue. I like you." She turned her head and looked as though she too paused a second to smell the summer on her own flesh. "I like the way you look." She saved it from embarrassing me with that factual tone of hers.

"Why?" I said.

"Where did you get those fine shoulders? Do you play something?"

"No," I said. "I just grew up and they came with me."

"I like your body. It's fine."

"I'm glad," I said.

"You like mine, don't you?"

"No," I said.

"Then it's denied you," she said.

I brushed her hair flat against her ear with the back of my hand and then we were silent a while.

"Brenda," I said, "you haven't asked me anything about me."

"How you feel? Do you want me to ask you how you feel?"

"Yes," I said, accepting the back door she gave me, though probably not for the same reasons she had offered it.

"How *do* you feel?"

"I want to swim."

"Okay," she said.

We spent the rest of the afternoon in the water. There were eight of those long lines painted down the length of the pool and by the end of the day I think we had parked for a while in every lane, close enough to the dark stripes to reach out and touch them. We came back to the chairs

now and then and sang hesitant, clever, nervous, gentle
dithyrambs about how we were beginning to feel towards
one another. Actually we did not have the feelings we said
we had until we spoke them — at least I didn't; to phrase
them was to invent them and own them. We whipped our
strangeness and newness into a froth that resembled love,
and we dared not play too long with it, talk too much of it,
or it would flatten and fizzle away. So we moved back
and forth from chairs to water, from talk to silence, and
considering my unshakable edginess with Brenda, and the
high walls of ego that rose, buttresses and all, between
her and her knowledge of herself, we managed pretty well.

At about four o'clock, at the bottom of the pool, Brenda
suddenly wrenched away from me and shot up to the sur-
face. I shot up after her.

"What's the matter?" I said.

First she whipped the hair off her forehead. Then she
pointed a hand down towards the base of the pool. "My
brother," she said, coughing some water free inside her.

And suddenly, like a crew-cut Proteus rising from the
sea, Ron Patimkin emerged from the lower depths we'd
just inhabited and his immensity was before us.

"Hey, Bren," he said, and pushed a palm flat into the
water so that a small hurricane beat up against Brenda
and me.

"What are you so happy about?" she said.

"The Yankees took two."

"Are we going to have Mickey Mantle for dinner?" she
said. "When the Yankees win," she said to me, treading
so easily she seemed to have turned the chlorine to marble
beneath her, "we set an extra place for Mickey Mantle."

"You want to race?" Ron asked.

"No, Ronald. Go race alone."

Nobody had as yet said a word about me. I treaded unobtrusively as I could, as a third party, unintroduced, will step back and say nothing, awaiting the amenities. I was tired, however, from the afternoon's sport, and wished to hell brother and sister would not tease and chat much longer. Fortunately Brenda introduced me. "Ronald, this is Neil Klugman. This is my brother, Ronald Patimkin."

Of all things there in the fifteen feet water, Ron reached out his hand to shake. I returned the shake, not quite as monumentally as he apparently expected; my chin slipped an inch into the water and all at once I was exhausted.

"Want to race?" Ron asked me good-naturedly.

"Go ahead, Neil, race with him. I want to call home and tell them you're coming to dinner."

"Am I? I'll have to call my aunt. You didn't say anything. My clothes —"

"We dine *au naturel*."

"What?" Ronald said.

"Swim, baby," Brenda said to him and it ached me some when she kissed him on the face.

I begged out of the race, saying I had to make a phone call myself, and once upon the tiled blue border of the pool, looked back to see Ron taking the length in sleek, immense strokes. He gave one the feeling that after swimming the length of the pool a half dozen times he would have earned the right to drink its contents; I imagined he had, like my Uncle Max, a colossal thirst and a gigantic bladder.

Aunt Gladys did not seem relieved when I told her she'd have only three feedings to prepare that night. "Fancyshmancy" was all she said to me on the phone.

We did not eat in the kitchen; rather, the six of us —
Brenda, myself, Ron, Mr. and Mrs. Patimkin, and
Brenda's little sister, Julie — sat around the dining room
table, while the maid, Carlota, a Navaho-faced Negro who
had little holes in her ears but no earrings, served us the
meal. I was seated next to Brenda, who was dressed in
what was *au naturel* for her: Bermudas, the close ones,
white polo shirt, tennis sneakers and white socks. Across
from me was Julie, ten, round-faced, bright, who before
dinner, while the other little girls on the street had been
playing with jacks and boys and each other, had been on
the back lawn putting golf balls with her father. Mr.
Patimkin reminded me of my father, except that when he
spoke he did not surround each syllable with a wheeze. He
was tall, strong, ungrammatical, and a ferocious eater.
When he attacked his salad — after drenching it in bottled
French dressing — the veins swelled under the heavy skin
of his forearm. He ate three helpings of salad, Ron had
four, Brenda and Julie had two, and only Mrs. Patimkin
and I had one each. I did not like Mrs. Patimkin, though
she was certainly the handsomest of all of us at the table.
She was disastrously polite to me, and with her purple eyes,
her dark hair, and large, persuasive frame, she gave me the
feeling of some captive beauty, some wild princess, who has
been tamed and made the servant to the king's daughter —
who was Brenda.

Outside, through the wide picture window, I could see
the back lawn with its twin oak trees. I say oaks, though
fancifully, one might call them sporting-goods trees. Beneath their branches, like fruit dropped from their limbs,
were two irons, a golf ball, a tennis can, a baseball bat,
basketball, a first-baseman's glove, and what was appar-

ently a riding crop. Further back, near the scrubs that
bounded the Patimkin property and in front of the small
basketball court, a square red blanket, with a white O
stitched in the center, looked to be on fire against the
green grass. A breeze must have blown outside, for the
net on the basket moved; inside we ate in the steady coolness of air by Westinghouse. It was a pleasure, except that
eating among those Brobdingnags, I felt for quite a while
as though four inches had been clipped from my shoulders,
three inches from my height, and for good measure, someone had removed my ribs and my chest had settled meekly
in towards my back.

There was not much dinner conversation; eating was
heavy and methodical and serious, and it would be just as
well to record all that was said in one swoop, rather than
indicate the sentences lost in the passing of food, the
words gurgled into mouthfuls, the syntax chopped and
forgotten in heapings, spillings, and gorgings.

To Ron: When's Harriet calling?

Ron: Five o'clock.

Julie: It *was* five o'clock.

Ron: Their time.

Julie: Why is it that it's earlier in Milwaukee? Suppose
you took a plane back and forth all day. You'd never get
older.

Brenda: That's right, sweetheart.

Mrs. P.: What do you give the child misinformation
for? Is that why she goes to school?

Brenda: I don't know why she goes to school.

Mr. P. (*lovingly*): College girl.

Ron: Where's Carlota? Carlota!

Mrs. P.: Carlota, give Ronald more.

CARLOTA (*calling*): More what?

RON: Everything.

MR. P.: Me too.

MRS. P.: They'll have to *roll* you on the links.

MR. P. (*pulling his shirt up and slapping his black, curved belly*): What are you talking about? Look at that?

RON (*yanking his T-shirt up*): Look at *this*.

BRENDA: (*to me*) Would you care to bare your middle?

ME (the choir boy again): No.

MRS. P.: That's right, Neil.

ME: Yes. Thank you.

CARLOTA (*over my shoulder, like an unsummoned spirit*): Would *you* like more?

ME: No.

MR. P.: He eats like a bird.

JULIE: Certain birds eat a lot.

BRENDA: Which ones?

MRS. P.: Let's not talk about animals at the dinner table. Brenda, why do you encourage her?

RON: Where's Carlota, I gotta play tonight.

MR. P.: Tape your wrist, don't forget.

MRS. P.: Where do you live, Bill?

BRENDA: Neil.

MRS. P.: Didn't I say Neil?

JULIE: You said "Where do you live, *Bill?*"

MRS. P.: I must have been thinking of something else.

RON: I hate tape. How the hell can I play in tape?

JULIE: Don't curse.

MRS. P.: That's right.

MR. P.: What is Mantle batting now?

JULIE: Three twenty-eight.

RON: Three twenty-five.

JULIE: Eight!

RON: Five, jerk! He got three for four in the second game.

JULIE: *Four* for four.

RON: That was an error, Minoso should have had it.

JULIE: *I* didn't think so.

BRENDA (*to me*): See?

MRS. P.: See what?

BRENDA: I was talking to Bill.

JULIE: Neil.

MR. P.: Shut up and eat.

MRS. P.: A little less talking, young lady.

JULIE: *I* didn't say anything.

BRENDA: She was talking to me, sweetie.

MR. P.: What's this *she* business. Is that how you call your mother? What's dessert?

The phone rings, and though we are awaiting dessert, the meal seems at a formal end, for Ron breaks for his room, Julie shouts "Harriet!" and Mr. Patimkin is not wholly successful in stifling a belch, though the failure even more than the effort ingratiates him to me. Mrs. Patimkin is directing Carlota not to mix the milk silverware and the meat silverware again, and Carlota is eating a peach while she listens; under the table I feel Brenda's fingers tease my calf. I am full.

We sat under the biggest of the oak trees while out on the basketball court Mr. Patimkin played five and two with Julie. In the driveway Ron was racing the motor of the Volkswagen. "Will somebody *please* move the Chrysler out from behind me?" he called angrily. "I'm late as it is."

"Excuse me," Brenda said, getting up.

"I think I'm behind the Chrysler," I said.

"Let's go," she said.

We backed the cars out so that Ron could hasten on to his game. Then we reparked them and went back to watching Mr. Patimkin and Julie.

"I like your sister," I said.

"So do I," she said. "I wonder what she'll turn out to be."

"Like you," I said.

"I don't know," she said. "Better probably." And then she added, "or maybe worse. How can you tell? My father's nice to her, but I'll give her another three years with my mother... Bill," she said, musingly.

"I didn't mind that," I said. "She's very beautiful, your mother."

"I can't even think of her as my mother. She hates me. Other girls, when they pack in September, at least their mothers help them. Not mine. She'll be busy sharpening pencils for Julie's pencil box while I'm carrying my trunk around upstairs. And it's so obvious why. It's practically a case study."

"Why?"

"She's jealous. It's so corny I'm ashamed to say it. Do you know my mother had the best back-hand in New Jersey? Really, she was the best tennis player in the state, man or woman. You ought to see the pictures of her when she was a girl. She was so healthy-looking. But not chubby or anything. She was soulful, truly. I love her in those pictures. Sometimes I say to her how beautiful the pictures are. I even asked to have one blown up so I could have it at school. 'We have other things to do with our money, young lady, than spend it on old photographs.'

Money! My father's up to here with it, but whenever I buy a coat you should hear her. 'You don't have to go to Bonwit's, young lady, Ohrbach's has the strongest fabrics of any of them.' Who *wants* a strong fabric! Finally I get what I want, but not till she's had a chance to aggravate me. Money is a waste for her. She doesn't even know how to enjoy it. She still thinks we live in Newark."

"But you get what you want," I said.

"Yes. Him," and she pointed out to Mr. Patimkin who had just swished his third straight set shot through the basket to the disgruntlement, apparently, of Julie, who stamped so hard at the ground that she raised a little dust storm around her perfect young legs.

"He's not too smart but he's sweet at least. He doesn't treat my brother the way she treats me. Thank God, for that. Oh, I'm tired of talking about them. Since my freshman year I think every conversation I've ever had has always wound up about my parents and how awful it is. It's universal. The only trouble is they don't know it."

From the way Julie and Mr. Patimkin were laughing now, out on the court, no problem could ever have seemed less universal; but, of course, it was universal for Brenda, more than that, cosmic — it made every cashmere sweater a battle with her mother, and her life, which, I was certain, consisted to a large part of cornering the market on fabrics that felt soft to the skin, took on the quality of a Hundred Years' War . . .

I did not intend to allow myself such unfaithful thoughts, to line up with Mrs. Patimkin while I sat beside Brenda, but I could not shake from my elephant's brain that she-still thinks-we-live-in-Newark remark. I did not speak, however, fearful that my tone would shatter our post-dinner ease and intimacy. It had been so simple to be intimate with water pounding and securing all our pores, and later, with the sun heating them and drugging our senses, but now, in the shade and the open, cool and clothed on her own grounds, I did not want to voice a word that would lift the cover and reveal that hideous emotion I always felt for her, and is the underside of love. It will not always *stay* the underside — but I am skipping ahead.

Suddenly, little Julie was upon us. "Want to play?" she said to me. "Daddy's tired."

"C'mon," Mr. Patimkin called. "Finish for me."

I hesitated — I hadn't held a basketball since high school — but Julie was dragging at my hand, and Brenda said, "Go ahead."

Mr. Patimkin tossed the ball towards me while I wasn't looking and it bounced off my chest, leaving a round dust spot, like the shadow of a moon, on my shirt. I laughed, insanely.

"Can't you catch?" Julie said.

Like her sister, she seemed to have a knack for asking practical, infuriating questions.

"Yes."

"Your turn," she said. "Daddy's behind forty-seven to thirty-nine. Two hundred wins."

For an instant, as I placed my toes in the little groove that over the years had been nicked into a foul line, I had one of those instantaneous waking dreams that plague me from time to time, and send, my friends tell me, deadly cataracts over my eyes: the sun had sunk, crickets had come and gone, the leaves had blackened, and still Julie and I stood alone on the lawn, tossing the ball at the basket; "Five hundred wins," she called, and then when she beat me to five hundred she called, "Now *you* have to reach it," and I did, and the night lengthened, and she called, "*Eight* hundred wins," and we played on and then it was eleven hundred that won and we played on and it never was morning.

"Shoot," Mr. Patimkin said. "You're me."

That puzzled me, but I took my set shot and, of course, missed. With the Lord's blessing and a soft breeze, I made the lay-up.

"You have forty-one. I go," Julie said.

Mr. Patimkin sat on the grass at the far end of the court. He took his shirt off, and in his undershirt, and his whole day's growth of beard, looked like a trucker. Brenda's old nose fitted him well. There was a bump in it, all right; up at the bridge it seemed as though a small eight-sided diamond had been squeezed in under the skin. I knew Mr. Patimkin would never bother to have that stone cut from his face, and yet, with joy and pride, no doubt, had paid to have Brenda's diamond removed and dropped down some toilet in Fifth Avenue Hospital.

Julie missed her set shot, and I admit to a slight, gay, flutter of heart.

"Put a little spin on it," Mr. Patimkin told her.

"Can I take it again?" Julie asked me.

"Yes." What with paternal directions from the sidelines and my own grudging graciousness on the court, there did not seem much of a chance for me to catch up. And I wanted to, suddenly, I wanted to win, to run little Julie into the ground. Brenda was back on one elbow, under the tree, chewing on a leaf, watching. And up in the house, at the kitchen window, I could see that the curtain had swished back — the sun too low now to glare off electrical

appliances — and Mrs. Patimkin was looking steadily out
at the game. And then Carlota appeared on the back steps,
eating a peach and holding a pail of garbage in her free
hand. She stopped to watch too.

It was my turn again. I missed the set shot and laugh-
ingly turned to Julie and said, "Can I take it again?"

"No!"

So I learned how the game was played. Over the years
Mr. Patimkin had taught his daughters that free throws
were theirs for the asking; he could afford to. However,
with the strange eyes of Short Hills upon me, matrons,
servants, and providers, I somehow felt I couldn't. But I
had to and I did.

"Thanks a lot, Neil," Julie said when the game was
ended — at 100 — and the crickets had come.

"You're welcome."

Under the trees, Brenda smiled. "Did you let her win?"

"I think so," I said. "I'm not sure."

There was something in my voice that prompted Brenda
to say, comfortingly, "Even Ron lets her win."

"It's all nice for Julie," I said.

3

The next morning I found a parking space on Washington
Street directly across from the library. Since I was twenty
minutes early I decided to stroll in the park rather than
cross over to work; I didn't particularly care to join my col-
leagues, who I knew would be sipping early morning coffee
in the binding room, smelling still of all the orange crush
they'd drunk that weekend at Asbury Park. I sat on a
bench and looked out towards Broad Street and the morn-

ing traffic. The Lackawanna commuter trains were rumbling in a few blocks to the north and I could hear them, I thought — the sunny green cars, old and clean, with windows that opened all the way. Some mornings, with time to kill before work, I would walk down to the tracks and watch the open windows roll in, on their sills the elbows of tropical suits and the edges of briefcases, the properties of businessmen arriving in town from Maplewood, the Oranges, and the suburbs beyond.

The park, bordered by Washington Street on the west and Broad on the east, was empty and shady and smelled of trees, night, and dog leavings; and there was a faint damp smell too, indicating that the huge rhino of a water cleaner had passed by already, soaking and whisking the downtown streets. Down Washington Street, behind me, was the Newark Museum — I could see it without even looking: two oriental vases in front like spittoons for a rajah, and next to it the little annex to which we had traveled on special buses as schoolchildren. The annex was a brick building, old and vine-covered, and always reminded me of New Jersey's link with the beginning of the country, with George Washington, who had trained his scrappy army — a little bronze tablet informed us children — in the very park where I now sat. At the far end of the park, beyond the Museum, was the bank building where I had gone to college. It had been converted some years before into an extension of Rutgers University; in fact, in what once had been the bank president's waiting room I had taken a course called Contemporary Moral Issues. Though it was summer now, and I was out of college three years, it was not hard for me to remember the other students, my friends, who had worked evenings in Bamberger's and

Kresge's and had used the commissions they'd earned pushing ladies' out-of-season shoes to pay their laboratory fees.
And then I looked out to Broad Street again. Jammed between a grimy-windowed bookstore and a cheesy luncheonette was the marquee of a tiny art theater — how many
years had passed since I'd stood beneath that marquee,
lying about the year of my birth so as to see Hedy Lamarr
swim naked in *Ecstasy*; and then, having slipped the ticket
taker an extra quarter, what disappointment I had felt at
the frugality of her Slavic charm . . . Sitting there in the
park, I felt a deep knowledge of Newark, an attachment
so rooted that it could not help but branch out into affection.

Suddenly it was nine o'clock and everything was scurrying. Wobbly-heeled girls revolved through the doors of
the telephone building across the way, traffic honked desperately, policeman barked, whistled, and waved motorists
to and fro. Over at St. Vincent's Church the huge dark
portals swung back and those bleary-eyes that had risen
early for Mass now blinked at the light. Then the wor-
shipers had stepped off the church steps and were racing
down the streets towards desks, filing cabinets, secretaries,
bosses, and — if the Lord had seen fit to remove a mite of
harshness from their lives — to the comfort of air-condi-
tioners pumping at their windows. I got up and crossed
over to the library, wondering if Brenda was awake yet.

The pale cement lions stood unconvincing guard on the
library steps, suffering their usual combination of elephan-
tiasis and arteriosclerosis, and I was prepared to pay them
as little attention as I had for the past eight months were
it not for a small colored boy who stood in front of one of
them. The lion had lost all of its toes the summer before

to a safari of juvenile delinquents, and now a new tor-
mentor stood before him, sagging a little in his knees, and
growling. He would growl, low and long, drop back,
wait, then growl again. Then he would straighten up, and,
shaking his head, he would say to the lion, "Man, you's
a coward ... " Then, once again, he'd growl.

The day began the same as any other. From behind the
desk on the main floor, I watched the hot high-breasted
teen-age girls walk twitchingly up the wide flight of marble
stairs that led to the main reading room. The stairs were
an imitation of a staircase somewhere in Versailles, though
in their toreador pants and sweaters these young daughters
of Italian leatherworkers, Polish brewery hands, and Jewish
furriers were hardly duchesses. They were not Brenda
either, and any lust that sparked inside me through the
dreary day was academic and time-passing. I looked at
my watch occasionally, thought of Brenda, and waited for
lunch and then for after lunch, when I would take over the
Information Desk upstairs and John McKee, who was only
twenty-one but wore elastic bands around his sleeves, would
march starchily down the stairs to work assiduously at
stamping books in and out. John McRubberbands was in
his last year at Newark State Teachers College where he was
studying at the Dewey Decimal System in preparation for
his lifework. The library was not going to be my lifework, I
knew it. Yet, there had been some talk — from Mr. Scapello, an old eunuch who had learned somehow to disguise
his voice as a man's — that when I returned from my summer vacation I would be put in charge of the Reference
Room, a position that had been empty ever since that morning when Martha Winney had fallen off a high stool in the
Encyclopedia Room and shattered all those frail bones that

come together to form what in a woman half her age we would call the hips.

I had strange fellows at the library and, in truth, there were many hours when I never quite knew how I'd gotten there or why I stayed. But I did stay and after a while waited patiently for that day when I would go into the men's room on the main floor for a cigarette and, studying myself as I expelled smoke into the mirror, would see that at some moment during the morning I had gone pale, and that under my skin, as under McKee's and Scapello's and Miss Winney's, there was a thin cushion of air separating the blood from the flesh. Someone had pumped it there while I was stamping out a book, and so life from now on would be not a throwing off, as it was for Aunt Gladys, and not a gathering in, as it was for Brenda, but a bouncing off, a numbness. I began to fear this, and yet, in my muscleless devotion to my work, seemed edging towards it, silently, as Miss Winney used to edge up to the *Britannica.* Her stool was empty now and awaited me.

Just before lunch the lion tamer came wide-eyed into the library. He stood still for a moment, only his fingers moving, as though he were counting the number of marble stairs before him. Then he walked creepily about on the marble floor, snickering at the clink of his taps and the way his little noise swelled up to the vaulted ceiling. Otto, the guard at the door, told him to make less noise with his shoes, but that did not seem to bother the little boy. He clacked on his tiptoes, high, secretively, delighted at the opportunity Otto had given him to practice this posture. He tiptoed up to me.

"Hey," he said, "where's the heart section?"

"The what?" I said.

"The heart section. Ain't you got no heart section?"

He had the thickest sort of southern Negro dialect and the only word that came clear to me was the one that sounded like heart.

"How do you spell it?" I said.

"*Heart.* Man, pictures. Drawing books. Where you got them?"

"You mean art books? Reproductions?"

He took my polysyllabic word for it. "Yea, they's them."

"In a couple places," I told him. "Which artist are you interested in?"

The boy's eyes narrowed so that his whole face seemed black. He started backing away, as he had from the lion. "All of them . . . " he mumbled.

"That's okay," I said. "You go look at whichever ones you want. The next flight up. Follow the arrow to where it says Stack Three. You remember that? Stack Three. Ask somebody upstairs."

He did not move; he seemed to be taking my curiosity about his taste as a kind of poll-tax investigation. "Go ahead," I said, slashing my face with a smile, "right up there . . . "

And like a shot he was scuffling and tapping up towards the heart section.

After lunch I came back to the in-and-out desk and there was John McKee, waiting, in his pale blue slacks, his black shoes, his barber-cloth shirt with the elastic bands, and a great knit tie, green, wrapped into a Windsor knot, that was huge and jumped when he talked. His breath smelled of hair oil and his hair of breath and when he spoke, spittle cobwebbed the corners of his mouth. I did not like him and at times had the urge to yank back on his armbands and slingshoot him out past Otto and the lions into the street.

"Has a little Negro boy passed the desk? With a thick accent? He's been hiding in the art books all morning. You know what those boys *do* in there."

"I saw him come in, John."

"So did I. Has he gone *out* though."

"I haven't noticed. I guess so."

"Those are *very* expensive books."

"Don't be so nervous, John. People are supposed to touch them."

"There is touching," John said sententiously, "and there is touching. Someone should check on him. I was afraid to leave the desk here. You know the way they treat the housing projects we give them."

"*You* give them?"

"The city. Have you seen what they do at Seth Boyden? They threw *beer* bottles, those big ones, on the *lawn*. They're taking over the city."

"Just the Negro sections."

"It's easy to laugh, you don't live near them. I'm going to call Mr. Scapello's office to check the Art Section. Where did he ever find out about art?"

"You'll give Mr. Scapello an ulcer, so soon after his egg-and-pepper sandwich. I'll check, I have to go upstairs anyway."

"You know what they do in there," John warned me.

"Don't worry, Johnny, *they're* the ones who'll get warts on their dirty little hands."

"Ha ha. Those books happen to cost — "

So that Mr. Scapello would not descend upon the boy

with his chalky fingers, I walked up the three flights to Stack Three, past the receiving room where rheumy-eyed Jimmy Boylen, our fifty-one-year-old boy, unloaded books from a cart; past the reading room, where bums off Mulberry Street slept over *Popular Mechanics*; past the smoking corridor where damp-browed summer students from the law school relaxed, some smoking, others trying to rub the colored dye from their tort texts off their fingertips; and finally, past the periodical room, where a few ancient ladies who'd been motored down from Upper Montclair now huddled in their chairs, pince-nezing over yellowed, fraying society pages in old old copies of the Newark *News*. Up on Stack Three I found the boy. He was seated on the glass-brick floor holding an open book in his lap, a book, in fact, that was bigger than his lap and had to be propped up by his knees. By the light of the window behind him I could see the hundreds of spaces between the hundreds of tiny black corkscrews that were his hair. He was very black and shiny, and the flesh of his lips did not so much appear to be a different color as it looked to be unfinished and awaiting another coat. The lips were parted, the eyes wide, and even the ears seemed to have a heightened receptivity. He looked ecstatic — until he saw me, that is. For all he knew I was John McKee.

"That's okay," I said before he could even move, "I'm just passing through. You read."

"Ain't nothing *to* read. They's pictures."

"Fine." I fished around the lowest shelves a moment, playing at work.

"Hey, mister," the boy said after a minute, "where is this?"

"Where is what?"

"Where is these pictures? These people, man, they sure does look cool. They ain't no yelling or shouting here, you could just see it."

He lifted the book so I could see. It was an expensive large-sized edition of Gauguin reproductions. The page he had been looking at showed an 8½ × 11 print, in color, of three native women standing knee-high in a rose-colored stream. It *was* a silent picture, he was right.

"That's Tahiti. That's an island in the Pacific Ocean."

"That ain't no place you could go, is it? Like a ree-*sort?*"

"You could go there, I suppose. It's very far. People live there . . ."

"Hey, *look*, look here at this one." He flipped back to a page where a young brown-skinned maid was leaning forward on her knees, as though to dry her hair. "Man," the boy said, "that's the fuckin life." The euphoria of his diction would have earned him eternal banishment from the Newark Public Library and its branches had John or Mr. Scapello — or, God forbid, the hospitalized Miss Winney — come to investigate.

"Who took these pictures?" he asked me.

"Gauguin. He didn't take them, he painted them. Paul Gauguin. He was a Frenchman."

"Is he a white man or a colored man?"

"He's white."

"Man," the boy smiled, chuckled almost, "I knew that. He don't *take* pictures like no colored men would. He's a good picture taker . . . *Look, look,* look here at this one. Ain't that the fuckin *life?*"

I agreed it was and left.

Later I sent Jimmy Boylen hopping down the stairs to tell McKee that everything was all right. The rest of the day was uneventful. I sat at the Information Desk thinking about Brenda and reminding myself that that evening I would have to get gas before I started up to Short Hills, which I could see now, in my mind's eye, at dusk, rose-colored, like a Gauguin stream.

When I pulled up to the Patimkin house that night, everybody but Julie was waiting for me on the front porch: Mr. and Mrs., Ron, and Brenda, wearing a dress. I had not seen her in a dress before and for an instant she did not look like the same girl. But that was only half the surprise. So many of those Lincolnesque college girls turn out to be limbed for shorts alone. Not Brenda. She looked, in a dress, as though she'd gone through life so attired, as though she'd never worn shorts, or bathing suits, or pajamas, or anything but that pale linen dress. I walked rather bouncingly up the lawn, past the huge weeping willow, towards the waiting Patimkins, wishing all the while that I'd had my car washed. Before I'd even reached them, Ron stepped forward and shook my hand, vigorously, as though he hadn't seen me since the Diaspora. Mrs. Patimkin smiled and Mr. Patimkin grunted something and continued twitching his wrists before him, then raising an imaginary golf club and driving a ghost of a golf ball up and away towards the Orange Mountains, that are called Orange, I'm convinced, because in that various suburban light that's the *only* color they do not come dressed in.

"We'll be right back," Brenda said to me. "You have to sit with Julie. Carlota's off."

"Okay," I said.

"We're taking Ron to the airport."

"Okay."

"Julie doesn't want to go. She says Ron pushed her in the pool this afternoon. We've been waiting for you, so we don't miss Ron's plane. Okay?"

"*Okay.*"

Mr. and Mrs. Patimkin and Ron moved off, and I flashed Brenda just the hint of a glare. She reached out and took my hand a moment.

"How do you like me?" she said.

"You're great to baby-sit for. Am I allowed all the milk and cake I want?"

"Don't be angry, baby. We'll be right back." Then she waited a moment, and when I failed to deflate the pout from my mouth, she gave *me* a glare, no hints about it. "I *meant* how do you like me in a dress!" Then she ran off towards the Chrysler, trotting in her high heels like a colt.

When I walked into the house, I slammed the screen door behind me.

"Close the other door too," a little voice shouted. "The air-conditioning."

I closed the other door, obediently.

"Neil?" Julie called.

"Yes."

"Hi. Want to play five and two?"

"No."

"Why not?"

I did not answer.

"I'm in the television room," she called.

"Good."

"Are you supposed to stay with me?"

"Yes."

She appeared unexpectedly through the dining room. "Want to read a book report I wrote?"

"Not now."

"What do you want to do?" she said.

"Nothing, honey. Why don't you watch TV?"

"All right," she said disgustedly, and kicked her way back to the television room.

For a while I remained in the hall, bitten with the urge to slide quietly out of the house, into my car, and back to Newark, where I might even sit in the alley and break candy with my own. I felt like Carlota; no, not even as comfortable as that. At last I left the hall and began to stroll in and out of rooms on the first floor. Next to the living room was the study, a small knotty-pine room jammed with cater-cornered leather chairs and a complete set of *Information Please Almanacs*. On the wall hung three colored photo-paintings; they were the kind which, regardless of the subjects, be they vital or infirm, old or youthful, are characterized by bud-cheeks, wet lips, pearly teeth, and shiny, metallized hair. The subjects in this case were Ron, Brenda, and Julie at about ages fourteen, thirteen, and two. Brenda had long auburn hair, her diamond-studded nose, and no glasses; all combined to make her look a regal thirteen-year-old who'd just gotten smoke in her eyes. Ron was rounder and his hairline was lower, but that love of spherical objects and lined courts twinkled in his boyish eyes. Poor little Julie was lost in the photo-painter's Platonic idea of childhood; her tiny humanity was smothered somewhere back of gobs of pink and white.

There were other pictures about, smaller ones, taken with a Brownie Reflex before photo-paintings had become fashionable. There was a tiny picture of Brenda on a horse;

another of Ron in bar mitzvah suit, *yamalkah*, and *tallas*;
and two pictures framed together — one of a beautiful,
faded woman, who must have been, from the eyes, Mrs.
Patimkin's mother, and the other of Mrs. Patimkin herself,
her hair in a halo, her eyes joyous and not those of a
slowly aging mother with a quick and lovely daughter.

I walked through the archway into the dining room and
stood a moment looking out at the sporting goods tree.
From the television room that winged off the dining room,
I could hear Julie listening to *This Is Your Life*. The kitchen, which winged off the other side, was empty, and apparently, with Carlota off, the Patimkins had had dinner
at the club. Mr. and Mrs. Patimkin's bedroom was in the
middle of the house, down the hall, next to Julie's, and
for a moment I wanted to see what size bed those giants
slept in — I imagined it wide and deep as a swimming pool
— but I postponed my investigation while Julie was in the
house, and instead opened the door in the kitchen that
led down to the basement.

The basement had a different kind of coolness from the
house, and it had a smell, which was something the upstairs was totally without. It felt cavernous down there,
but in a comforting way, like the simulated caves children
make for themselves on rainy days, in hall closets, under
blankets, or in between the legs of dining room tables. I
flipped on the light at the foot of the stairs and was not
surprised at the pine paneling, the bamboo furniture, the
ping-pong table, and the mirrored bar that was stocked
with every kind and size of glass, ice bucket, decanter,
mixer, swizzle stick, shot glass, pretzel bowl — all the
bacchanalian paraphernalia, plentiful, orderly, and un-
touched, as it can be only in the bar of a wealthy man who

never entertains drinking people, who himself does not drink, who, in fact, gets a fishy look from his wife when every several months he takes a shot of schnapps before dinner. I went behind the bar where there was an aluminum sink that had not seen a dirty glass, I'm sure, since Ron's bar mitzvah party, and would not see another, probably, until one of the Patimkin children was married or engaged. I would have poured myself a drink — just as a wicked wage for being forced into servantry — but I was uneasy about breaking the label on a bottle of whiskey. You had to break a label to get a drink. On the shelf back of the bar were two dozen bottles — twenty-three to be exact — of Jack Daniels, each with a little booklet tied to its collared neck informing patrons how patrician of them it was to drink the stuff. And over the Jack Daniels were more photos: there was a blown-up newspaper photo of Ron palming a basketball in one hand like a raisin; under the picture it said, "*Center*, Ronald Patimkin, Millburn High School, 6′4″, 217 pounds." And there was another picture of Brenda on a horse, and next to that, a velvet mounting board with ribbons and medals clipped to it: Essex County Horse Show 1949, Union County Horse Show 1950, Garden State Fair 1952, Morristown Horse Show 1953, and so on — all for Brenda, for jumping and running or galloping or whatever else young girls receive ribbons for. In the entire house I hadn't seen one picture of Mr. Patimkin.

The rest of the basement, back of the wide pine-paneled room, was gray cement walls and linoleum floor and contained innumerable electrical appliances, including a freezer big enough to house a family of Eskimos. Beside the freezer, incongruously, was a tall old refrigerator; its ancient presence was a reminder to me of the Patimkin roots in Newark. This same refrigerator had once stood in the kitchen of an apartment in some four-family house, probably in the same neighborhood where I had lived all my life, first with my parents and then, when the two of them went wheezing off to Arizona, with my aunt and uncle. After Pearl Harbor the refrigerator had made the move up to Short Hills; Patimkin Kitchen and Bathroom Sinks had gone to war: no new barracks was complete until it had a squad of Patimkin sinks lined up in its latrine.

I opened the door of the old refrigerator; it was not empty. No longer did it hold butter, eggs, herring in cream sauce, ginger ale, tuna fish salad, an occasional corsage — rather it was heaped with fruit, shelves swelled with it, every color, every texture, and hidden within, every kind of pit. There were greengage plums, black plums, red plums, apricots, nectarines, peaches, long horns of grapes, black, yellow, red, and cherries, cherries flowing out of boxes and staining everything scarlet. And there were melons — cantaloupes and honeydews — and on the top shelf, half of a huge watermelon, a thin sheet of wax paper clinging to its bare red face like a wet lip. Oh Patimkin! Fruit grew in their refrigerator and sporting goods dropped from their trees!

I grabbed a handful of cherries and then a nectarine, and I bit right down to its pit.

"You better wash that or you'll get diarrhea."

Julie was standing behind me in the pine-paneled room. She was wearing *her* Bermudas and *her* white polo shirt which was unlike Brenda's only in that it had a little dietary history of its own.

"What?" I said.

"They're not washed yet," Julie said, and in such a way that it seemed to place the refrigerator itself out-of-bounds, if only for me.

"That's all right," I said, and devoured the nectarine and put the pit in my pocket and stepped out of the refrigerator room, all in one second. I still didn't know what to do with the cherries. "I was just looking around," I said.

Julie didn't answer.

"Where's Ron going?" I asked, dropping the cherries into my pocket, among my keys and change.

"Milwaukee."

"For long?"

"To see Harriet. They're in love."

We looked at each other for longer than I could bear. "Harriet?" I asked.

"Yes."

Julie was looking at me as though she were trying to look behind me, and then I realized that I was standing with my hands out of sight. I brought them around to the front, and, I swear it, she did peek to see if they were empty.

We confronted one another again; she seemed to have a threat in her face.

Then she spoke. "Want to play ping-pong?"

"God, yes," I said, and made for the table with two long, bounding steps. "You can serve."

Julie smiled and we began to play.

I have no excuses to offer for what happened next. I began to win and I liked it.

"Can I take that one over?" Julie said. "I hurt my finger yesterday and it just hurt when I served."

"No."

I continued to win.

"That wasn't fair, Neil. My shoelace came untied. Can I take it —"

"No."

We played, I ferociously.

"Neil, you leaned over the table. That's illegal —"

"I didn't lean and it's not illegal."

I felt the cherries hopping among my nickels and pennies.

"Neil, you gypped me out of a point. You have nineteen and I have eleven —"

"Twenty and *ten*," I said. "Serve!"

She did and I smashed my return past her — it zoomed off the table and skittered into the refrigerator room.

"You're a cheater!" she screamed at me. "You cheat!" Her jaw was trembling as though she carried a weight on top of her pretty head. "*I hate* you!" And she threw her racket across the room and it clanged off the bar, just as, outside, I heard the Chrysler crushing gravel in the driveway.

"The game isn't over," I said to her.

"You cheat! And you were stealing fruit!" she said, and ran away before I had my chance to win.

Later that night, Brenda and I made love, our first time. We were sitting on the sofa in the television room and for some ten minutes had not spoken a word to each other. Julie had long since gone to a weepy bed, and though no one had said anything to me about her crying, I did not know if the child had mentioned my fistful of cherries, which, some time before, I had flushed down the toilet.

The television set was on and though the sound was off and the house quiet, the gray pictures still wiggled at the far end of the room. Brenda was quiet and her dress circled her legs, which were tucked back beneath her. We sat there for some while and did not speak. Then she went into the kitchen and when she came back she said that it sounded as though everyone was asleep. We sat a while longer, watching the soundless bodies on the screen eating a silent dinner in someone's silent restaurant. When I began to unbutton her dress she resisted me, and I like to think it was because she knew how lovely she looked in it. But she looked lovely, my Brenda, anyway, and we folded it carefully and held each other close and soon there we were, Brenda falling, slowly but with a smile, and me rising.

How can I describe loving Brenda? It was so sweet, as though I'd finally scored that twenty-first point.

When I got home I dialed Brenda's number, but not before my aunt heard and rose from her bed.

"Who are you calling at this hour? The doctor?"

"No."

"What kind phone calls, one o'clock at night?"

"Shhh!" I said.

"He tells *me* shhh. Phone calls one o'clock at night, we haven't got a big enough bill," and then she dragged herself back into the bed, where with a martyr's heart and bleary eyes she had resisted the downward tug of sleep until she'd heard my key in the door.

Brenda answered the phone.

"Neil?" she said.

"Yes," I whispered. "You didn't get out of bed, did you?"

"No," she said. "the phone is next to the bed."

"Good. How is it in bed?"

"Good. Are you in bed?"

"Yes," I lied, and tried to right myself by dragging the phone by its cord as close as I could to my bedroom.

"I'm in bed with you," she said.

"That's right," I said, "and I'm with you."

"I have the shades down, so it's dark and I don't see you."

"I don't see you either."

"That was so nice, Neil."

"Yes. Go to sleep, sweet, I'm here," and we hung up without goodbyes. In the morning, as planned, I called again, but I could hardly hear Brenda or myself for that matter, for Aunt Gladys and Uncle Max were going on a Workmen's Circle picnic in the afternoon, and there was some trouble about grape juice that had dripped all night from a jug in the refrigerator and by morning had leaked out onto the floor. Brenda was still in bed and so could play our game with some success, but I had to pull down all the shades of my senses to imagine myself beside her. I could only pray our nights and mornings would come, and soon enough they did.

4

Over the next week and a half there seemed to be only two people in my life: Brenda and the little colored kid who liked Gauguin. Every morning before the library opened, the boy was waiting; sometimes he seated himself on the lion's back, sometimes under his belly, sometimes he just stood around throwing pebbles at his mane. Then he would come inside, tap around the main floor until Otto stared him up on tiptoes, and finally headed up the long marble stairs that led to Tahiti. He did not always stay to

lunch time, but one very hot day he was there when I arrived in the morning and went through the door behind
me when I left at night. The next morning, it was, that
he did not show up, and as though in his place, a very old
man appeared, white, smelling of Life Savers, his nose and
jowls showing erupted veins beneath them. "Could you
tell me where I'd find the art section?"

"Stack Three," I said.

In a few minutes, he returned with a big brown-covered
book in his hand. He placed it on my desk, withdrew his
card from a long moneyless billfold and waited for me to
stamp out the book.

"Do you want to take this book *out*?" I said.

He smiled.

I took his card and jammed the metal edge into the
machine; but I did not stamp down. "Just a minute," I
said. I took a clipboard from under the desk and flipped
through a few pages, upon which were games of battleship
and tick-tack-toe that I'd been playing through the week
with myself. "I'm afraid there's a hold on this book."

"A what?"

"A hold. Someone's called up and asked that we hold
it for them. Can I take your name and address and drop
a card when it's free . . ."

And so I was able, not without flushing once or twice, to
get the book back in the stacks. When the colored kid
showed up later in the day, it was just where he'd left it the
afternoon before.

As for Brenda, I saw her every evening and when there
was not a night game that kept Mr. Patimkin awake and
in the TV room, or a Hadassah card party that sent Mrs.
Patimkin out of the house and brought her in at unpre-

dictable hours, we made love before the silent screen. One muggy, low-skied night Brenda took me swimming at the club. We were the only ones in the pool, and all the chairs, the cabañas, the lights, the diving boards, the very water seemed to exist only for our pleasure. She wore a blue suit that looked purple in the lights and down beneath the water it flashed sometimes green, sometimes black. Late in the evening a breeze came up off the golf course and we wrapped ourselves in one huge towel, pulled two chaise longues together, and despite the bartender, who was doing considerable pacing back and forth by the bar window, which overlooked the pool, we rested side by side on the chairs. Finally the bar light itself flipped off, and then, in a snap, the lights around the pool went down and out. My heart must have beat faster, or something, for Brenda seemed to guess my sudden doubt — *we should go,* I thought.

She said: "That's okay."

It was very dark, the sky was low and starless, and it took a while for me to see, once again, the diving board a shade lighter than the night, and to distinguish the water from the chairs that surrounded the far side of the pool.

I pushed the straps of her bathing suit down but she said no and rolled an inch away from me, and for the first time in the two weeks I'd known her she asked me a question about me.

"Where are your parents?" she said.

"Tucson," I said. "Why?"

"My mother asked me."

I could see the life guard's chair now, white almost.

"Why are you still here? Why aren't you with them?" she asked.

"I'm not a child any more, Brenda," I said, more sharply than I'd intended. "I just can't go wherever my parents are."

"But then why do you stay with your aunt and uncle?"

"They're not my parents."

"They're better?"

"No. Worse. I don't *know* why I stay with them."

"Why?" she said.

"Why don't I know?"

"Why do you stay? You do know, don't you?"

"My job, I suppose. It's convenient from there, and it's cheap, and it pleases my parents. My aunt's all right really ... Do I really have to explain to your mother why I live where I do?"

"It's not for my mother. I want to know. I wondered why you weren't with your parents, that's all."

"Are you cold?" I asked.

"No."

"Do you want to go home?"

"No, not unless you do. Don't you feel well, Neil?"

"I feel all right," and to let her know that I was still me, I held her to me, though that moment I was without desire.

"Neil?"

"What?"

"What about the library?"

"Who wants to know that?"

"My father," she laughed.

"And you?"

She did not answer a moment. "And me," she said finally.

"Well, what about it? Do I like it? It's okay. I sold shoes once and like the library better. After the Army they tried me for a couple months at Uncle Aaron's real estate company — Doris' father — and I like the library better than that..."

"How did you get a job *there?*"

"I worked there for a little while when I was in college, then when I quit Uncle Aaron's, oh, I don't know..."

"What did you take in college?"

"At Newark Colleges of Rutgers University I majored in philosophy. I am twenty-three years old. I—"

"Why do you sound nasty again?"

"Do I?"

"Yes."

I didn't say I was sorry.

"Are you planning on making a career of the library?"

"Bren, I'm not planning anything. I haven't planned a thing in three years. At least for the year I've been out of the Army. In the Army I used to plan to go away weekends. I'm — I'm not a planner." After all the truth I'd suddenly given her, I shouldn't have ruined it for myself with that final lie. I added, "I'm a liver."

"I'm a pancreas," she said.

"I'm a—"

And she kissed the absurd game away; she wanted to be serious.

"Do you love me, Neil?"

I did not answer.

"I'll sleep with you whether you do or not, so tell me the truth."

"That was pretty crude."

"Don't be prissy," she said.

"No, I mean a crude thing to say about me."

"I don't understand," she said, and she didn't, and that

she didn't pained me; I allowed myself the minor subter-
fuge, however, of forgiving Brenda her obtuseness. "Do
you?" she said.

"No."

"I want you to."

"What about the library?"

"What about it?" she said.

Was it obtuseness again? I thought not — and it wasn't,
for Brenda said, "When you love me, there'll be nothing
to worry about."

"Then of course I'll love you." I smiled.

"I know you will," she said. "Why don't you go in the
water, and I'll wait for you and close my eyes, and when
you come back you'll surprise me with the wet. Go
ahead."

"You like games, don't you?"

"Go ahead. I'll close my eyes."

I walked down to the edge of the pool and dove in. The
water felt colder than it had earlier, and when I broke
through and was headed blindly down I felt a touch of
panic. At the top again, I started to swim the length of the
pool and then turned at the end and started back, but suddenly I was sure that when I left the water Brenda would
be gone. I'd be alone in this damn place. I started for the
side and pulled myself up and ran to the chairs and
Brenda was there and I kissed her.

"God," she shivered, "You didn't stay long."

"I know."

"My turn," she said, and then she was up and a second
later I heard a little crack of water and then nothing.
Nothing for quite a while.

"Bren," I called softly, "are you all right?" but no one
answered.

I found her glasses on the chair beside me and held them
in my hands. "Brenda?"

Nothing.

"Brenda?"

"No fair calling," she said and gave me her drenched
self. "Your turn," she said.

This time I stayed below the water for a long while and
when I surfaced again my lungs were ready to pop. I threw
my head back for air and above me saw the sky, low like a
hand pushing down, and I began to swim as though to
move out from under its pressure. I wanted to get back to
Brenda, for I worried once again — and there was no evi-
dence, was there? — that if I stayed away too long she
would not be there when I returned. I wished that I had
carried her glasses away with me, so she would have to wait
for me to lead her back home. I was having crazy thoughts,
I knew, and yet they did not seem uncalled for in the darkness and strangeness of that place. Oh how I wanted to
call out to her from the pool, but I knew she would not
answer and I forced myself to swim the length a third
time, and then a fourth, but midway through the fifth I
felt a weird fright again, had momentary thoughts of my
own extinction, and that time when I came back I held her
tighter than either of us expected.

"Let go, let go," she laughed, "my turn — "

"But Brenda — "

But Brenda was gone and this time it seemed as though
she'd never come back. I settled back and waited for the
sun to dawn over the ninth hole, prayed it would if only
for the comfort of its light, and when Brenda finally returned to me I would not let her go, and her cold wetness
crept into me somehow and made me shiver. "That's it,
Brenda. Please, no more games," I said, and then when I

spoke again I held her so tightly I almost dug my body into hers, "I love you," I said, "I do."

So the summer went on. I saw Brenda every evening: we went swimming, we went for walks, we went for rides, up through the mountains so far and so long that by the time we started back the fog had begun to emerge from the trees and push out into the road, and I would tighten my hands on the wheel and Brenda would put on her glasses and watch the white line for me. And we would eat — a few nights after my discovery of the fruit refrigerator Brenda led me to it herself. We would fill huge soup bowls with cherries, and in serving dishes for roast beef we would heap slices of watermelon. Then we would go up and out the back doorway of the basement and onto the back lawn and sit under the sporting-goods tree, the light from the TV room the only brightness we had out there. All we would hear for a while were just the two of us spitting pits. "I wish they would take root overnight and in the morning there'd just be watermelons and cherries."

"If they took root in this yard, sweetie, they'd grow refrigerators and Westinghouse Preferred. I'm not being nasty," I'd add quickly, and Brenda would laugh, and say she felt like a greengage plum, and I would disappear down into the basement and the cherry bowl would now be a greengage plum bowl, and then a nectarine bowl, and then a peach bowl, until, I have to admit it, I cracked my frail bowel, and would have to spend the following night, sadly, on the wagon. And then too we went out for corned beef sandwiches, pizza, beer and shrimp, ice cream sodas, and hamburgers. We went to the Lions Club Fair one night and Brenda won a Lions Club ashtray by shooting three baskets in a row. And when Ron came home from Milwaukee we went from time to time to see him play basketball in the semi-pro summer league, and it was those evenings that I felt a stranger with Brenda, for she knew all the players' names, and though for the most part they were gawky-limbed and dull, there was one named Luther Ferrari who was neither, and whom Brenda had dated for a whole year in high school. He was Ron's closest friend and I remembered his name from the Newark *News*: he was one of the great Ferrari brothers, All State all of them in at least two sports. It was Ferrari who called Brenda Buck, a nickname which apparently went back to her ribbon-winning days. Like Ron, Ferrari was exceedingly polite, as though it were some affliction of those over six feet three; he was gentlemanly towards me and gentle towards Brenda, and after a while I balked when the suggestion was made that we go to see Ron play. And then one night we discovered that at eleven o'clock the cashier of the Hilltop Theatre went home and the manager disappeared into his office, and so that summer we saw the last quarter of at least fifteen movies, and then when we were driving home — driving Brenda home, that is — we would try to reconstruct the beginnings of the films. Our favorite last quarter of a movie was *Ma and Pa Kettle in the City*, our favorite fruit, greengage plums, and our favorite, our only, people, each other. Of course we ran into others from time to time, some of Brenda's friends, and occasionally, one or two of mine. One night in August we even went to a bar out on Route 6 with Laura Simpson Stolowitch and her fiancé, but it was a dreary evening. Brenda and I seemed untrained in talking to others, and so we danced a great deal, which we realized was one thing we'd never done before. Laura's boyfriend drank stingers pompously and Simp — Brenda wanted me to call her Stolo but I didn't — Simp drank a tepid combination of something like ginger ale and soda. Whenever we returned to the table, Simp would be talking about "the dance" and her fiancé about "the film," until finally Brenda asked him "Which film?" and then we danced till closing time. And when we went back to Brenda's we filled a bowl with cherries which we carried into the TV room and ate sloppily for a while; and later, on the sofa, we loved each other and when I moved from the darkened room to the bathroom I could always feel cherry pits against my bare soles. At home, undressing for the second time that night, I would find red marks on the undersides of my feet.

And how did her parents take all of this? Mrs. Patimkin continued to smile at me and Mr. Patimkin continued to think I ate like a bird. When invited to dinner I would, for his benefit, eat twice what I wanted, but the truth seemed to be that after he'd characterized my appetite that first time, he never really bothered to look again. I might have eaten ten times my normal amount, have finally killed myself with food, he would still have considered me not a man but a sparrow. No one seemed distressed by my presence, though Julie had cooled considerably; consequently, when Brenda suggested to her father that at the end of August I spend a week of my vacation at the Patimkin house, he pondered a moment, decided on the five iron, made his approach shot, and said yes. And when she passed on to her mother the decision of Patimkin Sink, there wasn't much Mrs. Patimkin could do. So, through Brenda's craftiness, I was invited.

On that Friday morning that was to be my last day of work, my Aunt Gladys saw me packing my bag and she

asked where I was going. I told her. She did not answer
and I thought I saw awe in those red-rimmed hysterical
eyes — I had come a long way since that day she'd said to
me on the phone, "Fancy-shmancy."

"How long you going, I should know how to shop I
wouldn't buy too much. You'll leave me with a refrigerator full of milk it'll go bad it'll stink up the refrigerator —"

"A week," I said.

"A *week?*" she said. "They got room for a week?"

"Aunt Gladys, they don't live over the store."

"I lived over a store I wasn't ashamed. Thank God we
always had a roof. We never went begging in the streets,"
she told me as I packed the Bermudas I'd just bought, "and
your cousin Susan we'll put through college, Uncle Max
should live and be well. We didn't send her away to camp
for August, she doesn't have shoes when she wants them,
sweaters she doesn't have a drawerful — "

"I didn't say anything, Aunt Gladys."

"You don't get enough to eat here? You leave over sometimes I show your Uncle Max your plate it's a shame. A
child in Europe could make a four-course meal from what
you leave over."

"Aunt Gladys." I went over to her. "I get everything I
want here. I'm just taking a vacation. Don't I deserve a
vacation?"

She held herself to me and I could feel her trembling.
"I told your mother I would take care of her Neil she
shouldn't worry. And now you go running — "

I put my arms around her and kissed her on the top of
her head. "C'mon," I said, "you're being silly. I'm not
running away. I'm just going away for a week, on a vacation."

"You'll leave their telephone number God forbid you should get sick."

"Okay."

"Millburn they live?"

"Short Hills. I'll leave the number."

"Since when do Jewish people live in Short Hills? They couldn't be real Jews believe me."

"They're real Jews," I said.

"I'll see it I'll believe it." She wiped her eyes with the corner of her apron, just as I was zipping up the sides of the suitcase. "Don't close the bag yet. I'll make a little package with some fruit in it, you'll take with you."

"Okay, Aunt Gladys," and on the way to work that morning I ate the orange and the two peaches that she'd put in a bag for me.

A few hours later Mr. Scapello informed me that when I returned from my vacation after Labor Day, I would be hoisted up onto Martha Winney's stool. He himself, he said, had made the same move some twelve years ago, and so it appeared that if I could manage to maintain my balance I might someday be Mr. Scapello. I would also get an eight-dollar increase in salary which was five dollars more than the increase Mr. Scapello had received years before. He shook my hand and then started back up the long flight of marble stairs, his behind barging against his suit jacket like a hoop. No sooner had he left my side then I smelled spearmint and looked up to see the old man with veiny nose and jowls.

"Hello, young man," he said pleasantly. "Is the book back?"

"What book?"

"The Gauguin. I was shopping and I thought I'd stop

by to ask. I haven't gotten the card yet. It's two weeks
already."

"No," I said, and as I spoke I saw that Mr. Scapello had
stopped midway up the stairs and turned as though he'd
forgotten to tell me something. "Look," I said to the old
man, "it should be back any day." I said it with a finality
that bordered on rudeness, and I alarmed myself, for suddenly I saw what would happen: the old man making a
fuss, Mr. Scapello gliding down the stairs, Mr. Scapello
scampering up to the stacks, Scapello scandalized, Scapello
profuse, Scapello presiding at the ascension of John Mc-
Kee to Miss Winney's stool. I turned to the old man,
"Why don't you leave your phone number and I'll try to
get a hold of it this afternoon —" but my attempt at concern and courtesy came too late, and the man growled
some words about public servants, a letter to the Mayor,
snotty kids, and left the library, thank God, only a second
before Mr. Scapello returned to my desk to remind me that
everyone was chipping in for a present for Miss Winney
and that if I liked I should leave a half dollar on his desk
during the day.

After lunch the colored kid came in. When he headed
past the desk for the stairs, I called over to him. "Come
here," I said. "Where are you going?"

"The heart section."

"What book are you reading?"

"That Mr. Go-again's book. Look, man, I ain't doing
nothing wrong. I didn't do *no* writing in *any*thing. You
could search me —"

"I know you didn't. Listen, if you like that book so much
why don't you please take it home? Do you have a library
card?"

"No, sir, I didn't take *nothing*."

"No, a library card is what we give to you so you can take books home. Then you won't have to come down here every day. Do you go to school?"

"Yes, sir. Miller Street School. But this here's summertime. It's okay I'm not in school. I ain't *supposed* to be in school."

"I know. As long as you go to school you can *have* a library card. You could take the book home."

"What you keep telling me take that book home for? At home somebody dee-*stroy* it."

"You could hide it someplace, in a desk — "

"Man," he said, squinting at me, "why don't you want me to come round here?"

"I didn't say you shouldn't."

"I *likes* to come here. I likes them stairs."

"I like them too," I said. "But the trouble is that someday somebody's going to take that book out."

He smiled. "Don't you worry," he said to me. "Ain't nobody done that yet," and he tapped off to the stairs and Stack Three.

Did I perspire that day! It was the coolest of the summer, but when I left work in the evening my shirt was sticking to my back. In the car I opened my bag, and while the rush-hour traffic flowed down Washington Street, I huddled in the back and changed into a clean shirt so that when I reached Short Hills I'd look as though I was deserving of an interlude in the suburbs. But driving up Central Avenue I could not keep my mind on my vacation, or for that matter on my driving: to the distress of pedestrians and motorists, I ground gears, overshot crosswalks, hesitated at green and red lights alike. I kept thinking that while I was on vacation that jowly bastard would return to the library, that the colored kid's book would disappear, that my new job would be taken away from me, that, in fact my old job — but then why should I worry about all that: the library wasn't going to be *my* life.

5

"Ron's getting married!" Julie screamed at me when I came through the door. "Ron's getting married!"

"Now?" I said.

"Labor Day! He's marrying Harriet, he's marrying Harriet." She began to sing it like a jump-rope song, nasal and rhythmic. "I'm going to be a sister-in-law!"

"Hi," Brenda said, "I'm going to be a sister-in-law."

"So I hear. When did it happen?"

"This afternoon he told us. They spoke long distance for forty minutes last night. She's flying here next week, and there's going to be a *huge* wedding. My parents are flittering all over the place. They've got to arrange everything in about a day or two. And my father's taking Ron in the business — but he's going to have to start at two hundred a week and then work himself up. That'll take till October."

"I thought he was going to be a gym teacher."

"He was. But now he has responsibilities . . ."

And at dinner Ron expanded on the subject of responsibilities and the future.

"We're going to have a boy," he said, to his mother's delight, "and when he's about six months old I'm going to sit him down with a basketball in front of him, and a football, and a baseball, and then whichever one he reaches for, that's the one we're going to concentrate on."

"Suppose he doesn't reach for any of them," Brenda said.

"Don't be funny, young lady," Mrs. Patimkin said.

"I'm going to be an aunt," Julie sang, and she stuck her tongue out at Brenda.

"When is Harriet coming?" Mr. Patimkin breathed through a mouthful of potatoes.

"A week from yesterday."

"Can she sleep in my room?" Julie cried. *"Can* she?"

"No, the guest room — " Mrs. Patimkin began, but then she remembered me — with a crushing side glance from those purple eyes, and said, "Of course."

Well, I did eat like a bird. After dinner my bag was carried — by me — up to the guest room which was across from Ron's room and right down the hall from Brenda. Brenda came along to show me the way.

"Let me see your bed, Bren."

"Later," she said.

"Can we? Up here?"

"I think so," she said. "Ron sleeps like a log."

"Can I stay the night?"

"I don't know."

"I could get up early and come back in here. We'll set the alarm."

"It'll wake everybody up."

"I'll remember to get up. I can do it."

"I better not stay up here with you too long," she said. "My mother'll have a fit. I think she's nervous about your being here."

"So am I. I hardly know them. Do you think I should really stay a whole week?"

"A whole week? Once Harriet gets here it'll be so chaotic you can probably stay two months."

"You think so?"

"Yes."

"Do you want me to?"

"Yes," she said, and went down the stairs so as to ease her mother's conscience.

I unpacked my bag and dropped my clothes into a drawer that was empty except for a packet of dress shields and a high school yearbook. In the middle of my unpacking, Ron came clunking up the stairs.

"Hi," he called into my room.

"Congratulations," I called back. I should have realized that any word of ceremony would provoke a handshake from Ron; he interrupted whatever it was he was about to do in his room, and came into mine.

"Thanks." He pumped me. "Thanks."

Then he sat down on my bed and watched me as I finished unpacking. I have one shirt with a Brooks Brothers label and I let it linger on the bed a while; the Arrows I heaped in the drawer. Ron sat there rubbing his forearm and grinning. After a while I was thoroughly unsettled by the silence.

"Well," I said, "that's something."

He agreed, to *what* I don't know.

"How does it feel?" I asked, after another longer silence.

"Better. Ferrari smacked it under the boards."

"Oh. Good," I said. "How does getting married feel?"

"Ah, okay, I guess."

I leaned against the bureau and counted stitches in the carpet.

Ron finally risked a journey into language. "Do you know anything about music?" he asked.

"Something, yes."

"You can listen to my phonograph if you want."

"Thanks, Ron. I didn't know you were interested in music.

"Sure. I got all the Andre Kostelanetz records ever made. You like Mantovani? I got all of him too. I like semi-classical a lot. You can hear my Columbus record if you want..." he dwindled off. Finally he shook my hand and left.

Downstairs I could hear Julie singing. "I'm going to be an a-a-aunt," and Mrs. Patimkin saying to her, "No, honey, you're going to be a sister-in-law. Sing that, sweetheart," but Julie continued to sing, "I'm going to be an a-a-aunt," and then I heard Brenda's voice joining hers, singing, "We're going to be an a-a-aunt," and then Julie joined that, and finally Mrs. Patimkin called to Mr. Patimkin, "Will you make her stop encouraging her..." and soon the duet ended.

And then I heard Mrs. Patimkin again. I couldn't make out the words but Brenda answered her. Their voices grew louder; finally I could hear perfectly. "I need a houseful of company at a time like this?" It was Mrs. Patimkin. "I asked you, Mother." "You asked your father. I'm the one you should have asked first. He doesn't know how much extra work this is for me..." "My God, Mother, you'd think we didn't have Carlota and Jenny." "Carlota and Jenny can't do everything. This is not the Salvation Army!" "What the hell does that mean?" "Watch your tongue, young lady. That may be very well for your college friends." "Oh, *stop* it, Mother!" "Don't raise your voice to me. When's the last time you lifted a finger to help around here?" "I'm not a slave ... I'm a daughter." "You ought to learn what a day's work means." "Why?" Brenda said. "*Why?*" "Because you're lazy,"

Mrs. Patimkin answered, "and you think the world owes you a living." "Whoever said *that?*" "You ought to earn some money and buy your own clothes." "Why? Good God, Mother, Daddy could live off the stocks alone, for God's sake. What are you complaining about?" "When's the last time you washed the dishes!" "Jesus Christ!" Brenda flared, "Carlota washes the dishes!" "Don't Jesus Christ me!" "Oh, Mother!" and Brenda was crying. "Why the hell are you like this!" "That's it," Mrs. Patimkin said "cry in front of your company..." "My *company* . . ." Brenda wept, "why don't you go yell at him too . . . why is everyone so nasty to me . . ."

From across the hall I heard Andre Kostelanetz let several thousand singing violins loose on "Night and Day." Ron's door was open and I saw he was stretched out, colossal, on his bed; he was singing along with the record. The words belonged to "Night and Day," but I didn't recognize Ron's tune. In a minute he picked up the phone and asked the operator for a Milwaukee number. While she connected him, he rolled over and turned up the volume on the record player, so that it would carry the nine hundred miles west.

I heard Julie downstairs. "Ha ha, Brenda's crying, ha ha, Brenda's crying."

And then Brenda was running up the stairs. "Your day'll come, you little bastard!" she called.

"*Brenda!*" Mrs. Patimkin called.

"*Mommy!*" Julie cried. "Brenda cursed at me!"

"What's going *on* here!" Mr. Patimkin shouted.

"You call *me*, Mrs. P?" Carlota shouted.

And Ron, in the other room, said, "Hello, Har, I told them . . ."

I sat down on my Brooks Brothers shirt and pronounced my own name out loud.

"Goddam her!" Brenda said to me as she paced up and down my room.

"Bren, do you think I should go — "

"Shhh..." She went to the door of my room and listened. "They're going visiting, thank God."

"Brenda — "

"Shhh ... They've gone."

"Julie too?"

"Yes," she said. "Is Ron in his room? His door is closed."

"He went out."

"You can't hear anybody move around here. They all creep around in *sneakers*. Oh Neil."

"Bren, I asked you, maybe I should just stay through tomorrow and then go."

"Oh, it isn't you she's angry about."

"I'm not helping any."

"It's Ron, really. That he's getting married just has her flipped. And me. Now with that goody-good Harriet around she'll just forget I ever exist."

"Isn't that okay with you?"

She walked off to the window and looked outside. It was dark and cool; the trees rustled and flapped as though they were sheets that had been hung out to dry. Everything outside hinted at September, and for the first time I realized how close we were to Brenda's departure for school.

"Is it, Bren?" but she was not listening to me.

She walked across the room to a door at the far end of the room. She opened it.

"I thought that was a closet," I said.

"Come here."

She held the door back and we leaned into the darkness and could hear the strange wind hissing in the eaves of the house.

"What's in here?" I said.

"Money."

Brenda went into the room. When the puny sixty-watt bulb was twisted on, I saw that the place was full of old furniture — two wing chairs with hair-oil lines at the back, a sofa with a paunch in its middle, a bridge table, two bridge chairs with their stuffing showing, a mirror whose backing had peeled off, shadeless lamps, lampless shades, a coffee table with a cracked glass top, and a pile of rolled up shades.

"What is this?" I said.

"A storeroom. Our old furniture."

"How old?"

"From Newark," she said. "Come here." She was on her hands and knees in front of the sofa and was holding up its paunch to peek beneath.

"Brenda, what the hell are we doing here? You're getting filthy."

"It's not here."

"*What?*"

"The money. I told you."

I sat down on a wing chair, raising some dust. It had begun to rain outside, and we could smell the fall dampness coming through the vent that was outlined at the far end of the storeroom. Brenda got up from the floor and sat down on the sofa. Her knees and Bermudas were dirty and when she pushed her hair back she dirtied her forehead. There among the disarrangement and dirt I had the strange experience of seeing us, *both* of us, placed among disarrangement and dirt: we looked like a young couple who had just moved into a new apartment; we had suddenly taken stock of our furniture, finances, and future, and all we could feel any pleasure about was the clean smell of outside, which reminded us we were alive, but which, in a pinch, would not feed us.

"What money?" I said again.

"The hundred-dollar bills. From when I was a little girl . . ." and she breathed deeply. "When I was little and we'd just moved from Newark, my father took me up here one day. He took me into this room and told me that if anything should ever happen to him, he wanted me to know where there was some money that I should have. He said it wasn't for anybody else but me, and that I should never tell anyone about it, not even Ron. Or my mother."

"How much was it?"

"Three hundred-dollar bills. I'd never seen them before. I was nine, around Julie's age. I don't think we'd been living here a month. I remember I used to come up here about once a week, when no one was home but Carlota, and crawl under the sofa and make sure it was still here. And it always was. He never mentioned it once again. Never."

"Where is it? Maybe someone stole it."

"I don't know, Neil. I suppose he took it back."

"When it was gone," I said, "my God, didn't you tell him? Maybe Carlota — "

"I never knew it was gone, until just now. I guess I stopped looking at one time or another . . . And then I forgot about it. Or just didn't think about it. I mean I always had enough, I didn't need this. I guess one day *he* figured I wouldn't need it."

Brenda paced up to the narrow, dust-covered window and drew her initials on it.

"Why did you want it now?" I said.

"I don't know..." she said and went over and twisted the bulb off.

I didn't move from the chair and Brenda, in her tight shorts and shirt, seemed naked standing there a few feet away. Then I saw her shoulders shaking. "I wanted to find it and tear it up in little pieces and put the goddam pieces in her purse! If it was there, I swear it, I would have done it."

"I wouldn't have let you, Bren."

"Wouldn't you have?"

"No."

"Make love to me, Neil. Right now."

"Where?"

"Do it! *Here.* On this cruddy cruddy cruddy sofa."

And I obeyed her.

The next morning Brenda made breakfast for the two of us. Ron had gone off to his first day of work — I'd heard him singing in the shower only an hour after I'd returned to my own room; in fact, I had still been awake when the Chrysler had pulled out of the garage, carrying boss and son down to the Patimkin works in Newark. Mrs. Patimkin wasn't home either; she had taken her car and had gone off to the Temple to talk to Rabbi Kranitz about the wedding. Julie was on the back lawn playing at helping Carlota hang the clothes.

"You know what I want to do this morning?" Brenda said. We were eating a grapefruit, sharing it rather sloppily, for Brenda couldn't find a paring knife, and so we'd decided to peel it down like an orange and eat the segments separately.

"What?" I said.

"Run," she said. "Do you ever run?"

"You mean on a track? God, yes. In high school we had to run a mile every month. So we wouldn't be Momma's boys. I think the bigger your lungs get the more you're supposed to hate your mother."

"I want to run," she said, "and I want you to run. Okay?"

"Oh, Brenda..."

But an hour later, after a breakfast that consisted of another grapefruit, which apparently is all a runner is supposed to eat in the morning, we had driven the Volkswagen over to the high school, behind which was a quarter-mile track. Some kids were playing with a dog out in the grassy center of the track, and at the far end, near the woods, a figure in white shorts with slits in the side, and no shirt, was twirling, twirling, and then flinging a shot put as far as he could. After it left his hand he did a little eagle-eyed tap dance while he watched it arch and bend and land in the distance.

"You know," Brenda said, "you look like me. Except bigger."

We were dressed similarly, sneakers, sweat socks, khaki Bermudas, and sweat shirts, but I had the feeling that Brenda was not talking about the accidents of our dress — if they were accidents. She meant, I was sure, that I was somehow beginning to look the way she wanted me to. Like herself.

"Let's see who's faster," she said, and then we started along the track. Within the first eighth of a mile the three little boys and their dog were following us. As we passed the corner where the shot putter was, he waved at us; Brenda called "Hi!" and I smiled, which, as you may or may not know, makes one engaged in serious running feel inordinately silly. At the quarter mile the kids dropped off and retired to the grass, the dog turned and started the other way, and I had a tiny knife in my side. Still I was abreast of Brenda, who as we started on the second lap, called "Hi!" once again to the lucky shot putter, who was reclining on the grass now, watching us, and rubbing his shot like a crystal ball. Ah, I thought, there's the sport.

"How about us throwing the shot put?" I panted.

"After," she said, and I saw beads of sweat clinging to the last strands of hair that shagged off her ear. When we approached the half mile Brenda suddenly swerved off the track onto the grass and tumbled down; her departure surprised me and I was still running.

"Hey, Bob Mathias," she called, "let's lie in the sun . . ."

But I acted as though I didn't hear her and though my heart pounded in my throat and my mouth was dry as a drought, I made my legs move, and swore I would not stop until I'd finished one more lap. As I passed the shot putter for the third time, I called "Hi!"

She was excited when I finally pulled up alongside of her. "You're good," she said. My hands were on my hips and I was looking at the ground and sucking air — rather, air was sucking me, I didn't have much to say about it.

"Uh-huh," I breathed.

"Let's do this every morning," she said. "We'll get up and have two grapefruit, and then you'll come out here and run. I'll time you. In two weeks you'll break four minutes, won't you, sweetie? I'll get Ron's stop watch." She was so excited — she'd slid over on the grass and was pushing my socks up against my wet ankles and calves. She bit my kneecap.

"Okay," I said.

"Then we'll go back and have a real breakfast."

"Okay."

"You drive back," she said, and suddenly she was up and running ahead of me, and then we were headed back in the car.

And the next morning, my mouth still edgy from the grapefruit segments, we were at the track. We had Ron's stop watch and a towel for me, for when I was finished.

"My legs are a little sore," I said.

"Do some exercises," Brenda said. "I'll do them with you." She heaped the towel on the grass and together we did deep knee bends, and sit-ups, and push-ups, and some high-knee raising in place. I felt overwhelmingly happy.

"I'm just going to run a half today, Bren. We'll see what I do..." and I heard Brenda click the watch, and then when I was on the far side of the track, the clouds trailing above me like my own white, fleecy tail, I saw that Brenda was on the ground, hugging her knees, and alternately checking the watch and looking out at me. We were the only ones there, and it all reminded me of one of those scenes in race-horse movies, where an old trainer like Walter Brennan and a young handsome man clock the beautiful girl's horse in the early Kentucky morning, to see if it really is the fastest two-year-old alive. There were differences all right — one being simply that at the quarter mile Brenda shouted out to me, "A minute and fourteen seconds," but it was pleasant and exciting and clean and when I was finished Brenda was standing up and waiting for me. Instead of a tape to break I had Brenda's sweet flesh to meet, and I did, and it was the first time she said that she loved me.

We ran — I ran — every morning, and by the end of the week I was running a 7:02 mile, and always at the end there was the little click of the watch and Brenda's arms.

At night, I would read in my pajamas, while Brenda, in her room, read, and we would wait for Ron to go to sleep. Some nights we had to wait longer than others, and I would hear the leaves swishing outside, for it had grown cooler at the end of August, and the air-conditioning was turned off at night and we were all allowed to open our windows. Finally Ron would be ready for bed. He would stomp around his room and then he would come to the door in his shorts and T-shirt and go into the bathroom where he would urinate loudly and brush his teeth. After he brushed his teeth I would go in to brush mine. We would pass in the hall and I would give him a hearty and sincere "Goodnight." Once in the bathroom, I would spend a moment admiring my tan in the mirror; behind me I could see Ron's jock straps hanging out to dry on the Hot and Cold knobs of the shower. Nobody ever questioned their tastefulness as adornment, and after a few nights I didn't even notice them.

While Ron brushed his teeth and I waited in my bed for my turn, I could hear the record player going in his room. Generally, after coming in from basketball, he would call Harriet — who was now only a few days away from us — and then would lock himself up with *Sports Illustrated* and

Mantovani; however, when he emerged from his room for his evening toilet, it was not a Mantovani record I would hear playing, but something else, apparently what he'd once referred to as his Columbus record. I *imagined* that was what I heard, for I could not tell much from the last moments of sound. All I heard were bells moaning evenly and soft patriotic music behind them, and riding over it all, a deep kind of Edward R. Murrow gloomy voice: "*And so goodbye, Columbus,*" the voice intoned, "*. . . goodbye, Columbus . . . goodbye . . .*" Then there would be silence and Ron would be back in his room; the light would switch off and in only a few minutes I would hear him rumbling down into that exhilarating, restorative, vitamin-packed sleep that I imagined athletes to enjoy.

One morning near sneaking-away time I had a dream and when I awakened from it, there was just enough dawn coming into the room for me to see the color of Brenda's hair. I touched her in her sleep, for the dream had unsettled me: it had taken place on a ship, an old sailing ship like those you see in pirate movies. With me on the ship was the little colored kid from the library — I was the captain and he my mate, and we were the only crew members. For a while it was a pleasant dream; we were anchored in the harbor of an island in the Pacific and it was very sunny. Up on the beach there were beautiful bare-skinned Negresses, and none of them moved; but suddenly *we* were moving, our ship, out of the harbor, and the Negresses moved slowly down to the shore and began to throw leis at us and say "Goodbye, Columbus . . . goodbye, Columbus . . . goodbye . . ." and though we did not want to go, the little boy and I, the boat was moving and there was nothing we could do about it, and he shouted at me that it was my fault and I shouted it was his for not having a library card, but

we were wasting our breath, for we were further and further
from the island, and soon the natives were nothing at all.
Space was all out of proportion in the dream, and things
were sized and squared in no way I'd ever seen before, and
I think it was that more than anything else that steered me
into consciousness. I did not want to leave Brenda's side
that morning, and for a while I played with the little point
at the nape of her neck, where she'd had her hair cut. I
stayed longer than I should have, and when finally I returned to my room I almost ran into Ron who was preparing for his day at Patimkin Kitchen and Bathroom Sinks.

6

That morning was supposed to have been my last at the
Patimkin house; however, when I began to throw my things
into my bag late in the day, Brenda told me I could unpack
— somehow she'd managed to inveigle another week out
of her parents, and I would be able to stay right through
till Labor Day, when Ron would be married; then, the following morning Brenda would be off to school and I would
go back to work. So we would be with each other until the
summer's last moment.

This should have made me overjoyed, but as Brenda
trotted back down the stairs to accompany her family to
the airport — where they were to pick up Harriet — I was
not joyful but disturbed, as I had been more and more with
the thought that when Brenda went back to Radcliffe, that
would be the end for me. I was convinced that even Miss
Winney's stool was not high enough for me to see clear up
to Boston. Nevertheless, I tossed my clothing back into
the drawer and was able, finally, to tell myself that there'd
been no hints of ending our affair from Brenda, and any

suspicions I had, any uneasiness, was spawned in my own uncertain heart. Then I went into Ron's room to call my aunt.

"Hello?" she said.

"Aunt Gladys," I said, "how are you?"

"You're sick."

"No, I'm having a fine time. I wanted to call you, I'm going to stay another week."

"Why?"

"I told you. I'm having a good time. Mrs. Patimkin asked me to stay until Labor Day."

"You've got clean underwear?"

"I'm washing it at night. I'm okay, Aunt Gladys."

"By hand you can't get it clean."

"It's clean enough. Look, Aunt Gladys, I'm having a wonderful time."

"*Shmutz* he lives in and I shouldn't worry."

"How's Uncle Max?" I asked.

"What should he be? Uncle Max is Uncle Max. You, I don't like the way your voice sounds."

"Why? Do I sound like I've got on dirty underwear?"

"Smart guy. Someday you'll learn."

"What?"

"What do you mean *what*? You'll find out. You'll stay there too long you'll be too good for us."

"Never, sweetheart," I said.

"I'll see it I'll believe it."

"Is it cool in Newark, Aunt Gladys?"

"It's snowing," she said.

"Hasn't it been cool all week?"

"You sit around all day it's cool. For me it's not February, believe me."

"Okay, Aunt Gladys. Say hello to everybody."

"You got a letter from your mother."

"Good. I'll read it when I get home."

"You couldn't take a ride down you'll read it?"

"It'll wait. I'll drop them a note. Be a good girl," I said.

"What about your socks?"

"I go barefoot. Goodbye, honey." And I hung up.

Down in the kitchen Carlota was getting dinner ready. I was always amazed at how Carlota's work never seemed to get in the way of her life. She made household chores seem like illustrative gestures of whatever it was she was singing, even, if as now, it was "I Get a Kick out of You." She moved from the oven to the automatic dishwasher — she pushed buttons, turned dials, peeked in the glass-doored oven, and from time to time picked a big black grape out of a bunch that lay on the sink. She chewed and chewed, humming all the time, and then, with a deliberated casualness, shot the skin and the pit directly into the garbage disposal unit. I said hello to her as I went out the back door, and though she did not return the greeting, I felt a kinship with one who, like me, had been partially wooed and won on Patimkin fruit.

Out on the lawn I shot baskets for a while; then I picked up an iron and drove a cotton golf ball limply up into the sunlight; then I kicked a soccer ball towards the oak tree; then I tried shooting foul shots again. Nothing diverted me — I felt open-stomached, as though I hadn't eaten for months, and though I went back inside and came out with my own handful of grapes, the feeling continued, and I knew it had nothing to do with my caloric intake; it was only a rumor of the hollowness that would come when Brenda was away. The fact of her departure had, of course, been on my mind for a while, but overnight it had taken on a darker hue. Curiously, the darkness seemed to have something to do with Harriet, Ron's intended, and I thought for a time that it was simply the reality of Harriet's arrival that had dramatized the passing of time: we had been talking about it and now suddenly it was here — just as Brenda's departure would be here before we knew it.

But it was more than that: the union of Harriet and Ron reminded me that separation need not be a permanent state. People could marry each other, even if they were young! And yet Brenda and I had never mentioned marriage, except perhaps for that night at the pool when she'd said, "When you love me, everything will be all right." Well, I loved her, and she me, and things didn't seem all right at all. Or was I inventing troubles again? I supposed I should really have thought my lot improved considerably; yet, there on the lawn, the August sky seemed too beautiful and temporary to bear, and I wanted Brenda to marry me. Marriage, though, was not what I proposed to her when she drove the car up the driveway, alone, some fifteen minutes later. That proposal would have taken a kind of courage that I did not think I had. I did not feel myself prepared for any answer but "Hallelujah!" Any other kind of yes wouldn't have satisfied me, and any kind of no, even one masked behind the words, "Let's wait, sweetheart," would have been my end. So I imagine that's why I proposed the surrogate, which turned out finally to be far more daring than I knew it to be at the time.

"Harriet's plane is late, so I drove home," Brenda called.

"Where's everyone else?"

"They're going to wait for her and have dinner at the airport. I have to tell Carlota," and she went inside.

In a few minutes she appeared on the porch. She wore a yellow dress that cut a wide-bottomed U across her shoulders and neck, and showed where the tanned flesh began above her breasts. On the lawn she stepped out of her heels and walked barefoot over to where I was sitting under the oak tree.

"Women who wear high heels all the time get tipped ovaries," she said.

"Who told you that?"

"I don't remember. I like to think everything's ship-shape in there."

"Brenda, I want to ask you something . . ."

She yanked the blanket with the big O on it over to us and sat down.

"What?" she said.

"I know this is out of the blue, though really it's not . . . I want you to buy a diaphragm. To go to a doctor and get one."

She smiled. "Don't worry, sweetie, we're careful. Everything is okay."

"But that's the safest."

"We're safe. It'd be a waste."

"Why take chances?"

"But we *aren't*. How many things do you need."

"Honey, it isn't bulk I'm interested in. It's not even safety," I added.

"You just want me to own one, is that it? Like a walking stick, or a pith helmet — "

"Brenda, I want you to own one for . . . for the sake of pleasure."

"Pleasure? Whose? The doctor's?"

"Mine," I said.

She did not answer me, but rubbed her fingers along the ridge of her collarbone to wipe away the tiny globes of perspiration that had suddenly formed there.

"No, Neil, it's silly."

"Why?"

"Why? It just is."

"You know why it's silly, Brenda — because I asked you to do it?"

"That's sillier."

"If you asked *me* to buy a diaphragm we'd have to go straight to the Yellow Pages and find a gynecologist open on Saturday afternoon."

"I would never ask you to do that, baby."

"It's the truth," I said, though I was smiling. "It's the truth."

"It's not," she said, and got up and walked over to the basketball court, where she walked on the white lines that Mr. Patimkin had laid the day before.

"Come back here," I said.

"Neil, it's silly and I don't want to talk about it."

"Why are you being so selfish?"

"Selfish? You're the one who's being selfish. It's your pleasure . . ."

"That's right. My pleasure. Why not!"

"Don't raise your voice. Carlota."

"Then get the hell over here," I said.

She walked over to me, leaving white footprints on the grass. "I didn't think you were such a creature of the flesh," she said.

"Didn't you?" I said. "I'll tell you something that you ought to know. It's not even the pleasures of the flesh I'm talking about."

"Then frankly, I don't know *what* you're talking about. Why you're even bothering. Isn't what we use sufficient?"

"I'm bothering just because I want you to go to a doctor and get a diaphragm. That's all. No explanation. Just do it. Do it because I asked you to."

"You're not being reasonable — "

"Goddamit, Brenda!"

"Goddamit yourself!" she said and went up into the house.

I closed my eyes and leaned back and in fifteen minutes, or maybe less, I heard somebody stroking at the cotton golf ball. She had changed into shorts and a blouse and was still barefoot.

We didn't speak with each other, but I watched her bring the club back of her ear, and then swing through, her chin tilted up with the line of flight a regular golf ball would have taken.

"That's five hundred yards," I said.

She didn't answer but walked after the cotton ball and then readied for another swing.

"Brenda. Please come here."

She walked over, dragging the club over the grass.

"What?"

"I don't want to argue with you."

"Nor I with you," she said. "It was the first time."

"Was it such an awful thing for me to ask?"

She nodded.

"Bren, I know it was probably a surprise. It was for me. But we're not children."

"Neil, I just don't want to. It's not because you asked me to, either. I don't know where you get that from. That's not it."

"Then why is it?"

"Oh everything. I just don't feel *old* enough for all that equipment."

"What does age have to do with it?"

"I don't mean age. I just mean — well, *me*. I mean it's so conscious a thing to do."

"Of course it's conscious. That's exactly it. Don't you see? It would change us."

"It would change me."

"Us. Together."

"Neil, how do you think I'd feel lying to some doctor."

"You can go to Margaret Sanger, in New York. They don't ask any questions."

"You've done this before?"

"No," I said. "I just know. I read Mary McCarthy."

"That's exactly right. That's just what I'd feel like, somebody out of *her*."

"Don't be dramatic," I said.

"You're the one who's being dramatic. You think there would be something affairish about it, then. Last summer I went with this whore who I sent out to buy — "

"Oh, Brenda, you're a selfish egotistical bitch! You're the one who's thinking about 'last summer,' about an end for us. In fact, that's the whole thing, isn't it — "

"That's right, I'm a bitch. I want this to end. That's why I ask you to stay another week, that's why I let you sleep with me in my own house. What's the *matter* with you! Why don't you and my mother take turns — one day she can plague me, the next you — "

"Stop it!"

"Go to hell, all of you!" Brenda said, and now she was

crying and I knew when she ran off I would not see her, as
I didn't, for the rest of the afternoon.

Harriet Ehrlich impressed me as a young lady singu-
larly unconscious of a motive in others or herself. All was
surfaces, and she seemed a perfect match for Ron, and too
for the Patimkins. Mrs. Patimkin, in fact, did just as
Brenda prophesied: Harriet appeared, and Brenda's
mother lifted one wing and pulled the girl in towards the
warm underpart of her body, where Brenda herself would
have liked to nestle. Harriet was built like Brenda, although a little chestier, and she nodded her head insist-
ently whenever anyone spoke. Sometimes she would even
say the last few words of your sentence with you, though
that was infrequent; for the most part she nodded and kept
her hands folded. All evening, as the Patimkins planned
where the newlyweds should live, what furniture they
should buy, how soon they should have a baby — all through
this I kept thinking that Harriet was wearing white gloves,
but she wasn't.

Brenda and I did not exchange a word or a glance;
we sat, listening, Brenda somewhat more impatient than
me. Near the end Harriet began calling Mrs. Patimkin
"Mother," and once, "Mother Patimkin," and that was
when Brenda went to sleep. I stayed behind, mesmerized
almost by the dissection, analysis, reconsideration, and
finally, the embracing of the trivial. At last Mr. and Mrs.
Patimkin tumbled off to bed, and Julie, who had fallen
asleep on her chair, was carried into her room by Ron.
That left us two non-Patimkins together.

"Ron tells me you have a very interesting job."

"I work in the library."

"I've always liked reading."

"That'll be nice, married to Ron."

"Ron likes music."

"Yes," I said. What had I *said?*

"You must get first crack at the best-sellers," she said.

"Sometimes." I said.

"Well," she said, flapping her hands on her knees, "I'm sure we'll all have a good time together. Ron and I hope you and Brenda will double with us soon."

"Not tonight." I smiled. "Soon. Will you excuse me?"

"Good night. I like Brenda very much."

"Thank you," I said as I started up the stairs.

I knocked gently on Brenda's door.

"I'm sleeping."

"Can I come in?" I asked.

Her door opened an inch and she said, "Ron will be up soon."

"We'll leave the door open. I only want to talk."

She let me in and I sat in the chair that faced the bed.

"How do you like your sister-in-law?"

"I've met her before."

"Brenda, you don't have to sound so damn terse."

She didn't answer and I just sat there yanking the string on the shade up and down.

"Are you still angry?" I asked at last.

"Yes."

"Don't be," I said. "You can forget about my suggestion. It's not worth it if this is what's going to happen."

"What did you expect to happen?"

"Nothing. I didn't think it would be so horrendous."

"That's because you can't understand my side."

"Perhaps."

"No perhaps about it."

"*Okay*," I said. "I just wish you'd realize what it is you're getting angry about. It's not my suggestion, Brenda."

"No? What is it?"

"It's me."

"Oh don't start that again, will you? I can't win, no matter what I say."

"Yes, you can," I said. "You have."

I walked out of her room, closing the door behind me for the night.

When I got downstairs the following morning there was a great deal of activity. In the living room I heard Mrs. Patimkin reading a list to Harriet while Julie ran in and out of rooms in search of a skate key. Carlota was vacuum ing the carpet; every appliance in the kitchen was bub bling, twisting, and shaking. Brenda greeted me with a perfectly pleasant smile and in the dining room, where I walked to look out at the back lawn and the weather, she kissed me on the shoulder.

"Hello," she said.

"Hello."

"I have to go with Harriet this morning," Brenda told me. "So we can't run. Unless you want to go alone."

"No. I'll read or something. Where are you going?"

"We're going to New York. Shopping. She's going to buy a wedding dress. For after the wedding. To go away in."

"What are *you* going to buy?"

"A dress to be maid of honor in. If I go with Harriet then I can go to Bergdorf's without all that Ohrbach's business with my mother."

"Get me something, will you?" I said.

"Oh, Neil, are you going to bring that up again!"

"I was only *fooling*. I wasn't even thinking about that."

"Then why did you say it?"

"Oh Jesus!" I said, and went outside and drove my car down into Millburn Center where I had some eggs and coffee.

When I came back, Brenda was gone, and there were only Carlota, Mrs. Patimkin, and myself in the house. I tried to stay out of whichever rooms they were in, but finally Mrs. Patimkin and I wound up sitting opposite each other in the TV room. She was checking off names on a long sheet of paper she held; next to her, on the table, were two thin phone books which she consulted from time to time.

"No rest for the weary," she said to me.

I smiled hugely, embracing the proverb as though Mrs. Patimkin had just then coined it. "Yes. Of course," I said. "Would you like some help? Maybe I could help you check something."

"Oh, no," she said with a little head-shaking dismissal, "it's for Hadassah."

"Oh," I said.

I sat and watched her until she asked, "Is your mother in Hadassah?"

"I don't know if she is now. She was in Newark."

"Was she an active member?"

"I guess so, she was always planting trees in Israel for someone."

"Really?" Mrs. Patimkin said. "What's her name?"

"Esther Klugman. She's in Arizona now. Do they have Hadassah there?"

"Wherever there are Jewish women."

"Then I guess she is. She's with my father. They went there for their asthma. I'm staying with my aunt in Newark. She's not in Hadassah. My Aunt Sylvia is, though. Do you know her, Aaron Klugman and Sylvia? They belong to your club. They have a daughter, my cousin Doris — " I couldn't stop myself " — They live in Livingston. Maybe it isn't Hadassah my Aunt Sylvia belongs to. I think it's some TB organization. Or cancer. Muscular dystrophy, maybe. I know she's interested in *some* disease."

"That's very nice," Mrs. Patimkin said.

"Oh yes."

"They do very good work."

"I know."

Mrs. Patimkin, I thought, had begun to warm to me; she let the purple eyes stop peering and just look out at the world for a while without judging. "Are you interested in B'nai Brith?" she asked me. "Ron is joining, you know, as soon as he gets married."

"I think I'll wait till then," I said.

Petulantly, Mrs. Patimkin went back to her lists, and I realized it had been foolish of me to risk lightheartedness with her about Jewish affairs. "You're active in the Temple, aren't you?" I asked with all the interest I could muster.

"Yes," she said.

"What Temple do *you* belong to?" she asked in a moment.

"We used to belong to Hudson Street Synagogue. Since my parents left, I haven't had much contact."

I didn't know whether Mrs. Patimkin caught a false tone in my voice. Personally I thought I had managed my rueful confession pretty well, especially when I recalled the decade of paganism prior to my parents' departure. Regardless, Mrs. Patimkin asked immediately — and strategically it seemed — "We're all going to Temple Friday night. Why don't you come with us? I mean, are you orthodox or conservative?"

I considered. "Well, I haven't gone in a long time ... I sort of switch ..." I smiled. "I'm just Jewish," I said wellmeaningly, but that too sent Mrs. Patimkin back to her Hadassah work. Desperately I tried to think of something that would convince her I wasn't an infidel. Finally I asked: "Do you know Martin Buber's work?"

"Buber ... Buber," she said, looking at her Hadassah list. "Is he orthodox or conservative?" she asked.

"... He's a philosopher."

"Is he *reformed?*" she asked, piqued either at my evasiveness or at the possibility that Buber attended Friday night services without a hat, and Mrs. Buber had only one set of dishes in her kitchen.

"Orthodox," I said faintly.

"That's very nice," she said.

"Yes."

"Isn't Hudson Street Synagogue orthodox?" she asked.

"I don't know."

"I thought you belonged."

"I was bar-mitzvahed there."

"And you don't know that it's orthodox?"

"Yes. I do. It is."

"Then *you* must be."

"Oh, yes, I am," I said. "What are you?" I popped, ushing.

"Orthodox. My husband is conservative," which meant,

I took it, that he didn't care. "Brenda is nothing, as you probably know."

"Oh?" I said. "No, I didn't know that."

"She was the best Hebrew student I've ever seen," Mrs. Patimkin said, "but then, of course, she got too big for her britches."

Mrs. Patimkin looked at me, and I wondered whether courtesy demanded that I agree. "Oh, I don't know," I said at last, "I'd say Brenda is conservative. Maybe a little reformed . . ."

The phone rang, rescuing me, and I spoke a silent orthodox prayer to the Lord.

"Hello," Mrs. Patimkin said. ". . . no . . . I can *not*, I have all the Hadassah calls to make . . ."

I acted as though I were listening to the birds outside, though the closed windows let no natural noises in.

"Have Ronald drive them up . . . But we can't wait, not if we want it on time . . ."

Mrs. Patimkin glanced up at me; then she put one hand over the mouthpiece. "Would you ride down to Newark for me?"

I stood. "Yes. Surely."

"Dear?" she said back into the phone, "Neil will come for it . . . No, *Neil*, Brenda's friend . . . Yes . . . Goodbye.

"Mr. Patimkin has some silver patterns I have to see. Would you drive down to his place and pick them up?"

"Of course."

"Do you know where the shop is?"

"Yes."

"Here," she said, handing a key ring to me, "take the Volkswagen."

"My car is right outside."

"Take these," she said.

Patimkin Kitchen and Bathroom Sinks was in the heart of the Negro section of Newark. Years ago, at the time of the great immigration, it had been the Jewish section, and still one could see the little fish stores, the kosher delicatessens, the Turkish baths, where my grandparents had shopped and bathed at the beginning of the century. Even the smells had lingered: whitefish, corned beef, sour tomatoes — but now, on top of these, was the grander greasier smell of auto wrecking shops, the sour stink of a brewery, the burning odor from a leather factory; and on the streets, instead of Yiddish, one heard the shouts of Negro children playing at Willie Mays with a broom handle and half a rubber ball. The neighborhood had changed: the old Jews like my grandparents had struggled and died, and their offspring had struggled and prospered, and moved further and further west, towards the edge of Newark, then out of it, and up the slope of the Orange Mountains, until they had reached the crest and started down the other side, pouring into Gentile territory as the Scotch-Irish had poured through the Cumberland Gap. Now, in fact, the Negroes were making the same migration, following the steps of the Jews, and those who remained in the Third Ward lived the most squalid of lives and dreamed in their fetid mattresses of the piny smell of Georgia nights.

I wondered, for an instant only, if I would see the colored kid from the library on the streets here. I didn't, of course, though I was sure he lived in one of the scabby, peeling buildings out of which dogs, children, and aproned women moved continually. On the top floors, windows were open, and the very old, who could no longer creak down the long

stairs to the street, sat where they had been put, in the
screenless windows, their elbows resting on fluffless pil-
lows, and their heads tipping forward on their necks, watching the push of the young and the pregnant and the unem-
ployed. Who would come after the Negroes? Who was
left? No one, I thought, and someday these streets, where
my grandmother drank hot tea from an old *jahrzeit* glass,
would be empty and we would all of us have moved to the
crest of the Orange Mountains, and wouldn't the dead stop
kicking at the slats in their coffins then?

I pulled the Volkswagen up in front of a huge garage
door that said across the front of it:

PATIMKIN KITCHEN AND BATHROOM SINKS
"Any Size — Any Shape"

Inside I could see a glass-enclosed office; it was in the center of an immense warehouse. Two trucks were being
loaded in the rear, and Mr. Patimkin, when I saw him, had
a cigar in his mouth and was shouting at someone. It was
Ron, who was wearing a white T-shirt that said Ohio State
Athletic Association across the front. Though he was
taller than Mr. Patimkin, and almost as stout, his hands
hung weakly at his sides like a small boy's; Mr. Patimkin's
cigar locomoted in his mouth. Six Negroes were loading
one of the trucks feverishly, tossing — my stomach
dropped — sink bowls at one another.

Ron left Mr. Patimkin's side and went back to directing
the men. He thrashed his arms about a good deal, and
though on the whole he seemed rather confused, he didn't
appear to be at all concerned about anybody dropping a
sink. Suddenly I could see myself directing the Negroes —

I would have an ulcer in an hour. I could almost hear the enamel surfaces shattering on the floor. And I could hear myself: "Watch it, you guys. Be careful, will you? *Whoops!* Oh, please be — *watch* it! Watch! Oh!" Suppose Mr. Patimkin should come up to me and say, "Okay, boy, you want to marry my daughter, let's see what you can do." Well, he would see: in a moment that floor would be a shattered mosaic, a crunchy path of enamel. "Klugman, what kind of worker are you? You work like you eat!" "That's right, that's right, I'm a sparrow, let me go." "Don't you even know how to load and unload?" "Mr. Patimkin, even breathing gives me trouble, sleep tires me out, let me go, let me go . . ."

Mr. Patimkin was headed back to the fish bowl to answer a ringing phone, and I wrenched myself free of my reverie and headed towards the office too. When I entered, Mr. Patimkin looked up from the phone with his eyes; the sticky cigar was in his free hand — he moved it at me, a greeting. From outside I heard Ron call in a high voice, "You can't all go to lunch at the same time. We haven't got all day!"

"Sit down," Mr. Patimkin shot at me, though when he went back to his conversation I saw there was only one chair in the office, his. People did not sit at Patimkin Sink — here you earned your money the hard way, standing up. I busied myself looking at the several calendars that hung from filing cabinets; they showed illustrations of women so dreamy, so fantastically thighed and uddered, that one could not think of them as pornographic. The artist who had drawn the calendar girls for "Lewis Construction Company," and "Earl's Truck and Auto Repair," and "Grossman and Son, Paper Box" had been painting some third sex I had never seen.

"Sure, sure, sure," Mr. Patimkin said into the phone "Tomorrow, don't tell me tomorrow. Tomorrow the world could blow up."

At the other end someone spoke. Who was it? Lewis from the construction company? Earl from truck repair?

"I'm running a business, Grossman, not a charity."

So it was Grossman being browbeaten at the other end.

"Shit on that," Mr. Patimkin said. "You're not the only one in town, my good friend," and he winked at me.

Ah-ha, a conspiracy against Grossman. Me and Mr. Patimkin. I smiled as collusively as I knew how.

"All right then, we're here till five . . . No later."

He wrote something on a piece of paper. It was only a big X.

"My kid'll be here," he said. "Yea, he's in the business."

Whatever Grossman said on the other end, it made Mr. Patimkin laugh. Mr. Patimkin hung up without a goodbye.

He looked out the back to see how Ron was doing. "Four years in college he can't unload a truck."

I didn't know what to say but finally chose the truth. "I guess I couldn't either."

"You could learn. What am I, a genius? I learned. Hard work never killed anybody."

To that I agreed.

Mr. Patimkin looked at his cigar. "A man works hard he's got something. You don't get anywhere sitting on your behind, you know . . . The biggest men in the country worked hard, believe me. Even Rockefeller. Success don't come easy . . ." He did not say this so much as he mused it out while he surveyed his dominion. He was not a man enamored of words, and I had the feeling that what had tempted him into this barrage of universals was probably the combination of Ron's performance and my presence — me, the outsider who might one day be an insider. But did Mr. Patimkin even consider that possibility? I did not know; I only knew that these few words he did speak could hardly transmit all the satisfaction and surprise he felt about the life he had managed to build for himself and his family.

He looked out at Ron again. "Look at him, if he played basketball like that they'd throw him the hell off the court." But he was smiling when he said it.

He walked over to the door. "Ronald, let them go to lunch."

Ron shouted back, "I thought I'd let some go now, and some later."

"Why?"

"Then somebody'll always be —"

"No fancy deals here," Mr. Patimkin shouted. "We all go to lunch at once."

Ron turned back. "All right, boys, lunch!"

His father smiled at me. "Smart boy? Huh?" He tapped his head. "That took brains, huh? He ain't got the stomach for business. He's an idealist," and then I think Mr. Patimkin suddenly realized who I was, and eagerly corrected himself so as not to offend. "That's all right, you know, if you're a schoolteacher, or like you, you know, a student or something like that. Here you need a little of the *gonif* in you. You know what that means? *Gonif?*"

"Thief," I said.

"You know more than my own kids. They're *goyim*, my kids, that's how much they understand." He watched the Negro loading gang walk past the office and shouted out to them, "You guys know how long an hour is? All right, you'll be back in an hour!"

Ron came into the office and of course shook my hand. "Do you have that stuff for Mrs. Patimkin?" I asked.

"Ronald, get him the silver patterns." Ron turned away and Mr. Patimkin said, "When I got married we had forks and knives from the five and ten. This kid needs gold to eat off," but there was no anger; far from it.

I drove to the mountains in my own car that afternoon, and stood for a while at the wire fence watching the deer lightly prance, coyly feed, under the protection of signs that read, Do Not Feed the Deer, *By Order of South Mountain Reservation.* Alongside me at the fence were dozens of kids; they giggled and screamed when the deer licked the popcorn from their hands, and then were sad when their own excitement sent the young loping away towards the far end of the field where their tawny-skinned mothers stood regally watching the traffic curl up the mountain road. Young white-skinned mothers, hardly older than I, and in many instances younger, chatted in their convertibles behind me, and looked down from time to time to see what their children were about. I had seen them before, when Brenda and I had gone out for a bite in the afternoon, or had driven up here for lunch: in clotches of three and four they sat in the rustic hamburger joints that dotted the Reservation area while their children gobbled hamburgers and malteds and were given dimes to feed the jukebox. Though none of the little ones were old enough to read the song titles, almost all of them could holler out the words, and they did, while the mothers, a few of whom I recognized as high school mates of mine, compared suntans, supermarkets, and vacations. They looked immortal sitting there. Their hair would always stay the color they desired, their clothes the right texture and shade; in their homes they would have simple Swedish modern when that was fashionable, and if huge, ugly baroque ever came back, out would go the long, midget-legged marble coffee table and in would come Louis Quatorze. These were the goddesses, and if I were Paris I could not have been able to choose among them, so microscopic were the differences. Their fates had collapsed them into one. Only Brenda shone. Money and comfort would not erase her singleness — they hadn't yet, or had they? What was I loving, I wondered, and since I am not one to stick scalpels into myself, I wiggled my hand in the fence and allowed a tiny-nosed buck to lick my thoughts away.

When I returned to the Patimkin house, Brenda was in the living room looking more beautiful than I had ever seen her. She was modeling her new dress for Harriet and her mother. Even Mrs. Patimkin seemed softened by the sight of her; it looked as though some sedative had been injected into her, and so relaxed the Brenda-hating muscles around her eyes and mouth.

Brenda, without glasses, modeled in place; when she looked at me it was a kind of groggy, half-waking look I got, and though others might have interpreted it as sleepiness it sounded in my veins as lust. Mrs. Patimkin told her finally that she'd bought a very nice dress and I told her she looked lovely and Harriet told her she was very beautiful and that *she* ought to be the bride, and then there was an uncomfortable silence while all of us wondered who ought to be the groom.

Then when Mrs. Patimkin had led Harriet out to the

kitchen, Brenda came up to me and said, "I *ought* to be
the bride."

"You ought, sweetheart." I kissed her, and suddenly she
was crying.

"What is it, honey?" I said.

"Let's go outside."

On the lawn, Brenda was no longer crying but her voice
sounded very tired.

"Neil, I called Margaret Sanger Clinic," she said.
"When I was in New York."

I didn't answer.

"Neil, they *did* ask if I was married. God, the woman
sounded like my mother . . ."

"What did you say?"

"I said *no*."

"What did she say?"

"I don't know. I hung up." She walked away and
around the oak tree. When she appeared again she'd
stepped out of her shoes and held one hand on the tree, as
though it were a Maypole she were circling.

"You can call them back," I said.

She shook her head. "No, I can't. I don't even know
why I called in the first place. We were shopping and I just
walked away, looked up the number, and called."

"Then you can go to a doctor."

She shook again.

"Look, Bren," I said, rushing to her, "we'll go together,
to a doctor. In New York —"

"I don't want to go to some dirty little office —"

"We won't. We'll go to the most posh gynecologist in
New York. One who gets *Harper's Bazaar* for the recep-
tion room. How does that sound?"

She bit her lower lip.

"You'll come with me?" she asked.

"I'll come with you."

"To the office?"

"Sweetie, your husband wouldn't come to the office."

"No?"

"He'd be working."

"But you're not," she said.

"I'm on vacation," I said, but I had answered the wrong question. "Bren, I'll wait and when you're all done we'll buy a drink. We'll go out to dinner."

"Neil, I shouldn't have called Margaret Sanger — it's not right."

"It is, Brenda. It's the most right thing we can do." She walked away and I was exhausted from pleading. Somehow I felt I could have convinced her had I been a bit more crafty; and yet I did not want it to be craftiness that changed her mind. I was silent when she came back, and perhaps it was just that, my *not* saying anything, that prompted her finally to say, "I'll ask Mother Patimkin if she wants us to take Harriet too . . ."

7

I shall never forget the heat and mugginess of that afternoon we drove into New York. It was four days after the day she'd called Margaret Sanger — she put it off and put it off, but finally on Friday, three days before Ron's wedding and four before her departure, we were heading through the Lincoln Tunnel, which seemed longer and fumier than ever, like Hell with tiled walls. Finally we were in New York and smothered again by the thick day. I pulled around the policeman who directed traffic in his shirt sleeves and up onto the Port Authority roof to park the car.

"Do you have cab fare?" I said.

"Aren't you going to come with me?"

"I thought I'd wait in the bar. Here, downstairs."

"You can wait in Central Park. His office is right across the street."

"Bren, what's the diff — " But when I saw the look that invaded her eyes I gave up the air-conditioned bar to accompany her across the city. There was a sudden shower while our cab went crosstown, and when the rain stopped the streets were sticky and shiny, and below the pavement was the rumble of the subways, and in all it was like entering the ear of a lion.

The doctor's office was in the Squibb Building, which is across from Bergdorf Goodman's and so was a perfect place for Brenda to add to her wardrobe. For some reason we had never once considered her going to a doctor in Newark, perhaps because it was too close to home and might allow for possibilities of discovery. When Brenda got to the revolving door she looked back at me; her eyes were very watery, even with her glasses, and I did not say a word, afraid what a word, any word, might do. I kissed her hair and motioned that I would be across the street by the Plaza fountain, and then I watched her revolve through the doors. Out on the street the traffic moved slowly as though the humidity were a wall holding everything back. Even the fountain seemed to be bubbling boiling water on the people who sat at its edge, and in an instant I decided against crossing the street, and turned south on Fifth and began to walk the steaming pavement towards St. Patrick's. On the north steps a crowd was gathered; everyone was watching a model being photographed. She was wearing a lemon-colored dress and had her feet pointed like a

ballerina, and as I passed into the church I heard some lady
say, "If I ate cottage cheese *ten* times a day, I couldn't be
that skinny."

It wasn't much cooler inside the church, though the still-
ness and the flicker of the candles made me think it was.
I took a seat at the rear and while I couldn't bring myself
to kneel, I did lean forward onto the back of the bench
before me, and held my hands together and closed my
eyes. I wondered if I looked like a Catholic, and in my
wonderment I began to make a little speech to myself. Can
I call the self-conscious words I spoke prayer? At any rate,
I called my audience God. God, I said, I am twenty-three
years old. I want to make the best of things. Now the
doctor is about to wed Brenda to me, and I am not entirely certain this is all for the best. What is it I love,
Lord? Why have I chosen? Who is Brenda? The race is
to the swift. Should I have stopped to think?

I was getting no answers, but I went on. If we meet You
at all, God, it's that we're carnal, and acquisitive, and
thereby partake of You. I am carnal, and I know You ap-
prove, I just know it. But how carnal can I get? I am acquisitive. Where do I turn now in my acquisitiveness?
Where do we meet? Which prize is You?

It was an ingenious meditation, and suddenly I felt
ashamed. I got up and walked outside, and the noise of
Fifth Avenue met me with an answer:

Which prize do you think, *schmuck?* Gold dinnerware,
sporting-goods trees, nectarines, garbage disposals, bump-
less noses, Patimkin Sink, Bonwit Teller —

But damn it, God, that *is* You!

And God only laughed, that clown.

On the steps around the fountain I sat in a small arc of

a rainbow that the sun had shot through the spray of the water. And then I saw Brenda coming out of the Squibb Building. She carried nothing with her, like a woman who's only been window shopping, and for a moment I was glad that in the end she had disobeyed my desire.

As she crossed the street, though, that little levity passed, and then I was myself again.

She walked up before me and looked down at where I sat; when she inhaled she filled her entire body, and then let her breath out with a "Whew!"

"Where is it?" I said.

My answer, at first, was merely that victorious look of hers, the one she'd given Simp the night she'd beaten her, the one I'd gotten the morning I finished the third lap alone. At last she said, "I'm wearing it."

"Oh, Bren."

"He said shall I wrap it or will you take it with you?"

"Oh Brenda, I love you."

We slept together that night, and so nervous were we about our new toy that we performed like kindergartners, or (in the language of that country) like a lousy double-play combination. And then the next day we hardly saw one another at all, for with the last-minute wedding preparations came scurrying, telegramming, shouting, crying, rushing — in short, lunacy. Even the meals lost their Patimkin fullness, and were tortured out of Kraft cheese, stale onion rolls, dry salami, a little chopped liver, and fruit cocktail. It was hectic all weekend, and I tried as best I could to keep clear of the storm, at whose eye, Ron, clumsy and smiling, and Harriet, flittering and courteous, were being pulled closer and closer together. By Sunday night fatigue had arrested hysteria and all of the Patimkins, Brenda included, had gone off to an early sleep. When Ron went into the bathroom to brush his teeth I decided to go in and brush mine. While I stood over the sink he checked his supports for dampness; then he hung them on the shower knobs and asked me if I would like to listen to his records for a while. It was not out of boredom and loneliness that I accepted; rather a brief spark of lockerroom comradery had been struck there among the soap and the water and the tile, and I thought that perhaps Ron's invitation was prompted by a desire to spend his last moments as a Single Man with another Single Man. If I was right, then it was the first real attestation he'd given to my masculinity. How could I refuse?

I sat on the unused twin bed.

"You want to hear Mantovani?"

"Sure," I said.

"Who do you like better, him or Kostelanetz?"

"It's a toss-up."

Ron went to his cabinet. "Hey, how about the Columbus record? Brenda ever play it for you?"

"No. I don't think so."

He extracted a record from its case, and like a giant with a sea shell, placed it gingerly on the phonograph. Then he smiled at me and leaned back onto his bed. His arms were behind his head and his eyes fixed on the ceiling. "They give this to all the seniors. With the yearbook —" but he hushed as soon as the sound began. I watched Ron and listened to the record.

At first there was just a roll of drums, then silence, then another drum roll — and then softly, a marching song, the melody of which was very familiar. When the song ended, I heard the bells, soft, loud, then soft again. And finally there came a Voice, bowel-deep and historic, the kind one associates with documentaries about the rise of Fascism.

"The year, 1956. The season, fall. The place, Ohio State University ..."

Blitzkrieg! Judgment Day! The Lord had lowered his baton, and the Ohio State Glee Club were lining out the Alma Mater as if their souls depended on it. After one desperate chorus, they fell, still screaming, into bottomless oblivion, and the Voice resumed:

"The leaves had begun to turn and redden on the trees. Smoky fires line Fraternity Row, as pledges rake the leaves and turn them to a misty haze. Old faces greet new ones, new faces meet old, and another year has begun ..."

Music. Glee Club in great comeback. Then the Voice: "The place, the banks of the Olentangy. The event, Homecoming Game, 1956. The opponent, the ever dangerous Illini ..."

Roar of crowd. New voice — Bill Stern: "Illini over the ball. The snap. Linday fading to pass, he finds a receiver, he passes long *long* down field — and IT'S INTERCEPTED BY NUMBER 43, HERB CLARK OF OHIO STATE! Clark evades one tackler, he evades another as he comes up to midfield. Now he's picking up blockers, he's down to the 45, the 40, the 35 — "

And as Bill Stern egged on Clark, and Clark, Bill Stern, Ron, on his bed, with just a little body-english, eased Herb Clark over the goal.

"And it's the Buckeyes ahead now, 21 to 19. *What a game!*"

The Voice of History baritoned in again: "But the season

was up and down, and by the time the first snow had covered the turf, it was the sound of dribbling and the cry *Up and In!* that echoed through the fieldhouse . . ."

Ron closed his eyes.

"The Minnesota game," a new, high voice announced, "and for some of our seniors, their last game for the red and white . . . The players are ready to come out on the floor and into the spotlight. There'll be a big hand of appreciation from this capacity crowd for some of the boys who won't be back next year. Here comes Larry Gardner, big Number 7, out onto the floor, Big Larry from Akron, Ohio . . ."

"Larry — " announced the P.A. system; "Larry," the crowd roared back.

"And here comes Ron Patimkin dribbling out. Ron, Number 11, from Short Hills, New Jersey. Big Ron's last game, and it'll be some time before Buckeye fans forget him . . ."

Big Ron tightened on his bed as the loudspeaker called his name; his ovation must have set the nets to trembling. Then the rest of the players were announced, and then basketball season was over, and it was Religious Emphasis Week, the Senior Prom (Billy May blaring at the gymnasium roof), Fraternity Skit Night, E. E. Cummings reading to students (verse, silence, applause); and then, finally, commencement:

"The campus is hushed this day of days. For several thousand young men and women it is a joyous yet a solemn occasion. And for their parents a day of laughter and a day of tears. It is a bright green day, it is June the seventh of the year one thousand nine hundred and fifty-seven and for these young Americans the most stirring day of their

lives. For many this will be their last glimpse of the
campus, of Columbus, for many many years. Life calls us,
and anxiously if not nervously we walk out into the world
and away from the pleasures of these ivied walls. But not
from its memories. They will be the concomitant, if not the
fundament, of our lives. We shall choose husbands and
wives, we shall choose jobs and homes, we shall sire children and grandchildren, but we will not forget you, Ohio
State. In the years ahead we will carry with us always
memories of thee, Ohio State . . ."

Slowly, softly, the OSU band begins the Alma Mater,
and then the bells chime that last hour. Soft, very soft, for
it is spring.

There was goose flesh on Ron's veiny arms as the Voice
continued. "We offer ourselves to you then, world, and
come at you in search of Life. And to you, Ohio State, to
you Columbus, we say thank you, thank you and goodbye.
We will miss you, in the fall, in the winter, in the spring,
but some day we shall return. Till then, goodbye, Ohio
State, goodbye, red and white, goodbye, Columbus . . .
goodbye, Columbus . . . goodbye . . ."

Ron's eyes were closed. The band was upending its last
truckload of nostalgia, and I tiptoed from the room, in step
with the 2163 members of the Class of '57.

I closed my door, but then opened it and looked back at
Ron: he was still humming on his bed. Thee! I thought,
my brother-in-law!

The wedding.
Let me begin with the relatives.
There was Mrs. Patimkin's side of the family: her sister
Molly, a tiny buxom hen whose ankles swelled and ringed

her shoes, and who would remember Ron's wedding if for
no other reason than she'd martyred her feet in three-inch
heels, and Molly's husband, the butter and egg man, Harry
Grossbart, who had earned his fortune with barley and corn
in the days of Prohibition. Now he was active in the
Temple and whenever he saw Brenda he swatted her on
the can; it was a kind of physical bootlegging that passed,
I guess, for familial affection. Then there was Mrs. Patimkin's brother, Marty Kreiger, the Kosher Hot-Dog King,
an immense man, as many stomachs as he had chins, and
already, at fifty-five, with as many heart attacks as chins
and stomachs combined. He had just come back from a
health cure in the Catskills, where he said he'd eaten
nothing but All-Bran and had won $1500 at gin rummy.
When the photographer came by to take pictures, Marty
put his hand on his wife's pancake breasts and said, "Hey,
how about a picture of this!" His wife, Sylvia, was a frail,
spindly woman with bones like a bird's. She had cried
throughout the ceremony, and sobbed openly, in fact, when
the rabbi had pronounced Ron and Harriet "man and
wife in the eyes of God and the State of New Jersey."
Later, at dinner, she had hardened enough to slap her
husband's hand as it reached out for a cigar. However,
when he reached across to hold her breast she just looked
aghast and said nothing.

Also there were Mrs. Patimkin's twin sisters, Rose and
Pearl, who both had white hair, the color of Lincoln convertibles, and nasal voices, and husbands who followed
after them but talked only to each other, as though, in
fact, sister had married sister, and husband had married
husband. The husbands, named Earl Klein and Manny
Kartzman, sat next to each other during the ceremony, then

at dinner, and once, in fact, while the band was playing
between courses, they rose, Klein and Kartzman, as though
to dance, but instead walked to the far end of the hall
where together they paced off the width of the floor. Earl,
I learned later, was in the carpet business, and apparently
he was trying to figure how much money he would make
if the Hotel Pierre favored him with a sale.

On Mr. Patimkin's side there was only Leo, his half-
brother. Leo was married to a woman named Bea whom
nobody seemed to talk to. Bea kept hopping up and
down during the meal and running over to the kiddie table
to see if her little girl, Sharon, was being taken care of.
"I told her not to take the kid. Get a baby-sitter, I said."
Leo told me this while Brenda danced with Ron's best man,
Ferrari. "She says what are we, millionaires? No, for
Christ sake, but my brother's kids gets married, I can have
a little celebration. No, we gotta *shlep* the kid with us.
Aah, it gives her something to do! ..." He looked around
the hall. Up on the stage Harry Winters (né Weinberg)
was leading his band in a medley from *My Fair Lady*; on the
floor, all ages, all sizes, all shapes were dancing. Mr. Patimkin was dancing with Julie, whose dress had slipped
down from her shoulders to reveal her soft small back, and
long neck, like Brenda's. He danced in little squares and
was making considerable effort not to step on Julie's toes.
Harriet, who was, as everyone said, a beautiful bride, was
dancing with her father. Ron danced with Harriet's mother,
Brenda with Ferrari, and I had sat down for a while in the
empty chair beside Leo so as not to get maneuvered into
dancing with Mrs. Patimkin, which seemed to be the direction towards which things were moving.

"You're Brenda's boy friend? Huh?" Leo said.

I nodded — earlier in the evening I'd stopped giving blushing explanations. "You gotta deal there, boy," Leo said, "you don't louse it up."

"She's very beautiful," I said.

Leo poured himself a glass of champagne, and then waited as though he expected a head to form on it; when one didn't, he filled the glass to the brim.

"Beautiful, not beautiful, what's the difference. I'm a practical man. I'm on the bottom, so I gotta be. You're Aly Khan you worry about marrying movie stars. I wasn't born yesterday... You know how old I was when I got married? Thirty-five years old. I don't know what the hell kind of hurry I was in." He drained his glass and refilled it. "I'll tell you something, one good thing happened to me in my whole life. Two maybe. Before I came back from overseas I got a letter from my wife — she wasn't my wife then. My mother-in-law found an apartment for us in Queens. Sixty-two fifty a month it cost. That's the last good thing that happened."

"What was the first?"

"What first?"

"You said *two* things," I said.

"I don't remember. I say two because my wife tells me I'm sarcastic and a cynic. That way maybe she won't think I'm such a wise guy."

I saw Brenda and Ferrari separate, and so excused myself and started for Brenda, but just then Mr. Patimkin separated from Julie and it looked as though the two men were going to switch partners. Instead the four of them stood on the dance floor and when I reached them they were laughing and Julie was saying, "What's so funny!" Ferrari said "Hi" to me and whisked Julie away, which sent her into peals of laughter.

Mr. Patimkin had one hand on Brenda's back and suddenly the other one was on mine. "You kids having a good
time?" he said.

We were sort of swaying, the three of us, to "Get Me to
the Church on Time."

Brenda kissed her father. "Yes," she said. "I'm so
drunk my head doesn't even need my neck."

"It's a fine wedding, Mr. Patimkin."

"You want anything just ask me . . ." he said, a little
drunken himself. "You're two good kids . . . How do you
like that brother of yours getting married? . . . Huh? . . . Is
that a girl or is that a girl?"

Brenda smiled, and though she apparently thought her
father had spoken of her, I was sure he'd been referring to
Harriet.

"You like weddings, Daddy?" Brenda said.

"I like my kids' weddings . . ." He slapped me on the
back. "You two kids, you want anything? Go have a good
time. Remember," he said to Brenda, "you're my
honey . . ." Then he looked at me. "Whatever my Buck
wants is good enough for me. There's no business too big
it can't use another head."

I smiled, though not directly at him, and beyond I could
see Leo sopping up champagne and watching the three of
us; when he caught my eye he made a sign with his hand,
a circle with his thumb and forefinger, indicating, "That a
boy, that a boy!"

After Mr. Patimkin departed, Brenda and I danced
closely, and we only sat down when the waiters began to cir-
culate with the main course. The head table was noisy,
particularly at our end where the men were almost all team-
mates of Ron's, in one sport or another; they ate a fan-
tastic number of rolls. Tank Feldman, Ron's roommate

who had flown in from Toledo, kept sending the waiter
back for rolls, for celery, for olives, and always to the
squealing delight of Gloria Feldman, his wife, a nervous,
undernourished girl who continually looked down the front
of her gown as though there was some sort of construction
project going on under her clothes. Gloria and Tank, in
fact, seemed to be self-appointed precinct captains at our
end. They proposed toasts, burst into wild song, and continually referred to Brenda and me as "love birds." Brenda
smiled at this with her eyeteeth and I brought up a cheery
look from some fraudulent auricle of my heart.

And the night continued: we ate, we drank, we danced
— Rose and Pearl did the Charleston with one another
(while their husbands examined woodwork and chande-
liers), and then I did the Charleston with none other than
Gloria Feldman, who made coy, hideous faces at me all
the time we danced. Near the end of the evening, Brenda,
who'd been drinking champagne like her Uncle Leo, did a
Rita Hayworth tango with herself, and Julie fell asleep on
some ferns she'd whisked off the head table and made into
a mattress at the far end of the hall. I felt a numbness
creep into my hard palate, and by three o'clock people
were dancing in their coats, shoeless ladies were wrapping
hunks of wedding cake in napkins for their children's
lunch, and finally Gloria Feldman made her way over to our
end of the table and said, freshly, "Well, our little Radcliffe
smarty, what have *you* been doing all summer?"

"Growing a penis."

Gloria smiled and left as quickly as she'd come, and
Brenda without another word headed shakily away for the
ladies' room and the rewards of overindulgence. No sooner
had she left than Leo was beside me, a glass in one hand, a
new bottle of champagne in the other.

"No sign of the bride and groom?" he said, leering.
He'd lost most of his consonants by this time and was doing the best he could with long, wet vowels. "Well, you're
next, kid, I see it in the cards...You're nobody's
sucker..." And he stabbed me in the side with the top
of the bottle, spilling champagne onto the side of my
rented tux. He straightened up, poured more onto his
hand and glass, but then suddenly he stopped. He was
looking into the lights which were hidden beneath a long
bank of flowers that adorned the front of the table. He
shook the bottle in his hand as though to make it fizz.
"The son of a bitch who invented the fluorescent bulb
should drop dead!" He set the bottle down and drank.

Up on the stage Harry Winters brought his musicians to
a halt. The drummer stood up, stretched, and they all
began to open up cases and put their instruments away.
On the floor, relatives, friends, associates, were holding each
other around the waists and the shoulders, and small children huddled around their parents' legs. A couple of kids
ran in and out of the crowd, screaming at tag, until one was
grabbed by an adult and slapped soundly on the behind.
He began to cry, and couple by couple the floor emptied.
Our table was a tangle of squashed everything: napkins,
fruits, flowers; there were empty whiskey bottles, droopy
ferns, and dishes puddled with unfinished cherry jubilee,
gone sticky with the hours. At the end of the table Mr.
Patimkin was sitting next to his wife, holding her hand.
Opposite them, on two bridge chairs that had been pulled
up, sat Mr. and Mrs. Ehrlich. They spoke quietly and
evenly, as though they had known each other for years
and years. Everything had slowed down now, and from
time to time people would come up to the Patimkins and
Ehrlichs, wish them *mazel tov*, and then drag themselves

and their families out into the September night, which was
cool and windy, someone said, and reminded me that soon
would come winter and snow.

"They never wear out, those things, you know that."
Leo was pointing to the fluorescent lights that shone
through the flowers. "They last for years. They could
make a car like that if they wanted, that could never wear
out. It would run on water in the summer and snow in the
winter. But they wouldn't do it, the big boys ... Look at
me," Leo said, splashing his suit front with champagne,
"I sell a good bulb. You can't get the kind of bulb I sell
in the drugstores. It's a quality bulb. But I'm the little
guy. I don't even own a car. His brother, and I don't even
own an automobile. I take a train wherever I go. I'm the
only guy I know who wears out three pairs of rubbers every
winter. Most guys get new ones when they lose the old
ones. I wear them out, like shoes. Look," he said, leaning
into me, "I could sell a crappy bulb, it wouldn't break my
heart. But it's not good business."

The Ehrlichs and Patimkins scraped back their chairs
and headed away, all except Mr. Patimkin who came down
the table towards Leo and me.

He slapped Leo on the back. "Well, how you doing,
shtarke?"

"All right, Ben. All right . . ."

"You have a good time?"

"You had a nice affair, Ben, it must've cost a pretty
penny, believe me . . ."

Mr. Patimkin laughed. "When I make out my income
tax I go to see Leo. He knows just how much money I
spent . . . You need a ride home?" he asked me.

"No, thanks. I'm waiting for Brenda. We have my car."

"Good night," Mr. Patimkin said.

I watched him step down off the platform that held the head table, and then start towards the exit. Now the only people in the hall — the shambles of a hall — were myself, Leo, and his wife and child who slept, both of them, with their heads pillowed on a crumpled tablecloth at a table down on the floor before us. Brenda still wasn't around.

"When you got it," Leo said, rubbing his fingers together, "you can afford to talk like a big shot. Who needs a guy like me any more. Salesmen, you spit on them. You can go to the supermarket and buy anything. Where my wife shops you can buy sheets and pillowcases. Imagine, a grocery store! Me, I sell to gas stations, factories, small businesses, all up and down the east coast. Sure, you can sell a guy in a gas station a crappy bulb that'll burn out in a week. For inside the pumps I'm talking, it takes a certain kind of bulb. A utility bulb. All right, so you sell him a crappy bulb, and then a week later he puts in a new one, and while he's screwing it in he still remembers your name. Not me. I sell a quality bulb. It lasts a month, five weeks, before it even flickers, then it gives you another couple days, dim maybe, but so you shouldn't go blind. It hangs on, it's a quality bulb. Before it even burns out you notice it's getting darker, so you put a new one in. What people don't like is when one minute it's sunlight and the next dark. Let it glimmer a few days and they don't feel so bad. Nobody ever throws out my bulb — they figure they'll save them, can always use them in a pinch. Sometimes I say to a guy, you ever throw out a bulb you bought from Leo Patimkin? You gotta use psychology. That's why I'm sending my kid to college. You don't know a little psychology these days, you're licked..."

He lifted an arm and pointed out to his wife; then he

slumped down in his seat. "Aaach!" he said, and drank off half a glass of champagne. "I'll tell you, I go as far as New London, Connecticut. That's as far as I'll go, and when I come home at night I stop first for a couple drinks. Martinis. Two I have, sometimes three. That seems fair, don't it? But to her a little sip or a bathtubful, it smells the same. She says it's bad for the kid if I come home smelling. The kid's a baby, for God's sake, she thinks that's the way I'm *supposed* to smell. A forty-eight-year-old man with a three-year-old kid! She'll give me a thrombosis that kid. My wife, she wants me to come home early and play with the kid before she goes to bed. Come home, she says, and *I'll* make you a drink. Hah! I spend all day sniffing gas, leaning under hoods with grimy *poilishehs* in New London, trying to force a lousy bulb into a socket —I'll screw it in myself, I tell them — and she thinks I want to come home and drink a martini from a jelly glass! How long are you going to stay in bars, she says. Till a Jewish girl is Miss Rheingold!

"Look," he went on after another drink, "I love my kid like Ben loves his Brenda. It's not that I don't want to play with her. But if I play with the kid and then at night get into bed with my wife, then she can't expect fancy things from me. It's one or the other. I'm no movie star."

Leo looked at his empty glass and put it on the table; he tilted the bottle up and drank the champagne like soda water. "How much do you think I make a week?" he said.

"I don't know."

"Take a guess."

"A hundred dollars."

"Sure, and tomorrow they're gonna let the lions out of the cage in Central Park. What do you think I make?"

"I can't tell."

"A cabdriver makes more than me. That's a fact. My wife's brother is a cabdriver, *he* lives in Kew Gardens. And he don't take no crap, no sir, not those cabbies. Last week it was raining one night and I said the hell with it, I'm taking a cab. I'd been all day in Newton, Mass. I don't usually go so far, but on the train in the morning I said to myself, stay on, go further, it'll be a change. And I know all the time I'm kidding myself. I wouldn't even make up the extra fare it cost me. But I stay on. And at night I still had a couple boxes with me, so when the guy pulls up at Grand Central there's like a genie inside me says get in. I even threw the bulbs in, not even caring if they broke. And this cabbie says, Whatya want to do, buddy, rip the leather? Those are brand new seats I got. No, I said. Jesus Christ, he says, some goddam people. I get in and give him a Queens address which ought to shut him up, but no, all the way up the Drive he was Jesus Christing me. It's hot in the cab, so I open a window and *then* he turns around and says, Whatya want to do, give me a cold in the neck? I just got over a goddam cold . . ." Leo looked at me, bleary-eyed. "This city is crazy! If I had a little money I'd get out of here in a minute. I'd go to California. They don't need bulbs out there it's so light. I went to New Guinea during the war from San Francisco. *There*," he burst, "there is the other good thing that happened to me, that night in San Francisco with this Hannah Schreiber. That's the both of them, you asked me I'm telling you — the apartment my mother-in-law got us, and this Hannah Schreiber. One night was all. I went to a B'nai Brith dance for servicemen in the basement of some big temple, and I met her. I wasn't married then, so don't make faces."

"I'm not."

"She had a nice little room by herself. She was going to school to be a teacher. Already I knew something was up because she let me feel inside her slip in the cab. Listen to me, I sound like I'm always in cabs. Maybe two other times in my life. To tell the truth I don't even enjoy it. All the time I'm riding I'm watching the meter. Even the pleasures I can't enjoy!"

"What about Hannah Schreiber?"

He smiled, flashing some gold in his mouth. "How do you like that name? She was only a girl, but she had an old lady's name. In the room she says to me she believes in oral love. I can still hear her: Leo Patimkin, I believe in oral love. I don't know what the hell she means. I figure she was one of those Christian Scientists or some cult or something. So I said, But what about for soldiers, guys going overseas who may get killed, God forbid." He shrugged his shoulders. "The smartest guy in the world I wasn't. But that's twenty years almost, I was still wet behind the ears. I'll tell you, every once in a while my wife — you know, she does for me what Hannah Schreiber did. I don't like to force her, she works hard. That to her is like a cab to me. I wouldn't force her. I can remember every time, I'll bet. Once after a Seder, my mother was still living, she should rest in peace. My wife was up to here with Mogen David. In fact, *twice* after Seders. Aachhh! Everything good in my life I can count on my fingers! God forbid some one should leave me a million dollars, I wouldn't even have to take off my shoes. I got a whole other hand yet."

He pointed to the fluorescent bulbs with the nearly empty champagne bottle. "You call that a light? That's a light to *read* by? It's purple, for God's sake! Half the blind men in the world ruined themselves by those damn things. You know who's behind them? The optometrists! I'll tell you, if I could get a couple hundred for all my stock and the territory, I'd sell tomorrow. That's right, Leo A. Patimkin, one semester accounting, City College nights, will sell equipment, territory, good name. I'll buy two inches in the *Times*. The territory is from here to everywhere. I go where I want, my own boss, no one tells me what to do. You know the Bible? 'Let there be light — and there's Leo Patimkin!' That's my trademark, I'll sell that too. I tell them that slogan, the *poilishehs*, they think I'm making it up. What good is it to be smart unless you're in on the ground floor! I got more brains in my pinky than Ben got in his whole *head*. Why is it he's on top and I'm on the bottom! *Why!* Believe me, if you're born lucky, you're lucky!" And then he exploded into silence.

I had the feeling that he was going to cry, so I leaned over and whispered to him, "You better go home." He agreed, but I had to raise him out of his seat and steer him by one arm down to his wife and child. The little girl could not be awakened, and Leo and Bea asked me to watch her while they went out into the lobby to get their coats. When they returned, Leo seemed to have dragged himself back to the level of human communication. He shook my hand with real feeling. I was very touched.

"You'll go far," he said to me. "You're a smart boy, you'll play it safe. Don't louse things up."

"I won't."

"Next time we see you it'll be *your* wedding," and he winked at me. Bea stood alongside, muttering goodbye all the while he spoke. He shook my hand again and then picked the child out of her seat, and they turned towards the door. From the back, round-shouldered, burdened, child-carrying, they looked like people fleeing a captured city.

Brenda, I discovered, was asleep on a couch in the lobby. It was almost four o'clock and the two of us and the desk clerk were the only ones in the hotel lobby. At first I did not waken Brenda, for she was pale and wilted and I knew she had been sick. I sat beside her, smoothing her hair back off her ears. How would I ever come to know her, I wondered, for as she slept I felt I knew no more of her than what I could see in a photograph. I stirred her gently and in a half-sleep she walked beside me out to the car.

It was almost dawn when we came out of the Jersey side of the Lincoln Tunnel. I switched down to my parking lights, and drove on to the Turnpike, and there out before me I could see the swampy meadows that spread for miles and miles, watery, blotchy, smelly, like an oversight of God. I thought of that other oversight, Leo Patimkin, half-brother to Ben. In a few hours he would be on a train heading north, and as he passed Scarsdale and White Plains, he would belch and taste champagne and let the flavor linger in his mouth. Alongside him on the seat, like another passenger, would be cartons of bulbs. He would get off at New London, or maybe, inspired by the sight of his half-brother, he would stay on again, hoping for some new luck further north. For the world was Leo's territory, every city, every swamp, every road and highway. He could go on to Newfoundland if he wanted, Hudson Bay, and on up to Thule, and then slide down the other side of the globe and rap on frosted windows on the Russian steppes, if he wanted. But he wouldn't. Leo was forty-eight years old and he had learned. He pursued discomfort and sorrow, all right, but if you had a heartful by the time you reached New London, what new awfulness could you look forward to in Vladivostok?

The next day the wind was blowing the fall in and the branches of the weeping willow were fingering at the Patim-kin front lawn. I drove Brenda to the train at noon, and she left me.

8

Autumn came quickly. It was cold and in Jersey the leaves turned and fell overnight. The following Saturday I took a ride up to see the deer, and did not even get out of the car, for it was too brisk to be standing at the wire fence, and so I watched the animals walk and run in the dimness of the late afternoon, and after a while everything, even the objects of nature, the trees, the clouds, the grass, the weeds, reminded me of Brenda, and I drove back down to Newark. Already we had sent our first letters and I had called her late one night, but in the mail and on the phone we had some difficulty discovering one another; we had not the style yet. That night I tried her again, and someone on her floor said she was out and would not be in till late.

Upon my return to the library I was questioned by Mr. Scapello about the Gauguin book. The jowly gentleman *had* sent a nasty letter about my discourtesy, and I was only able to extricate myself by offering a confused story in an indignant tone. In fact, I even managed to turn it around so that Mr. Scapello was apologizing to me as he led me up to my new post, there among the encyclopedias, the bibliographies, the indexes and guides. My bullying surprised me, and I wondered if some of it had not been learned from Mr. Patimkin that morning I'd heard him giving Grossman

an earful on the phone. Perhaps I was more of a business-
man than I thought. Maybe I could learn to become a
Patimkin with ease . . .

Days passed slowly; I never did see the colored kid again,
and when, one noon, I looked in the stacks, Gauguin was
gone, apparently charged out finally by the jowly man. I
wondered what it had been like that day the colored kid
had discovered the book was gone. Had he cried? For some
reason I imagined that he had blamed it on me, but then
I realized that I was confusing the dream I'd had with
reality. Chances were he had discovered someone else, Van
Gogh, Vermeer . . . But no, they were not his kind of
artists. What had probably happened was that he'd given
up on the library and gone back to playing Willie Mays
in the streets. He was better off, I thought. No sense
carrying dreams of Tahiti in your head, if you can't afford
the fare.

Let's see, what else did I do? I ate, I slept, I went to the
movies, I sent broken-spined books to the bindery — I did
everything I'd ever done before, but now each activity was
surrounded by a fence, existed alone, and my life consisted
of jumping from one fence to the next. There was no flow,
for that had been Brenda.

And then Brenda wrote saying that she could be coming
in for the Jewish holidays which were only a week away. I
was so overjoyed I wanted to call Mr. and Mrs. Patimkin,
just to tell them of my pleasure. However, when I got to
the phone and had actually dialed the first two letters, I
knew that at the other end there would be silence; if there
was anything said, it would only be Mrs. Patimkin asking,
"What is it you want?" Mr. Patimkin had probably forgotten my name.

That night, after dinner, I gave Aunt Gladys a kiss and told her she shouldn't work so hard.

"In less than a week it's Rosh Hashana and he thinks I should take a vacation. Ten people I'm having. What do you think, a chicken cleans itself? Thank God, the holidays come once a year, I'd be an old woman before my time."

But then it was only nine people Aunt Gladys was having, for only two days after her letter Brenda called.

"Oy, Gut!" Aunt Gladys called. "Long *distance!*"

"Hello?" I said.

"Hello, sweetie?"

"Yes," I said.

"What *is* it?" Aunt Gladys tugged at my shirt. "What is it?"

"It's for me."

"Who?" Aunt Gladys said, pointing into the receiver.

"Brenda," I said.

"Yes?" Brenda said.

"Brenda?" Aunt Gladys said. "What does she call long distance, I almost had a heart attack."

"Because she's in Boston," I said. "Please, Aunt Gladys . . ."

And Aunt Gladys walked off, mumbling, "These kids . . ."

"Hello," I said again into the phone.

"Neil, how are you?"

"I love you."

"Neil, I have bad news. I can't come in this week."

"But, honey, it's the Jewish holidays."

"Sweet*heart*," she laughed.

"Can't you say that, for an excuse?"

"I have a test Saturday, and a paper, and you know if I went home I wouldn't get anything done . . ."

"You would."

"Neil, I just *can't*. My mother'd make me go to Temple, and I wouldn't even have enough time to see *you*."

"Oh God, Brenda."

"Sweetie?"

"Yes?"

"Can't you come up here?" she asked.

"I'm working."

"The Jewish holidays," she said.

"Honey, I can't. Last year I didn't take them off, I can't all—"

"You can say you had a conversion."

"Besides, my aunt's having all the family for dinner, and you know what with my parents — "

"Come up, Neil."

"I can't just take two days off, Bren. I just got promoted and a raise — "

"The hell with the raise."

"Baby, it's my job."

"Forever?" she said.

"No."

"Then come. I've got a hotel room."

"For me?"

"For us."

"Can you do that?"

"No and yes. People do it."

"Brenda, you tempt me."

"Be tempted."

"I could take a train Wednesday right from work."

"You could stay till Sunday night."

"Bren, I can't. I still have to be back to work on Saturday."

"Don't you ever get a day *off?*" she said.

"Tuesdays," I said glumly.

"God."

"And Sunday," I added.

Brenda said something but I did not hear her, for Aunt Gladys called, "You talk all day long distance?"

"Quiet!" I shouted back to her.

"Neil, will you?"

"Damn it, yes," I said.

"Are you angry?"

"I don't think so. I'm going to come up."

"Till Sunday."

"We'll see."

"Don't feel upset, Neil. You sound upset. It is the Jewish holidays. I mean you *should* be off."

"That's right," I said. "I'm an orthodox Jew, for God's sake, I ought to take advantage of it."

"That's right," she said.

"Is there a train around six?"

"Every hour, I think."

"Then I'll be on the one that leaves at six."

"I'll be at the station," she said. "How will I know you?"

"I'll be disguised as an orthodox Jew."

"Me too," she said.

"Good night, love," I said.

Aunt Gladys cried when I told her I was going away for Rosh Hashana.

"And I was preparing a big meal," she said.

"You can still prepare it."

"What will I tell your mother?"

"I'll tell her, Aunt Gladys. Please. You have no right to get upset . . ."

"Someday you'll have a family you'll know what it's like."

"I have a family now."

"What's a matter," she said, blowing her nose, "That girl couldn't come home to see her family it's the holidays?"

"She's in school, she just can't — "

"If she loved her family she'd find time. We don't live six hundred years."

"She does love her family."

"Then one day a year you could break your heart and pay a visit."

"Aunt Gladys, you don't understand."

"Sure," she said, "when I'm twenty-three years old I'll understand everything."

I went to kiss her and she said, "Go away from me, go run to Boston . . ."

The next morning I discovered that Mr. Scapello didn't want me to leave on Rosh Hashana either, but I unnerved him, I think, by hinting that his coldness about my taking the two days off might just be so much veiled anti-Semitism, so on the whole he was easier to manage. At lunch time I took a walk down to Penn Station and picked up a train schedule to Boston. That was my bedtime reading for the next three nights.

She did not look like Brenda, at least for the first minute. And probably to her I did not look like me. But we kissed and held each other, and it was strange to feel the thickness of our coats between us.

"I'm letting my hair grow," she said in the cab, and that in fact was all she said. Not until I helped her out of the cab did I notice the thin gold band shining on her left hand.

She hung back, strolling casually about the lobby while I signed the register "Mr. and Mrs. Neil Klugman," and then in the room we kissed again.

"Your heart's pounding," I said to her.

"I know," she said.

"Are you nervous?"

"No."

"Have you done this before?" I said.

"I read Mary McCarthy."

She took off her coat and instead of putting it in the closet, she tossed it across the chair. I sat down on the bed; she didn't.

"What's the matter?"

Brenda took a deep breath and walked over to the window, and I thought that perhaps it would be best for me to ask nothing — for us to get used to each other's presence in quiet. I hung her coat and mine in the empty closet, and left the suitcases — mine and hers — standing by the bed.

Brenda was kneeling backwards in the chair, looking out the window as though out the window was where she'd rather be. I came up behind her and put my hands around her body and held her breasts, and when I felt the cool draft that swept under the sill, I realized how long it had been since that first warm night when I had put my arms around her and felt the tiny wings beating in her back. And then I realized why I'd really come to Boston — it had

[handwritten margin note: pg 14]

[handwritten note at bottom: Did he go to Boston to propose or break it off]

been long enough. It was time to stop kidding about marriage.

"Is something the matter?" I said.

"Yes."

It wasn't the answer I'd expected; I wanted no answer really, only to soothe her nervousness with my concern.

But I asked, "What is it? Why didn't you mention it on the phone?"

"It only happened today."

"School?"

"Home. They found out about us."

I turned her face up to mine. "That's okay. I told my aunt I was coming here too. What's the difference?"

"About the summer. About our sleeping together."

"Oh?"

"Yes."

". . . Ron?"

"No."

"That night, you mean, did Julie — "

"No," she said, "it wasn't *anybody*."

"I don't get it."

Brenda got up and walked over to the bed where she sat down on the edge. I sat in the chair.

"My mother found the thing."

"The diaphragm?"

She nodded.

"When?" I asked.

"The other day, I guess." She walked to the bureau and opened her purse. "Here, you can read them in the order I got them." She tossed an envelope at me; it was dirty-edged and crumpled, as though it had been in and out of her pockets a good many times. "I got this one this morning," she said. "Special delivery."

I took out the letter and read:

PATIMKIN KITCHEN AND BATHROOM SINKS

"Any Size — Any Shape"

Dear Brenda —

Don't pay any Attention to your Mother's Letter when
you get it. I love you honey if you want a coat I'll buy
You a coat. You could always have anything you wanted.
We have every faith in you so you won't be too upset by
what your mother says in her Letter. Of course she is a little
hystericall because of the shock and she has been Working
so hard for Hadassah. She is a Woman and it is hard for her
to understand some of the Shocks in life. Of course I can't
say We weren't all surprised because from the beginning I
was nice to him and Thought he would appreciate the nice
vacation we supplied for him. Some People never turn out
the way you hope and pray but I am willing to forgive and
call Buy Gones, Buy Gones, You have always up till now
been a good Buck and got good scholastic Grades and Ron
has always been what we wanted a Good Boy, most important, and a Nice boy. This late in my life believe me I am
not going to start hating my own flesh and blood. As for your
mistake it takes Two to make a mistake and now that you
will be away at school and from him and what you got
involved in you will probably do all right I have every faith
you will. You have to have faith in your children like in a
Business or any serious undertaking and there is nothing
that is so bad that we can't forgive especially when Our
own flesh and blood is involved. We have a nice close nitt
family and why not???? Have a nice Holiday and in
Temple I will say a Prayer for you as I do every year.
On Monday I want you to go into Boston and buy a coat.

Whatever you need because I know how Cold it gets up where you are . . . Give my regards to Linda and remember to bring her home with you on Thanksgiving like last year. You two had such a nice time. I have always never said bad things about any of your friends or Rons and that this should happen is only the exception that proves the rule. Have a Happy Holiday.

YOUR FATHER

And then it was signed BEN PATIMKIN, but that was crossed out and written beneath "Your Father" were again, like an echo, the words, "Your Father."

"Who's Linda?" I asked.

"My roommate, last year." She tossed another envelope to me. "Here. I got this one in the afternoon. Air Mail."

The letter was from Brenda's mother. I started to read it and then put it down a moment. "You got this *after?*"

"Yes," she said. "When I got his I didn't know what was happening. Read hers."

I began again.

Dear Brenda:

I don't even know how to begin. I have been crying all morning and have had to skip my board meeting this afternoon because my eyes are so red. I never thought this would happen to a daughter of mine. I wonder if you know what I mean, if it is at least on your conscience, so I won't have to degrade either of us with a description. All I can say is that this morning when I was cleaning out the drawers and putting away your summer clothing I came upon something in your bottom drawer, *under* some sweaters which you probably remember leaving there. I cried the minute I saw it and I haven't stopped crying yet. Your father called a while ago and now he is driving home because he heard how upset I was on the phone.

I don't know what we ever did that you should reward us this way. We gave you a nice home and all the love and respect a child needs. I always was proud when you were a little girl that you could take care of yourself so well. You took care of Julie so beautifully it was a treat to see, when you were only fourteen years old. But you drifted away from your family, even though we sent you to the best schools and gave you the best money could buy. Why you should reward us this way is a question I'll carry with me to the grave.

About your friend I have no words. He is his parents' responsibility and I cannot imagine what kind of home life he had that he could act that way. Certainly that was a fine way to repay us for the hospitality we were nice enough to show to him, a perfect stranger. That the two of you should be carrying on like that in our very house I will never in my life be able to understand. Times certainly have changed since I was a girl that this kind of thing could go on. I keep asking myself if at least you didn't think of us while you were doing that. If not for me, how could you do this to your father? God forbid Julie should ever learn of this.

God only knows what you have been doing all these years we put our trust in you.

You have broken your parents' hearts and you should know that. This is some thank you for all we gave you.

MOTHER

She only signed "Mother" once, and that was in an extraordinarily miniscule hand, like a whisper.

"Brenda," I said.

"What?"

"Are you starting to cry?"

"No. I cried already."

"Don't start again."

"I'm trying not to, for God's sake."

"Okay . . . Brenda, can I ask you one question?"

"What?"

"Why did you leave it home?"

"Because I didn't plan on using it here, that's why."

"Suppose I'd come up. I mean I have come up, what about that?"

"I thought I'd come down first."

"So then couldn't you have carried it down then? Like a toothbrush?"

"Are you trying to be funny?"

"No. I'm just asking you why you left it home."

"I told you," Brenda said. "I thought I'd come home."

"But, Brenda, that doesn't make any sense. Suppose you did come home, and then you came back again. Wouldn't you have taken it with you then?"

"I don't *know*."

"Don't get angry," I said.

"You're the one who's angry."

"I'm upset, I'm not angry."

"I'm upset then too."

I did not answer but walked to the window and looked out. The stars and moon were out, silver and hard, and from the window I could see over to the Harvard campus where lights burned and then seemed to flicker when the trees blew across them.

"Brenda . . ."

"What?"

"Knowing how your mother feels about you, wasn't it silly to leave it home? Risky?"

"What does how she feels about me have to do with it?"

"You can't trust her."

"Why can't I?"

"Don't you see. You *can't*."

"Neil, she was only cleaning out the drawers."

"Didn't you know she would?"

"She never did before. Or maybe she did. Neil, I couldn't think of everything. We slept together night after night and nobody heard or noticed — "

"Brenda, why the hell are you willfully confusing things?"

"I'm not!"

"Okay," I said softly. "All right."

"It's you who's confusing things," Brenda said. "You act as though I wanted her to find it."

I didn't answer.

"Do you believe *that*?" she said, after neither of us had spoken for a full minute.

"I don't know."

"Oh, Neil, you're *crazy*."

"What was crazier than leaving that damn thing around?"

"It was an oversight."

"Now it's an oversight, before it was deliberate."

"It was an oversight about the drawer. It wasn't an oversight about leaving it," she said.

"Brenda, sweetheart, wouldn't the safest, smartest, easiest, simplest thing been to have taken it with you? Wouldn't it?"

"It didn't make any difference either way."

"Brenda, this is the most frustrating argument of my life!"

"You keep making it seem as though I *wanted* her to

find it. Do you think I need this? Do you? I can't even go home any more."

"Is that so?"

"Yes!"

"No," I said. "You can go home — your father will be waiting with two coats and a half-dozen dresses."

"What about my mother?"

"It'll be the same with her."

"Don't be absurd. How can I face them!"

"Why can't you face them? Did you do anything wrong?"

"Neil, look at the reality of the thing, will you?"

"*Did* you do anything wrong?"

"Neil, *they* think it's wrong. They're my parents."

"But do you think it's wrong — "

"That doesn't *matter*."

"It does to me, Brenda . . ."

"Neil, why are *you* confusing things? You keep accusing me of things."

"Damn it, Brenda, you're guilty of some things."

"*What?*"

"Of leaving that damn diaphragm there. How can you call it an oversight!"

"Oh, Neil, don't start any of that psychoanalytic crap!"

"Then why else did you do it? You wanted her to find it!"

"Why?"

"I don't know, Brenda, *why?*"

"Oh!" she said, and she picked up the pillow and threw it back on to the bed.

"What happens now, Bren?" I said.

"What does that mean?"

"Just that. What happens now?"

She rolled over on to the bed and buried her head in it.

"Don't start crying," I said.

"I'm *not*."

I was still holding the letters and took Mr. Patimkin's from its envelope.

"Why does your father capitalize all these letters?"

She didn't answer.

" 'As for your mistake,' " I read aloud to Brenda, " 'it takes Two to make a mistake and now that you will be away at school and from him and what you got involved in you will probably do all right I have every faith you will. Your father. Your father.' "

She turned and looked at me; but silently.

" 'I have always never said bad things about any of your friends or Rons and that this should happen is only the exception that proves the rule. Have a Happy Holiday.' " I stopped; in Brenda's face there was positively no threat of tears; she looked, suddenly, solid and decisive. "Well, what are you going to do?" I asked.

"Nothing."

"Who are you going to bring home Thanksgiving — Linda?" I said, "or me?"

"Who *can* I bring home, Neil?"

"I don't know, who can you?"

"Can I bring you home?"

"I don't know," I said, "can you?"

"Stop repeating the question!"

"I sure as hell can't give you the answer."

"Neil, be realistic. After this, can I bring you home? Can you see us all sitting around the table?"

"I can't if you can't, and I can if you can."

"Are you going to speak Zen, for God's sake!"

[handwritten margin notes: feel is burning any bridges between them — he realizes marriage will not work / he has no compassion here]

[handwritten note at bottom: Neil attacks — could have salvaged things but he didn't try]

"Brenda, the choices aren't mine. You can bring Linda or me. You can go home or not go home. That's another choice. Then you don't even have to worry about choosing between me and Linda."

"Neil, you don't understand. They're still my parents. They did send me to the best schools, didn't they? They have given me everything I've wanted, haven't they?"

"Yes."

"Then how can I not go home? I *have* to go home."

"Why?"

"You don't understand. Your parents don't bother you any more. You're lucky."

"Oh, sure. I live with my crazy aunt, that's a real bargain."

"Families are different. You don't understand."

"Goddamit, I understand more than you think. I understand why the hell you left that thing lying around. Don't you? Can't you put two and two together?"

"Neil, what are you talking about! You're the one who doesn't understand. You're the one who from the very beginning was accusing me of things? Remember? Isn't it so? Why don't you have your eyes fixed? Why don't you have this fixed, that fixed? As if it were my fault that I *could* have them fixed. You kept acting as if I was going to run away from you every minute. And now you're doing it again, telling me I planted that thing on purpose."

"I loved you, Brenda, so I cared."

"I loved *you*. That's why I got that damn thing in the first place."

And then we heard the tense in which we'd spoken and we settled back into ourselves and silence.

A few minutes later I picked up my bag and put on my

coat. I think Brenda was crying too when I went out the door.

Instead of grabbing a cab immediately, I walked down the street and out towards the Harvard Yard which I had never seen before. I entered one of the gates and then headed out along a path, under the tired autumn foliage and the dark sky. I wanted to be alone, in the dark; not because I wanted to think about anything, but rather because, for just a while, I wanted to think about nothing. I walked clear across the Yard and up a little hill and then I was standing in front of the Lamont Library, which, Brenda had once told me, had Patimkin Sinks in its rest rooms. From the light of the lamp on the path behind me I could see my reflection in the glass front of the building. Inside, it was dark and there were no students to be seen, no librarians. Suddenly, I wanted to set down my suitcase and pick up a rock and heave it right through the glass, but of course I didn't. I simply looked at myself in the mirror the light made of the window. I was only that substance, I thought, those limbs, that face that I saw in front of me. I looked, but the outside of me gave up little information about the inside of me. I wished I could scoot around to the other side of the window, faster than light or sound or Herb Clark on Homecoming Day, to get behind that image and catch whatever it was that looked through those eyes. What was it inside me that had turned pursuit and clutching into love, and then turned it inside out again? What was it that had turned winning into losing, and losing — who knows — into winning? I was sure I had loved Brenda, though standing there, I knew I couldn't any longer. And I knew it would be a long while before I

He is drawn immediately to the library

made love to anyone the way I had made love to her. With anyone else, could I summon up such a passion? Whatever spawned my love for her, had that spawned such lust too? If she had only been slightly *not* Brenda . . . but then would I have loved her? I looked hard at the image of me, at that darkening of the glass, and then my gaze pushed through it, over the cool floor, to a broken wall of books, imperfectly shelved.

I did not look very much longer, but took a train that got me into Newark just as the sun was rising on the first day of the Jewish New Year. I was back in plenty of time for work.

He is choosing to reject Brenda & her Jewishness, so he can return to the safeness of the library, to his safe predictable life

line top of page "made love" – he missed the whole point of loving Brenda

He hasn't gone with his parents because he doesn't want change – he is very static – he is an inadequate person. He feels safe & Gladys in Newark

THE

CONVERSION

OF THE JEWS

Y OU'RE a real one for opening your mouth in the first place," Itzie said. "What do you open your mouth all the time for?"

"I didn't bring it up, Itz, I didn't," Ozzie said.

"What do you care about Jesus Christ for anyway?"

"I didn't bring up Jesus Christ. He did. I didn't even know what he was talking about. Jesus is historical, he kept saying. Jesus is historical." Ozzie mimicked the monumental voice of Rabbi Binder.

"Jesus was a person that lived like you and me," Ozzie continued. "That's what Binder said —"

"Yeah? . . . So what! What do I give two cents whether he lived or not. And what do you gotta open your mouth!" Itzie Lieberman favored closed-mouthedness, especially when it came to Ozzie Freedman's questions. Mrs. Freedman had to see Rabbi Binder twice before about Ozzie's questions and this Wednesday at four-thirty would be the third time. Itzie preferred to keep *his* mother in the kitchen; he settled for behind-the-back subtleties such as gestures, faces, snarls and other less delicate barnyard noises.

"He was a real person, Jesus, but he wasn't like God, and we don't believe he is God." Slowly, Ozzie was explaining Rabbi Binder's position to Itzie, who had been absent from Hebrew School the previous afternoon.

"The Catholics," Itzie said helpfully, "they believe in Jesus Christ, that he's God." Itzie Lieberman used "the Catholics" in its broadest sense — to include the Protestants.

Ozzie received Itzie's remark with a tiny head bob, as though it were a footnote, and went on. "His mother was Mary, and his father probably was Joseph," Ozzie said. "But the New Testament says his real father was God."

"His *real* father?"

"Yeah," Ozzie said, "that's the big thing, his father's supposed to be God."

"Bull."

"That's what Rabbi Binder says, that it's impossible — "

"Sure it's impossible. That stuff's all bull. To have a baby you gotta get laid," Itzie theologized. "Mary hadda get laid."

"That's what Binder says: 'The only way a woman can have a baby is to have intercourse with a man.' "

"He said *that*, Ozz?" For a moment it appeared that Itzie had put the theological question aside. "He said that, intercourse?" A little curled smile shaped itself in the lower half of Itzie's face like a pink mustache. "What you guys do, Ozz, you laugh or something?"

"I raised my hand."

"Yeah? Whatja say?"

"That's when I asked the question."

Itzie's face lit up. "Whatja ask about — intercourse?"

"No, I asked the question about God, how if He could create the heaven and earth in six days, and make all the animals and the fish and the light in six days — the light especially, that's what always gets me, that He could make the light. Making fish and animals, that's pretty good — "

"That's damn good." Itzie's appreciation was honest but unimaginative: it was as though God had just pitched a one-hitter.

"But making light . . . I mean when you think about it, it's really something," Ozzie said. "Anyway, I asked Binder if He could make all that in six days, and He could *pick* the six days he wanted right out of nowhere, why couldn't He let a woman have a baby without having intercourse."

"You said intercourse, Ozz, to Binder?"

"Yeah."

"Right in class?"

"Yeah."

Itzie smacked the side of his head.

"I mean, no kidding around," Ozzie said, "that'd really be nothing. After all that other stuff, that'd practically be nothing."

Itzie considered a moment. "What'd Binder say?"

"He started all over again explaining how Jesus was historical and how he lived like you and me but he wasn't God. So I said I under*stood* that. What I wanted to know was different."

What Ozzie wanted to know was always different. The first time he had wanted to know how Rabbi Binder could call the Jews "The Chosen People" if the Declaration of Independence claimed all men to be created equal. Rabbi Binder tried to distinguish for him between political equality and spiritual legitimacy, but what Ozzie wanted to know, he insisted vehemently, was different. That was the first time his mother had to come.

Then there was the plane crash. Fifty-eight people had

been killed in a plane crash at La Guardia. In studying a casualty list in the newspaper his mother had discovered among the list of those dead eight Jewish names (his grandmother had nine but she counted Miller as a Jewish name); because of the eight she said the plane crash was "a tragedy." During free-discussion time on Wednesday Ozzie had brought to Rabbi Binder's attention this matter of "some of his relations" always picking out the Jewish names. Rabbi Binder had begun to explain cultural unity and some other things when Ozzie stood up at his seat and said that what he wanted to know was different. Rabbi Binder insisted that he sit down and it was then that Ozzie shouted that he wished all fifty-eight were Jews. That was the second time his mother came.

"And he kept explaining about Jesus being historical, and so I kept asking him. No kidding, Itz, he was trying to make me look stupid."

"So what he finally do?"

"Finally he starts screaming that I was deliberately simple-minded and a wise guy, and that my mother had to come, and this was the last time. And that I'd never get bar-mitzvahed if he could help it. Then, Itz, then he starts talking in that voice like a statue, real slow and deep, and he says that I better think over what I said about the Lord. He told me to go to his office and think it over." Ozzie leaned his body towards Itzie. "Itz, I thought it over for a solid hour, and now I'm convinced God could do it."

Ozzie had planned to confess his latest transgression to his mother as soon as she came home from work. But it was a Friday night in November and already dark, and when Mrs. Freedman came through the door she tossed off her coat, kissed Ozzie quickly on the face, and went to the kitchen table to light the three yellow candles, two for the Sabbath and one for Ozzie's father.

When his mother lit the candles she would move her two arms slowly towards her, dragging them through the air, as though persuading people whose minds were half made up. And her eyes would get glassy with tears. Even when his father was alive Ozzie remembered that her eyes had gotten glassy, so it didn't have anything to do with his dying. It had something to do with lighting the candles.

As she touched the flaming match to the unlit wick of a Sabbath candle, the phone rang, and Ozzie, standing only a foot from it, plucked it off the receiver and held it muffled to his chest. When his mother lit candles Ozzie felt there should be no noise; even breathing, if you could manage it, should be softened. Ozzie pressed the phone to his breast and watched his mother dragging whatever she was dragging, and he felt his own eyes get glassy. His mother was a round, tired, gray-haired penguin of a woman whose gray skin had begun to feel the tug of gravity and the weight of her own history. Even when she was dressed up she didn't look like a chosen person. But when she lit candles she looked like something better; like a woman who knew momentarily that God could do anything.

After a few mysterious minutes she was finished. Ozzie hung up the phone and walked to the kitchen table where she was beginning to lay the two places for the four-course Sabbath meal. He told her that she would have to see Rabbi Binder next Wednesday at four-thirty, and then he told her why. For the first time in their life together she hit Ozzie across the face with her hand.

All through the chopped liver and chicken soup part of

the dinner Ozzie cried; he didn't have any appetite for the rest.

On Wednesday, in the largest of the three basement class-rooms of the synagogue, Rabbi Marvin Binder, a tall, hand-some, broad-shouldered man of thirty with thick strong-fibered black hair, removed his watch from his pocket and saw that it was four o'clock. At the rear of the room Yakov Blotnik, the seventy-one-year-old custodian, slowly polished the large window, mumbling to himself, unaware that it was four o'clock or six o'clock, Monday or Wednesday. To most of the students Yakov Blotnik's mumbling, along with his brown curly beard, scythe nose, and two heel-trailing black cats, made of him an object of wonder, a for-eigner, a relic, towards whom they were alternately fearful and disrespectful. To Ozzie the mumbling had always seemed a monotonous, curious prayer; what made it curi-ous was that old Blotnik had been mumbling so steadily for so many years, Ozzie suspected he had memorized the prayers and forgotten all about God.

"It is now free-discussion time," Rabbi Binder said. "Feel free to talk about any Jewish matter at all — re-ligion, family, politics, sports — "

There was silence. It was a gusty, clouded November afternoon and it did not seem as though there ever was or could be a thing called baseball. So nobody this week said a word about that hero from the past, Hank Greenberg — which limited free discussion considerably.

And the soul-battering Ozzie Freedman had just re-ceived from Rabbi Binder had imposed its limitation. When it was Ozzie's turn to read aloud from the Hebrew book the rabbi had asked him petulantly why he didn't read more rapidly. He was showing no progress. Ozzie said he could read faster but that if he did he was sure not to understand what he was reading. Nevertheless, at the rabbi's repeated suggestion Ozzie tried, and showed a great talent, but in the midst of a long passage he stopped short and said he didn't understand a word he was reading, and started in again at a drag-footed pace. Then came the soul-battering.

Consequently when free-discussion time rolled around none of the students felt too free. The rabbi's invitation was answered only by the mumbling of feeble old Blotnik.

"Isn't there anything at all you would like to discuss?" Rabbi Binder asked again, looking at his watch. "No questions or comments?"

There was a small grumble from the third row. The rabbi requested that Ozzie rise and give the rest of the class the advantage of his thought.

Ozzie rose. "I forget it now," he said, and sat down in his place.

Rabbi Binder advanced a seat towards Ozzie and poised himself on the edge of the desk. It was Itzie's desk and the rabbi's frame only a dagger's-length away from his face snapped him to sitting attention.

"Stand up again, Oscar," Rabbi Binder said calmly, "and try to assemble your thoughts."

Ozzie stood up. All his classmates turned in their seats and watched as he gave an unconvincing scratch to his forehead.

"I can't assemble any," he announced, and plunked himself down.

"Stand up!" Rabbi Binder advanced from Itzie's desk to the one directly in front of Ozzie; when the rabbinical back was turned Itzie gave it five-fingers off the tip of his nose, causing a small titter in the room. Rabbi Binder was too absorbed in squelching Ozzie's nonsense once and for all to bother with titters. "Stand up, Oscar. What's your question about?"

Ozzie pulled a word out of the air. It was the handiest word. "Religion."

"Oh, now you remember?"

"Yes."

"What is it?"

Trapped, Ozzie blurted the first thing that came to him. "Why can't He make anything He wants to make!"

As Rabbi Binder prepared an answer, a final answer, Itzie, ten feet behind him, raised one finger on his left hand, gestured it meaningfully towards the rabbi's back, and brought the house down.

Binder twisted quickly to see what had happened and in the midst of the commotion Ozzie shouted into the rabbi's back what he couldn't have shouted to his face. It was a loud, toneless sound that had the timbre of something stored inside for about six days.

"You don't know! You don't know anything about God!"

The rabbi spun back towards Ozzie. "What?"

"You don't know — you don't — "

"Apologize, Oscar, apologize!" It was a threat.

"You don't — "

Rabbi Binder's hand flicked out at Ozzie's cheek. Perhaps it had only been meant to clamp the boy's mouth shut, but Ozzie ducked and the palm caught him squarely on the nose.

The blood came in a short, red spurt on to Ozzie's shirt front.

The next moment was all confusion. Ozzie screamed,
"You bastard, you bastard!" and broke for the classroom
door. Rabbi Binder lurched a step backwards, as though
his own blood had started flowing violently in the opposite
direction, then gave a clumsy lurch forward and bolted out
the door after Ozzie. The class followed after the rabbi's
huge blue-suited back, and before old Blotnik could turn
from his window, the room was empty and everyone was
headed full speed up the three flights leading to the roof.

If one should compare the light of day to the life of man:
sunrise to birth; sunset — the dropping down over the edge
— to death; then as Ozzie Freedman wiggled through the
trapdoor of the synagogue roof, his feet kicking backwards bronco-style at Rabbi Binder's outstretched arms —
at that moment the day was fifty years old. As a rule, fifty
or fifty-five reflects accurately the age of late afternoons in
November, for it is in that month, during those hours, that
one's awareness of light seems no longer a matter of seeing, but of hearing: light begins clicking away. In fact, as
Ozzie locked shut the trapdoor in the rabbi's face, the
sharp click of the bolt into the lock might momentarily
have been mistaken for the sound of the heavier gray that
had just throbbed through the sky.
    With all his weight Ozzie kneeled on the locked door;
any instant he was certain that Rabbi Binder's shoulder
would fling it open, splintering the wood into shrapnel and
catapulting his body into the sky. But the door did not
move and below him he heard only the rumble of feet,
first loud then dim, like thunder rolling away.
    A question shot through his brain. "Can this be *me*?"
For a thirteen-year-old who had just labeled his religious
leader a bastard, twice, it was not an improper question.

Louder and louder the question came to him —"Is it me? Is it me?" — until he discovered himself no longer kneeling, but racing crazily towards the edge of the roof, his eyes crying, his throat screaming, and his arms flying everywhichway as though not his own.

"Is it me? Is it me Me Me Me Me! It has to be me — but is it!"

It is the question a thief must ask himself the night he jimmies open his first window, and it is said to be the question with which bridegrooms quiz themselves before the altar.

In the few wild seconds it took Ozzie's body to propel him to the edge of the roof, his self-examination began to grow fuzzy. Gazing down at the street, he became confused as to the problem beneath the question: was it, is-it-me-who-called-Binder-a-bastard? or, is-it-me-prancing-around-on-the-roof? However, the scene below settled all, for there is an instant in any action when whether it is you or somebody else is academic. The thief crams the money in his pockets and scoots out the window. The bridegroom signs the hotel register for two. And the boy on the roof finds a streetful of people gaping at him, necks stretched backwards, faces up, as though he were the ceiling of the Hayden Planetarium. Suddenly you know it's you.

"Oscar! Oscar Freedman!" A voice rose from the center of the crowd, a voice that, could it have been seen, would have looked like the writing on scroll. "Oscar Freedman, get down from there. Immediately!" Rabbi Binder was pointing one arm stiffly up at him; and at the end of that arm, one finger aimed menacingly. It was the attitude of a dictator, but one — the eyes confessed all — whose personal valet had spit neatly in his face.

Ozzie didn't answer. Only for a blink's length did he look towards Rabbi Binder. Instead his eyes began to fit together the world beneath him, to sort out people from places, friends from enemies, participants from spectators. In little jagged starlike clusters his friends stood around Rabbi Binder, who was still pointing. The topmost point on a star compounded not of angels but of five adolescent boys was Itzie. What a world it was, with those stars below, Rabbi Binder below ... Ozzie, who a moment earlier hadn't been able to control his own body, started to feel the meaning of the word control: he felt Peace and he felt Power.

"Oscar Freedman, I'll give you three to come down."

Few dictators give their subjects three to do anything; but, as always, Rabbi Binder only looked dictatorial.

"Are you ready, Oscar?"

Ozzie nodded his head yes, although he had no intention in the world — the lower one of the celestial one he'd just entered — of coming down even if Rabbi Binder should give him a million.

"All right then," said Rabbi Binder. He ran a hand through his black Samson hair as though it were the gesture prescribed for uttering the first digit. Then, with his other hand cutting a circle out of the small piece of sky around him, he spoke. "One!"

There was no thunder. On the contrary, at that moment, as though "one" was the cue for which he had been waiting, the world's least thunderous person appeared on the synagogue steps. He did not so much come out the synagogue door as lean out, onto the darkening air. He clutched at the doorknob with one hand and looked up at the roof.

"Oy!"

Yakov Blotnik's old mind hobbled slowly, as if on crutches, and though he couldn't decide precisely what the boy was doing on the roof, he knew it wasn't good — that is, it wasn't-good-for-the-Jews. For Yakov Blotnik life had fractionated itself simply: things were either good-for-the-Jews or no-good-for-the-Jews.

He smacked his free hand to his in-sucked cheek, gently. "Oy, Gut!" And then quickly as he was able, he jacked down his head and surveyed the street. There was Rabbi Binder (like a man at an auction with only three dollars in his pocket, he had just delivered a shaky "Two!"); there were the students, and that was all. So far it-wasn't-so-bad-for-the-Jews. But the boy had to come down immediately, before anybody saw. The problem: how to get the boy off the roof?

Anybody who has ever had a cat on the roof knows how to get him down. You call the fire department. Or first you call the operator and you ask her for the fire department. And the next thing there is great jamming of brakes and clanging of bells and shouting of instructions. And then the cat is off the roof. You do the same thing to get a boy off the roof.

That is, you do the same thing if you are Yakov Blotnik and you once had a cat on the roof.

When the engines, all four of them, arrived, Rabbi Binder had four times given Ozzie the count of three. The big hook-and-ladder swung around the corner and one of the firemen leaped from it, plunging headlong towards the yellow fire hydrant in front of the synagogue. With a huge wrench he began to unscrew the top nozzle. Rabbi Binder raced over to him and pulled at his shoulder.

"There's no fire..."

The fireman mumbled back over his shoulder and, heat-edly, continued working at the nozzle.

"But there's no fire, there's no fire..." Binder shouted. When the fireman mumbled again, the rabbi grasped his face with both his hands and pointed it up at the roof.

To Ozzie it looked as though Rabbi Binder was trying to tug the fireman's head out of his body, like a cork from a bottle. He had to giggle at the picture they made: it was a family portrait — rabbi in black skullcap, fireman in red fire hat, and the little yellow hydrant squatting beside like a kid brother, bareheaded. From the edge of the roof Ozzie waved at the portrait, a one-handed, flapping, mock-ing wave; in doing it his right foot slipped from under him. Rabbi Binder covered his eyes with his hands.

Firemen work fast. Before Ozzie had even regained his balance, a big, round, yellowed net was being held on the synagogue lawn. The firemen who held it looked up at Ozzie with stern, feelingless faces.

One of the firemen turned his head towards Rabbi Binder. "What, is the kid nuts or something?"

Rabbi Binder unpeeled his hands from his eyes, slowly, painfully, as if they were tape. Then he checked: nothing on the sidewalk, no dents in the net.

"Is he gonna jump, or what?" the fireman shouted.

In a voice not at all like a statue, Rabbi Binder finally answered. "Yes, Yes, I think so... He's been threatening to..."

Threatening to? Why, the reason he was on the roof, Ozzie remembered, was to get away; he hadn't even thought about jumping. He had just run to get away, and the truth was that he hadn't really headed for the roof as much as he'd been chased there.

"What's his name, the kid?"

"Freedman," Rabbi Binder answered. "Oscar Freed-man."

The fireman looked up at Ozzie. "What is it with you, Oscar? You gonna jump, or what?"

Ozzie did not answer. Frankly, the question had just arisen.

"Look, Oscar, if you're gonna jump, jump — and if you're not gonna jump, don't jump. But don't waste our time, willya?"

Ozzie looked at the fireman and then at Rabbi Binder. He wanted to see Rabbi Binder cover his eyes one more time.

"I'm going to jump."

And then he scampered around the edge of the roof to the corner, where there was no net below, and he flapped his arms at his sides, swishing the air and smacking his palms to his trousers on the downbeat. He began screaming like some kind of engine, "Wheeeee . . . wheeeeee," and leaning way out over the edge with the upper half of his body. The firemen whipped around to cover the ground with the net. Rabbi Binder mumbled a few words to Some-body and covered his eyes. Everything happened quickly, jerkily, as in a silent movie. The crowd, which had arrived with the fire engines, gave out a long, Fourth-of-July fire-works oooh-aahhh. In the excitement no one had paid the crowd much heed, except, of course, Yakov Blotnik, who swung from the doorknob counting heads. "Fier und tsvansik . . . finf und tsvantsik . . . Oy, Gut!" It wasn't like this with the cat.

Rabbi Binder peeked through his fingers, checked the sidewalk and net. Empty. But there was Ozzie racing to the other corner. The firemen raced with him but were unable to keep up. Whenever Ozzie wanted to he might jump and splatter himself upon the sidewalk, and by the time the firemen scooted to the spot all they could do with their net would be to cover the mess.

"Wheeeee... wheeeee..."

"Hey, Oscar," the winded fireman yelled, "What the hell is this, a game or something?"

"Wheeeee... wheeeee..."

"Hey, Oscar — "

But he was off now to the other corner, flapping his wings fiercely. Rabbi Binder couldn't take it any longer — the fire engines from nowhere, the screaming suicidal boy, the net. He fell to his knees, exhausted, and with his hands curled together in front of his chest like a little dome, he pleaded, "Oscar, stop it, Oscar. Don't jump, Oscar. Please come down... Please don't jump."

And further back in the crowd a single voice, a single young voice, shouted a lone word to the boy on the roof.

"Jump!"

It was Itzie. Ozzie momentarily stopped flapping.

"Go ahead, Ozz — jump!" Itzie broke off his point of the star and courageously, with the inspiration not of a wise-guy but of a disciple, stood alone. "Jump, Ozz, jump!"

Still on his knees, his hands still curled, Rabbi Binder twisted his body back. He looked at Itzie, then, agonizingly, back to Ozzie.

"Oscar, Don't jump! Please, Don't Jump ... please please..."

"Jump!" This time it wasn't Itzie but another point of the star. By the time Mrs. Freedman arrived to keep her four-thirty appointment with Rabbi Binder, the whole little upside down heaven was shouting and pleading for Ozzie to jump, and Rabbi Binder no longer was pleading with him not to jump, but was crying into the dome of his hands.

Understandably Mrs. Freedman couldn't figure out what her son was doing on the roof. So she asked.

"Ozzie, my Ozzie, what are you doing? My Ozzie, what is it?"

Ozzie stopped wheeeeeing and slowed his arms down to a cruising flap, the kind birds use in soft winds, but he did not answer. He stood against the low, clouded, darkening sky — light clicked down swiftly now, as on a small gear — flapping softly and gazing down at the small bundle of a woman who was his mother.

"What are you doing, Ozzie?" She turned towards the kneeling Rabbi Binder and rushed so close that only a paper-thickness of dusk lay between her stomach and his shoulders.

"What is my baby doing?"

Rabbi Binder gaped up at her but he too was mute. All that moved was the dome of his hands; it shook back and forth like a weak pulse.

"Rabbi, get him down! He'll kill himself. Get him down, my only baby . . ."

"I can't," Rabbi Binder said, "I can't . . ." and he turned his handsome head towards the crowd of boys behind him. "It's them. Listen to them."

And for the first time Mrs. Freedman saw the crowd of boys, and she heard what they were yelling.

"He's doing it for them. He won't listen to me. It's them." Rabbi Binder spoke like one in a trance.

"For them?"

"Yes."

"Why for them?"

"They want him to ..."

Mrs. Freedman raised her two arms upward as though she were conducting the sky. "For them he's doing it!" And then in a gesture older than pyramids, older than prophets and floods, her arms came slapping down to her sides. "A martyr I have. Look!" She tilted her head to the roof. Ozzie was still flapping softly. "My martyr."

"Oscar, come down, *please*," Rabbi Binder groaned.

In a startlingly even voice Mrs. Freedman called to the boy on the roof. "Ozzie, come down, Ozzie. Don't be a martyr, my baby."

As though it were a litany, Rabbi Binder repeated her words. "Don't be a martyr, my baby. Don't be a martyr."

"Gawhead, Ozz — *be* a Martin!" It was Itzie. "Be a Martin, be a Martin," and all the voices joined in singing for Martindom, whatever *it* was. "Be a Martin, be a Martin ..."

Somehow when you're on a roof the darker it gets the less you can hear. All Ozzie knew was that two groups wanted two new things: his friends were spirited and musical about what they wanted; his mother and the rabbi were even-toned, chanting, about what they didn't want. The rabbi's voice was without tears now and so was his mother's.

The big net stared up at Ozzie like a sightless eye. The big, clouded sky pushed down. From beneath it looked like a gray corrugated board. Suddenly, looking up into that un-sympathetic sky, Ozzie realized all the strangeness of what these people, his friends, were asking: they wanted him to jump, to kill himself; they were singing about it now — it made them that happy. And there was an even greater strangeness: Rabbi Binder was on his knees, trembling. If there was a question to be asked now it was not "Is it me?" but rather "Is it us? . . . Is it us?"

Being on the roof, it turned out, was a serious thing. If he jumped would the singing become dancing? Would it? What would jumping stop? Yearningly, Ozzie wished he could rip open the sky, plunge his hands through, and pull out the sun; and on the sun, like a coin, would be stamped JUMP or DON'T JUMP.

Ozzie's knees rocked and sagged a little under him as though they were setting him for a dive. His arms tight-ened, stiffened, froze, from shoulders to fingernails. He felt as if each part of his body were going to vote as to whether he should kill himself or not — and each part as though it were independent of *him*.

The light took an unexpected click down and the new darkness, like a gag, hushed the friends singing for this and the mother and rabbi chanting for that.

Ozzie stopped counting votes, and in a curiously high voice, like one who wasn't prepared for speech, he spoke.

"Mamma?"

"Yes, Oscar."

"Mamma, get down on your knees, like Rabbi Binder."

"Oscar —"

"Get down on your knees," he said, "or I'll jump."

Ozzie heard a whimper, then a quick rustling, and when he looked down where his mother had stood he saw the top of a head and beneath that a circle of dress. She was kneeling beside Rabbi Binder.

He spoke again. "Everybody kneel." There was the sound of everybody kneeling.

Ozzie looked around. With one hand he pointed towards the synagogue entrance. "Make *him* kneel."

There was a noise, not of kneeling, but of body-and-cloth stretching. Ozzie could hear Rabbi Binder saying in a gruff whisper, ". . . or he'll *kill* himself," and when next he looked there was Yakov Blotnik off the doorknob and for the first time in his life upon his knees in the Gentile posture of prayer.

As for the firemen — it is not as difficult as one might imagine to hold a net taut while you are kneeling.

Ozzie looked around again; and then he called to Rabbi Binder.

"Rabbi?"

"Yes, Oscar."

"Rabbi Binder, do you believe in God."

"Yes."

"Do you believe God can do Anything?" Ozzie leaned his head out into the darkness. "Anything?"

"Oscar, I think — "

"Tell me you believe God can do Anything."

There was a second's hesitation. Then: "God can do Anything."

"Tell me you believe God can make a child without intercourse."

"He can."

"Tell me!"

"God," Rabbi Binder admitted, "can make a child without intercourse."

"Mamma, you tell me."

"God can make a child without intercourse," his mother said.

"Make *him* tell me." There was no doubt who *him* was.

In a few moments Ozzie heard an old comical voice say something to the increasing darkness about God.

Next, Ozzie made everybody say it. And then he made them all say they believed in Jesus Christ — first one at a time, then all together.

When the catechizing was through it was the beginning of evening. From the street it sounded as if the boy on the roof might have sighed.

"Ozzie?" A woman's voice dared to speak. "You'll come down now?"

There was no answer, but the woman waited, and when a voice finally did speak it was thin and crying, and exhausted as that of an old man who has just finished pulling the bells.

"Mamma, don't you see — you shouldn't hit me. He shouldn't hit me. You shouldn't hit me about God, Mamma. You should never hit anybody about God — "

"Ozzie, please come down now."

"Promise me, promise me you'll never hit anybody about God."

He had asked only his mother, but for some reason everyone kneeling in the street promised he would never hit anybody about God.

Once again there was silence.

"I can come down now, Mamma," the boy on the roof finally said. He turned his head both ways as though checking the traffic lights. "Now I can come down . . ."

And he did, right into the center of the yellow net that glowed in the evening's edge like an overgrown halo.

DEFENDER

OF

THE FAITH

Mary defending Jewish faith?
Mary changes thru/out
Grossbart never changes
Grossbart manipulates of his faith
Mary defends the faith by not
    letting Grossbart use the faith
    to manipulate.

In MAY of 1945, only a few weeks after the fighting had ended in Europe, I was rotated back to the States, where I spent the remainder of the war with a training company at Camp Crowder, Missouri. Along with the rest of the Ninth Army, I had been racing across Germany so swiftly during the late winter and spring that when I boarded the plane, I couldn't believe its destination lay to the west. My mind might inform me otherwise, but there was an inertia of the spirit that told me we were flying to a new front, where we would disembark and continue our push eastward — eastward until we'd circled the globe, marching through villages along whose twisting, cobbled streets crowds of the enemy would watch us take possession of what, up till then, they'd considered their own. I had changed enough in two years not to mind the trembling of the old people, the crying of the very young, the uncertainty and fear in the eyes of the once arrogant. I had been fortunate enough to develop an infantryman's heart, which, like his feet, at first aches and swells but finally grows horny enough for him to travel the weirdest paths without feeling a thing.

Captain Paul Barrett was my C.O. in Camp Crowder. The day I reported for duty, he came out of his office to shake my hand. He was short, gruff, and fiery, and — indoors or out — he wore his polished helmet liner pulled down to his little eyes. In Europe, he had received a battlefield commission and a serious chest wound, and he'd been returned to the States only a few months before. He spoke easily to me, and at the evening formation he introduced me to the troops. "Gentlemen," he said, "Sergeant Thurston, as you know, is no longer with this company. Your new first sergeant is Sergeant Nathan Marx, here. He is a veteran of the European theater, and consequently will expect to find a company of soldiers here, and not a company of *boys*."

I sat up late in the orderly room that evening, trying half-heartedly to solve the riddle of duty rosters, personnel forms, and morning reports. The Charge of Quarters slept with his mouth open on a mattress on the floor. A trainee stood reading the next day's duty roster, which was posted on the bulletin board just inside the screen door. It was a warm evening, and I could hear radios playing dance music over in the barracks. The trainee, who had been staring at me whenever he thought I wouldn't notice, finally took a step in my direction.

"Hey, Sarge — we having a G.I. party tomorrow night?" he asked. A G.I. party is a barracks cleaning.

"You usually have them on Friday nights?" I asked him.

"Yes," he said, and then he added, mysteriously, "that's the whole thing."

"Then you'll have a G.I. party."

He turned away, and I heard him mumbling. His

shoulders were moving, and I wondered if he was crying.

"What's your name, soldier?" I asked.

He turned, not crying at all. Instead, his green-speckled eyes, long and narrow, flashed like fish in the sun. He walked over to me and sat on the edge of my desk. He reached out a hand. "Sheldon," he said.

"Stand on your feet, Sheldon."

Getting off the desk, he said, "Sheldon Grossbart." He smiled at the familiarity into which he'd led me.

"You against cleaning the barracks Friday night, Grossbart?" I said. "Maybe we shouldn't have G.I. parties. Maybe we should get a maid." My tone startled me. I felt I sounded like every top sergeant I had ever known.

"No, Sergeant." He grew serious, but with a seriousness that seemed to be only the stifling of a smile. "It's just — G.I. parties on Friday night, of all nights."

He slipped up onto the corner of the desk again — not quite sitting, but not quite standing, either. He looked at me with those speckled eyes flashing, and then made a gesture with his hand. It was very slight — no more than a movement back and forth of the wrist — and yet it managed to exclude from our affairs everything else in the orderly room, to make the two of us the center of the world. It seemed, in fact, to exclude everything even about the two of us except our hearts.

"Sergeant Thurston was one thing," he whispered, glancing at the sleeping C.Q., "but we thought that with you here things might be a little different."

"We?"

"The Jewish personnel."

"Why?" I asked, harshly. "What's on your mind?"

Whether I was still angry at the "Sheldon" business, or now at something else, I hadn't time to tell, but clearly I was angry.

"We thought you — Marx, you know, like Karl Marx. The Marx Brothers. Those guys are all — M-a-r-x. Isn't that how *you* spell it, Sergeant?"

"M-a-r-x."

"Fishbein said — " He stopped. "What I mean to say, Sergeant — " His face and neck were red, and his mouth moved but no words came out. In a moment, he raised himself to attention, gazing down at me. It was as though he had suddenly decided he could expect no more sympathy from me than from Thurston, the reason being that I was of Thurston's faith, and not his. The young man had managed to confuse himself as to what my faith really was, but I felt no desire to straighten him out. Very simply, I didn't like him.

When I did nothing but return his gaze, he spoke, in an altered tone. "You see, Sergeant," he explained to me, "Friday nights, Jews are supposed to go to services."

"Did Sergeant Thurston tell you you couldn't go to them when there was a G.I. party?"

"No."

"Did he say you had to stay and scrub the floors?"

"No, Sergeant."

"Did the Captain say you had to stay and scrub the floors?"

"That isn't it, Sergeant. It's the other guys in the barracks." He leaned toward me. "They think we're goofing off. But we're not. That's when Jews go to services, Friday night. We have to."

"Then go."

"But the other guys make accusations. They have no right."

"That's not the Army's problem, Grossbart. It's a personal problem you'll have to work out yourself."

"But it's un*fair*."

I got up to leave. "There's nothing I can do about it," I said.

Grossbart stiffened and stood in front of me. "But this is a matter of *religion,* sir."

"Sergeant," I said.

"I mean 'Sergeant,'" he said, almost snarling.

"Look, go see the chaplain. You want to see Captain Barrett, I'll arrange an appointment."

"No, no. I don't want to make trouble, Sergeant. That's the first thing they throw up to you. I just want my rights!"

"Damn it, Grossbart, stop whining. You have your rights. You can stay and scrub floors or you can go to shul — "

The smile swam in again. Spittle gleamed at the corners of his mouth. "You mean church, Sergeant."

"I mean shul, Grossbart!"

I walked past him and went outside. Near me, I heard the scrunching of a guard's boots on gravel. Beyond the lighted windows of the barracks, young men in T shirts and fatigue pants were sitting on their bunks, polishing their rifles. Suddenly there was a light rustling behind me. I turned and saw Grossbart's dark frame fleeing back to the barracks, racing to tell his Jewish friends that they were right — that, like Karl and Harpo, I was one of them.

The next morning, while chatting with Captain Barrett, I recounted the incident of the previous evening. Somehow, in the telling, it must have seemed to the Captain that I was not so much explaining Grossbart's position as defending it. "Marx, I'd fight side by side with a nigger if the fella proved to me he was a man. I pride myself," he said, looking out the window, "that I've got an open mind. Consequently, Sergeant, nobody gets special treatment here, for the good *or* the bad. All a man's got to do is prove himself. A man fires well on the range, I give him a weekend pass. He scores high in P.T., he gets a weekend pass. He *earns* it." He turned from the window and pointed a finger at me. "You're a Jewish fella, am I right, Marx?"

"Yes, sir."

"And I admire you. I admire you because of the ribbons on your chest. I judge a man by what he shows me on the field of battle, Sergeant. It's what he's got *here*," he said, and then, though I expected he would point to his chest, he jerked a thumb toward the buttons straining to hold his blouse across his belly. "Guts," he said.

"O.K., sir. I only wanted to pass on to you how the men felt."

"Mr. Marx, you're going to be old before your time if you worry about how the men feel. Leave that stuff to the chaplain — that's his business, not yours. Let's us train these fellas to shoot straight. If the Jewish personnel feels the other men are accusing them of goldbricking — well, I just don't know. Seems awful funny that suddenly the Lord is calling so loud in Private Grossman's ear he's just got to run to church."

"Synagogue," I said.

"Synagogue is right, Sergeant. I'll write that down for handy reference. Thank you for stopping by."

That evening, a few minutes before the company gathered outside the orderly room for the chow formation, I called the C.Q., Corporal Robert LaHill, in to see me. LaHill was a dark, burly fellow whose hair curled out of his clothes wherever it could. He had a glaze in his eyes that made one think of caves and dinosaurs. "LaHill," I said, "when you take the formation, remind the men that they're free to attend church services *whenever* they are held, provided they report to the orderly room before they leave the area."

LaHill scratched his wrist, but gave no indication that he'd heard or understood.

"LaHill," I said, "*church*. You remember? Church, priest, Mass, confession."

He curled one lip into a kind of smile; I took it for a signal that for a second he had flickered back up into the human race.

"Jewish personnel who want to attend services this evening are to fall out in front of the orderly room at 1900," I said. Then, as an afterthought, I added, "By order of Captain Barrett."

A little while later, as the day's last light — softer than any I had seen that year — began to drop over Camp Crowder, I heard LaHill's thick, inflectionless voice outside my window: "Give me your ears, troopers. Toppie says for me to tell you that at 1900 hours all Jewish personnel is to fall out in front, here, if they want to attend the Jewish Mass."

At seven o'clock, I looked out the orderly-room window and saw three soldiers in starched khakis standing on the dusty quadrangle. They looked at their watches and fidgeted while they whispered back and forth. It was getting dimmer, and, alone on the otherwise deserted field, they looked tiny. When I opened the door, I heard the noises of the G.I. party coming from the surrounding barracks — bunks being pushed to the walls, faucets pounding water into buckets, brooms whisking at the wooden floors, cleaning the dirt away for Saturday's inspection. Big puffs of cloth moved round and round on the windowpanes. I walked outside, and the moment my foot hit the ground I thought I heard Grossbart call to the others, " 'Ten-*hut!*" Or maybe, when they all three jumped to attention, I imagined I heard the command.

Grossbart stepped forward. "Thank you, sir," he said.

" 'Sergeant,' Grossbart," I reminded him. "You call officers 'sir.' I'm not an officer. You've been in the Army three weeks — you know that."

He turned his palms out at his sides to indicate that, in truth, he and I lived beyond convention. "Thank you, anyway," he said.

"Yes," a tall boy behind him said. "Thanks a lot."

And the third boy whispered, "Thank you," but his mouth barely fluttered, so that he did not alter by more than a lip's movement his posture of attention.

"For what?" I asked.

Grossbart snorted happily. "For the announcement. The Corporal's announcement. It helped. It made it — "

"Fancier." The tall boy finished Grossbart's sentence.

Grossbart smiled. "He means formal, sir. Public," he said to me. "Now it won't seem as though we're just taking off — goldbricking because the work has begun."

"It was by order of Captain Barrett," I said.

"Aaah, but you pull a little weight," Grossbart said. "So we thank you." Then he turned to his companions. "Sergeant Marx, I want you to meet Larry Fishbein."

The tall boy stepped forward and extended his hand. I shook it. "You from New York?" he asked.

"Yes."

"Me, too." He had a cadaverous face that collapsed inward from his cheekbone to his jaw, and when he smiled — as he did at the news of our communal attachment — revealed a mouthful of bad teeth. He was blinking his eyes a good deal, as though he were fighting back tears. "What borough?" he asked.

I turned to Grossbart. "It's five after seven. What time are services?"

"Shul," he said, smiling, "is in ten minutes. I want you to meet Mickey Halpern. This is Nathan Marx, our sergeant."

The third boy hopped forward. "Private Michael Halpern." He saluted.

"Salute officers, Halpern," I said. The boy dropped his hand, and, on its way down, in his nervousness, checked to see if his shirt pockets were buttoned.

"Shall I march them over, sir?" Grossbart asked. "Or are you coming along?"

From behind Grossbart, Fishbein piped up. "Afterward, they're having refreshments. A ladies' auxiliary from St. Louis, the rabbi told us last week."

"The chaplain," Halpern whispered.

"You're welcome to come along," Grossbart said.

To avoid his plea, I looked away, and saw, in the windows of the barracks, a cloud of faces staring out at the four of us. "Hurry along, Grossbart," I said.

"O.K., then," he said. He turned to the others. "Double time, *march!*"

They started off, but ten feet away Grossbart spun

around and, running backward, called to me, "Good *shabbus*, sir!" And then the three of them were swallowed into the alien Missouri dusk.

Even after they had disappeared over the parade ground, whose green was now a deep blue, I could hear Grossbart singing the double-time cadence, and as it grew dimmer and dimmer, it suddenly touched a deep memory — as did the slant of the light — and I was remembering the shrill sounds of a Bronx playground where, years ago, beside the Grand Concourse, I had played on long spring evenings such as this. It was a pleasant memory for a young man so far from peace and home, and it brought so many recollections with it that I began to grow exceedingly tender about myself. In fact, I indulged myself in a reverie so strong that I felt as though a hand were reaching down inside me. It had to reach so very far to touch me! It had to reach past those days in the forests of Belgium, and past the dying I'd refused to weep over; past the nights in German farmhouses whose books we'd burned to warm us; past endless stretches when I had shut off all softness I might feel for my fellows, and had managed even to deny myself the posture of a conqueror — the swagger that I, as a Jew, might well have worn as my boots whacked against the rubble of Wesel, Münster, and Braunschweig.

But now one night noise, one rumor of home and time past, and memory plunged down through all I had anesthetized, and came to what I suddenly remembered was myself. So it was not altogether curious that, in search of more of me, I found myself following Grossbart's tracks to Chapel No. 3, where the Jewish services were being held.

I took a seat in the last row, which was empty. Two rows

in front of me sat Grossbart, Fishbein, and Halpern, holding little white Dixie cups. Each row of seats was raised higher than the one in front of it, and I could see clearly what was going on. Fishbein was pouring the contents of his cup into Grossbart's, and Grossbart looked mirthful as the liquid made a purple arc between Fishbein's hand and his. In the glaring yellow light, I saw the chaplain standing on the platform at the front; he was chanting the first line of the responsive reading. Grossbart's prayer book remained closed on his lap; he was swishing the cup around. Only Halpern responded to the chant by praying. The fingers of his right hand were spread wide across the cover of his open book. His cap was pulled down low onto his brow, which made it round, like a yarmulke. From time to time, Grossbart wet his lips at the cup's edge; Fishbein, his long yellow face a dying light bulb, looked from here to there, craning forward to catch sight of the faces down the row, then of those in front of him, then behind. He saw me, and his eyelids beat a tattoo. His elbow slid into Grossbart's side, his neck inclined toward his friend, he whispered something, and then, when the congregation next responded to the chant, Grossbart's voice was among the others. Fishbein looked into his book now, too; his lips, however, didn't move.

Finally, it was time to drink the wine. The chaplain smiled down at them as Grossbart swigged his in one long gulp, Halpern sipped, meditating, and Fishbein faked devotion with an empty cup. "As I look down amongst the congregation" — the chaplain grinned at the word — "this night, I see many new faces, and I want to welcome you to Friday-night services here at Camp Crowder. I am Major Leo Ben Ezra, your chaplain." Though an American, the chaplain spoke deliberately — syllable by syllable, almost — as though to communicate, above all, with the lip readers in his audience. "I have only a few words to say before we adjourn to the refreshment room, where the kind ladies of the Temple Sinai, St. Louis, Missouri, have a nice setting for you."

Applause and whistling broke out. After another momentary grin, the chaplain raised his hands, palms out, his eyes flicking upward a moment, as if to remind the troops where they were and Who Else might be in attendance. In the sudden silence that followed, I thought I heard Grossbart cackle, "Let the goyim clean the floors!" Were those the words? I wasn't sure, but Fishbein, grinning, nudged Halpern. Halpern looked dumbly at him, then went back to his prayer book, which had been occupying him all through the rabbi's talk. One hand tugged at the black kinky hair that stuck out under his cap. His lips moved.

The rabbi continued. "It is about the food that I want to speak to you for a moment. I know, I know, I know," he intoned, wearily, "how in the mouths of most of you the *trafe* food tastes like ashes. I know how you gag, some of you, and how your parents suffer to think of their children eating foods unclean and offensive to the palate. What can I tell you? I can only say, close your eyes and swallow as best you can. Eat what you must to live, and throw away the rest. I wish I could help more. For those of you who find this impossible, may I ask that you try and try, but then come to see me in private. If your revulsion is so great, we will have to seek aid from those higher up."

A round of chatter rose and subsided. Then everyone sang "Ain Kelohainu"; after all those years, I discovered I still knew the words. Then, suddenly, the service over,

Grossbart was upon me. "Higher up? He means the General?"

"Hey, Shelly," Fishbein said, "he means God." He smacked his face and looked at Halpern. "How high can you go!"

"Sh-h-h!" Grossbart said. "What do you think, Sergeant?"

"I don't know," I said. "You better ask the chaplain."

"I'm going to. I'm making an appointment to see him in private. So is Mickey."

Halpern shook his head. "No, no, Sheldon — "

"You have rights, Mickey," Grossbart said. "They can't push us around."

"It's O.K.," said Halpern. "It bothers my mother, not me."

Grossbart looked at me. "Yesterday he threw up. From the hash. It was all ham and God knows what else."

"I have a cold — that was why," Halpern said. He pushed his yarmulke back into a cap.

"What about you, Fishbein?" I asked. "You kosher, too?"

He flushed. "A little. But I'll let it ride. I have a very strong stomach, and I don't eat a lot anyway." I continued to look at him, and he held up his wrist to reinforce what he'd just said; his watch strap was tightened to the last hole, and he pointed that out to me.

"But services are important to you?" I asked him.

He looked at Grossbart. "Sure, sir."

" 'Sergeant.' "

"Not so much at home," said Grossbart, stepping between us, "but away from home it gives one a sense of his Jewishness."

"We have to stick together," Fishbein said.

I started to walk toward the door; Halpern stepped back to make way for me.

"That's what happened in Germany," Grossbart was saying, loud enough for me to hear. "They didn't stick together. They let themselves get pushed around."

I turned. "Look, Grossbart. This is the Army, not summer camp."

He smiled. "So?"

Halpern tried to sneak off, but Grossbart held his arm.

"Grossbart, how old are you?" I asked.

"Nineteen."

"And you?" I said to Fishbein.

"The same. The same month, even."

"And what about him?" I pointed to Halpern, who had by now made it safely to the door.

"Eighteen," Grossbart whispered. "But like he can't tie his shoes or brush his teeth himself. I feel sorry for him."

"I feel sorry for all of us, Grossbart," I said, "but just act like a man. Just don't overdo it."

"Overdo what, sir?"

"The 'sir' business, for one thing. Don't overdo that," I said.

I left him standing there. I passed by Halpern, but he did not look at me. Then I was outside, but, behind, I heard Grossbart call, "Hey, Mickey, my *leben*, come on back. Refreshments!"

"*Leben!*" My grandmother's word for me!

One morning a week later, while I was working at my desk, Captain Barrett shouted for me to come into his office. When I entered, he had his helmet liner squashed down so far on his head that I couldn't even see his eyes. He was on the phone, and when he spoke to me, he cupped one hand over the mouthpiece. "Who the hell is Grossbart?"

"Third platoon, Captain," I said. "A trainee."

"What's all this stink about food? His mother called a goddam congressman about the food." He uncovered the mouthpiece and slid his helmet up until I could see his bottom eyelashes. "Yes, sir," he said into the phone. "Yes, sir. I'm still here, sir. I'm asking Marx, here, right now — "

He covered the mouthpiece again and turned his head back toward me. "Lightfoot Harry's on the phone," he said, between his teeth. "This congressman calls General Lyman, who calls Colonel Sousa, who calls the Major, who calls me. They're just dying to stick this thing on me. Whatsa matter?" He shook the phone at me. "I don't feed the troops? What is this?"

"Sir, Grossbart is strange — " Barrett greeted that with a mockingly indulgent smile. I altered my approach. "Captain, he's a very orthodox Jew, and so he's only allowed to eat certain foods."

"He throws up, the congressman said. Every time he eats something, his mother says, he throws up!"

"He's accustomed to observing the dietary laws, Captain."

"So why's his old lady have to call the White House?"

"Jewish parents, sir — they're apt to be more protective than you expect. I mean, Jews have a very close family life. A boy goes away from home, sometimes the mother is liable to get very upset. Probably the boy mentioned something in a letter, and his mother misinterpreted."

"I'd like to punch him one right in the mouth," the

Captain said. "There's a war on, and he wants a silver platter!"

"I don't think the boy's to blame, sir. I'm sure we can straighten it out by just asking him. Jewish parents worry —"

"*All* parents worry, for Christ's sake. But they don't get on their high horse and start pulling strings —"

I interrupted, my voice higher, tighter than before. "The home life, Captain, is very important — but you're right, it may sometimes get out of hand. It's a very wonderful thing, Captain, but because it's so close, this kind of thing . . ."

He didn't listen any longer to my attempt to present both myself and Lightfoot Harry with an explanation for the letter. He turned back to the phone. "Sir?" he said. "Sir — Marx, here, tells me Jews have a tendency to be pushy. He says he thinks we can settle it right here in the company. . . . Yes, sir. . . . I *will* call back, sir, soon as I can." He hung up. "Where are the men, Sergeant?"

"On the range."

With a whack on the top of his helmet, he crushed it down over his eyes again, and charged out of his chair. "We're going for a ride," he said.

The Captain drove, and I sat beside him. It was a hot spring day, and under my newly starched fatigues I felt as though my armpits were melting down onto my sides and chest. The roads were dry, and by the time we reached the firing range, my teeth felt gritty with dust, though my mouth had been shut the whole trip. The Captain slammed the brakes on and told me to get the hell out and find Grossbart.

I found him on his belly, firing wildly at the five-hundred-feet target. Waiting their turns behind him were Halpern and Fishbein. Fishbein, wearing a pair of steel-rimmed G.I. glasses I hadn't seen on him before, had the appearance of an old peddler who would gladly have sold you his rifle and the cartridges that were slung all over him. I stood back by the ammo boxes, waiting for Grossbart to finish spraying the distant targets. Fishbein straggled back to stand near me.

"Hello, Sergeant Marx," he said.

"How are you?" I mumbled.

"Fine, thank you. Sheldon's really a good shot."

"I didn't notice."

"I'm not so good, but I think I'm getting the hang of it now. Sergeant, I don't mean to, you know, ask what I shouldn't — " The boy stopped. He was trying to speak intimately, but the noise of the shooting forced him to shout at me.

"What is it?" I asked. Down the range, I saw Captain Barrett standing up in the jeep, scanning the line for me and Grossbart.

"My parents keep asking and asking where we're going," Fishbein said. "Everybody says the Pacific. I don't care, but my parents — If I could relieve their minds, I think I could concentrate more on my shooting."

"I don't know where, Fishbein. Try to concentrate anyway."

"Sheldon says you might be able to find out."

"I don't know a thing, Fishbein. You just take it easy, and don't let Sheldon — "

"*I'm* taking it easy, Sergeant. It's at home — "

Grossbart had finished on the line, and was dusting his fatigues with one hand. I called to him. "Grossbart, the Captain wants to see you."

He came toward us. His eyes blazed and twinkled. "Hi!"

"Don't point that rifle!" I said.

"I wouldn't shoot you, Sarge." He gave me a smile as wide as a pumpkin, and turned the barrel aside.

"Damn you, Grossbart, this is no joke! Follow me."

I walked ahead of him, and had the awful suspicion that, behind me, Grossbart was *marching*, his rifle on his shoulder, as though he were a one-man detachment. At the jeep, he gave the Captain a rifle salute. "Private Sheldon Grossbart, sir."

"At ease, Grossman." The Captain sat down, slid over into the empty seat, and, crooking a finger, invited Grossbart closer.

"Bart, sir. Sheldon Gross*bart*. It's a common error." Grossbart nodded at me; *I* understood, he indicated. I looked away just as the mess truck pulled up to the range, disgorging a half-dozen K.P.s with rolled-up sleeves. The mess sergeant screamed at them while they set up the chow-line equipment.

"Grossbart, your mama wrote some congressman that we don't feed you right. Do you know that?" the Captain said.

"It was my father, sir. He wrote to Representative Franconi that my religion forbids me to eat certain foods."

"What religion is that, Grossbart?"

"Jewish."

" 'Jewish, *sir*,' " I said to Grossbart.

"Excuse me, sir. Jewish, sir."

"What have you been living on?" the Captain asked.

"You've been in the Army a month already. You don't look to me like you're falling to pieces."

"I eat because I have to, sir. But Sergeant Marx will testify to the fact that I don't eat one mouthful more than I need to in order to survive."

"Is that so, Marx?" Barrett asked.

"I've never seen Grossbart eat, sir," I said.

"But you heard the rabbi," Grossbart said. "He told us what to do, and I listened."

The Captain looked at me. "Well, Marx?"

"I still don't know what he eats and doesn't eat, sir."

Grossbart raised his arms to plead with me, and it looked for a moment as though he were going to hand me his weapon to hold. "But, Sergeant — "

"Look, Grossbart, just answer the Captain's questions," I said sharply.

Barrett smiled at me, and I resented it. "All right, Grossbart," he said. "What is it you want? The little piece of paper? You want out?"

"No, sir. Only to be allowed to live as a Jew. And for the others, too."

"What others?"

"Fishbein, sir, and Halpern."

"They don't like the way we serve, either?"

"Halpern throws up, sir. I've seen it."

"I thought *you* throw up."

"Just once, sir. I didn't know the sausage was sausage."

"We'll give menus, Grossbart. We'll show training films about the food, so you can identify when we're trying to poison you."

Grossbart did not answer. The men had been organized

into two long chow lines. At the tail end of one, I spotted Fishbein — or, rather, his glasses spotted me. They winked sunlight back at me. Halpern stood next to him, patting the inside of his collar with a khaki handkerchief. They moved with the line as it began to edge up toward the food. The mess sergeant was still screaming at the K.P.s. For a moment, I was actually terrified by the thought that somehow the mess sergeant was going to become involved in Grossbart's problem.

"Marx," the Captain said, "you're a Jewish fella — am I right?"

I played straight man. "Yes, sir."

"How long you been in the Army? Tell this boy."

"Three years and two months."

"A year in combat, Grossbart. Twelve goddam months in combat all through Europe. I admire this man." The Captain snapped a wrist against my chest. "Do you hear him peeping about the food? Do you? I want an answer, Grossbart. Yes or no."

"No, sir."

"And why not? He's a Jewish fella."

"Some things are more important to some Jews than other things to other Jews."

Barrett blew up. "Look, Grossbart. Marx, here, is a good man — a goddam hero. When you were in high school, Sergeant Marx was killing Germans. Who does more for the Jews — you, by throwing up over a lousy piece of sausage, a piece of first-cut meat, or Marx, by killing those Nazi bastards? If I was a Jew, Grossbart, I'd kiss this man's feet. He's a goddam hero, and *he* eats what we give him. Why do you have to cause trouble is what I want to know! What is it you're buckin' for — a discharge?"

"No, sir."

"I'm talking to a wall! Sergeant, get him out of my way."
Barrett swung himself back into the driver's seat. "I'm going to see the chaplain." The engine roared, the jeep spun
around in a whirl of dust, and the Captain was headed back
to camp.

For a moment, Grossbart and I stood side by side, watching the jeep. Then he looked at me and said, "I don't want
to start trouble. That's the first thing they toss up to us."

When he spoke, I saw that his teeth were white and
straight, and the sight of them suddenly made me understand that Grossbart actually did have parents — that once
upon a time someone had taken little Sheldon to the den-
tist. He was their son. Despite all the talk about his parents, it was hard to believe in Grossbart as a child, an heir
— as related by blood to anyone, mother, father, or, above
all, to me. This realization led me to another.

"What does your father do, Grossbart?" I asked as we
started to walk back toward the chow line.

"He's a tailor."

"An American?"

"Now, yes. A son in the Army," he said, jokingly.

"And your mother?" I asked.

He winked. "A *ballabusta*. She practically sleeps with a
dustcloth in her hand."

"She's also an immigrant?"

"All she talks is Yiddish, still."

"And your father, too?"

"A little English. 'Clean,' 'Press,' 'Take the pants in.'
That's the extent of it. But they're good to me."

"Then, Grossbart — " I reached out and stopped him.
He turned toward me, and when our eyes met, his seemed

to jump back, to shiver in their sockets. "Grossbart — you were the one who wrote that letter, weren't you?"

It took only a second or two for his eyes to flash happy again. "Yes." He walked on, and I kept pace. "It's what my father *would* have written if he had known how. It was his name, though. *He* signed it. He even mailed it. I sent it home. For the New York postmark."

I was astonished, and he saw it. With complete seriousness, he thrust his right arm in front of me. "Blood is blood, Sergeant," he said, pinching the blue vein in his wrist.

"What the hell *are* you trying to do, Grossbart?" I asked. "I've seen you eat. Do you know that? I told the Captain I don't know what you eat, but I've seen you eat like a hound at chow."

"We work hard, Sergeant. We're in training. For a furnace to work, you've got to feed it coal."

"Why did you say in the letter that you threw up all the time?"

"I was really talking about Mickey there. I was talking *for* him. He would never write, Sergeant, though I pleaded with him. He'll waste away to nothing if I don't help. Sergeant, I used my name — my father's name — but it's Mickey, and Fishbein, too, I'm watching out for."

"You're a regular Messiah, aren't you?"

We were at the chow line now.

"That's a good one, Sergeant," he said, smiling. "But who knows? Who can tell? Maybe you're the Messiah — a little bit. What Mickey says is the Messiah is a collective idea. He went to Yeshiva, Mickey, for a while. He says *together* we're the Messiah. Me a little bit, you a little bit.

You should hear that kid talk, Sergeant, when he gets going."

"Me a little bit, you a little bit," I said. "You'd like to believe that, wouldn't you, Grossbart? That would make everything so clean for you."

"It doesn't seem too bad a thing to believe, Sergeant. It only means we should all *give* a little, is all."

I walked off to eat my rations with the other noncoms.

Two days later, a letter addressed to Captain Barrett passed over my desk. It had come through the chain of command — from the office of Congressman Franconi, where it had been received, to General Lyman, to Colonel Sousa, to Major Lamont, now to Captain Barrett. I read it over twice. It was dated May 14, the day Barrett had spoken with Grossbart on the rifle range.

Dear Congressman:

First let me thank you for your interest in behalf of my son, Private Sheldon Grossbart. Fortunately, I was able to speak with Sheldon on the phone the other night, and I think I've been able to solve our problem. He is, as I mentioned in my last letter, a very religious boy, and it was only with the greatest difficulty that I could persuade him that the religious thing to do — what God Himself would want Sheldon to do — would be to suffer the pangs of religious remorse for the good of his country and all mankind. It took some doing, Congressman, but finally he saw the light. In fact, what he said (and I wrote down the words on a scratch pad so as never to forget), what he said was "I guess you're right, Dad. So many millions of my

*fellow-Jews gave up their lives to the enemy, the least I
can do is live for a while minus a bit of my heritage so as
to help end this struggle and regain for all the children of
God dignity and humanity." That, Congressman, would
make any father proud.*

*By the way, Sheldon wanted me to know — and to pass
on to you — the name of a soldier who helped him reach
this decision: SERGEANT NATHAN MARX. Sergeant
Marx is a combat veteran who is Sheldon's first sergeant.
This man has helped Sheldon over some of the first hur-
dles he's had to face in the Army, and is in part responsible
for Sheldon's changing his mind about the dietary laws. I
know Sheldon would appreciate any recognition Marx
could receive.*

*Thank you and good luck. I look forward to seeing your
name on the next election ballot.*

> *Respectfully,*
> *Samuel E. Grossbart*

Attached to the Grossbart communiqué was another,
addressed to General Marshall Lyman, the post com-
mander, and signed by Representative Charles E. Franconi, of the House of Representatives. The communiqué
informed General Lyman that Sergeant Nathan Marx was
a credit to the U.S. Army and the Jewish people.

What was Grossbart's motive in recanting? Did he feel
he'd gone too far? Was the letter a strategic retreat — a
crafty attempt to strengthen what he considered our alli-
ance? Or had he actually changed his mind, via an imaginary dialogue between Grossbart *père* and Grossbart *fils*?
I was puzzled, but only for a few days — that is, only until
I realized that, whatever his reasons, he had actually de-

cided to disappear from my life; he was going to allow
himself to become just another trainee. I saw him at inspection, but he never winked; at chow formations, but he
never flashed me a sign. On Sundays, with the other trainees, he would sit around watching the noncoms' softball
team, for which I pitched, but not once did he speak an
unnecessary word to me. Fishbein and Halpern retreated,
too — at Grossbart's command, I was sure. Apparently he
had seen that wisdom lay in turning back before he plunged
over into the ugliness of privilege undeserved. Our separation allowed me to forgive him our past encounters, and,
finally, to admire him for his good sense.

Meanwhile, free of Grossbart, I grew used to my job and
my administrative tasks. I stepped on a scale one day, and
discovered I had truly become a noncombatant; I had
gained seven pounds. I found patience to get past the first
three pages of a book. I thought about the future more and
more, and wrote letters to girls I'd known before the war.
I even got a few answers. I sent away to Columbia for a
Law School catalogue. I continued to follow the war in
the Pacific, but it was not my war. I thought I could see
the end, and sometimes, at night, I dreamed that I was
walking on the streets of Manhattan — Broadway, Third
Avenue, 116th Street, where I had lived the three years I
attended Columbia. I curled myself around these dreams
and I began to be happy.

And then, one Sunday, when everybody was away and
I was alone in the orderly room reading a month-old copy
of the *Sporting News*, Grossbart reappeared.

"You a baseball fan, Sergeant?"

I looked up. "How are you?"

"Fine," Grossbart said. "They're making a soldier out of me."

"How are Fishbein and Halpern?"

"Coming along," he said. "We've got no training this afternoon. They're at the movies."

"How come you're not with them?"

"I wanted to come over and say hello."

He smiled — a shy, regular-guy smile, as though he and I well knew that our friendship drew its sustenance from unexpected visits, remembered birthdays, and borrowed lawnmowers. At first it offended me, and then the feeling was swallowed by the general uneasiness I felt at the thought that everyone on the post was locked away in a dark movie theater and I was here alone with Grossbart. I folded up my paper.

"Sergeant," he said, "I'd like to ask a favor. It is a favor, and I'm making no bones about it."

He stopped, allowing me to refuse him a hearing — which, of course, forced me into a courtesy I did not intend. "Go ahead."

"Well, actually it's two favors."

I said nothing.

"The first one's about these rumors. Everybody says we're going to the Pacific."

"As I told your friend Fishbein, I don't know," I said. "You'll just have to wait to find out. Like everybody else."

"You think there's a chance of any of us going East?"

"Germany?" I said. "Maybe."

"I meant New York."

"I don't think so, Grossbart. Offhand."

"Thanks for the information, Sergeant," he said.

"It's not information, Grossbart. Just what I surmise."

"It certainly would be good to be near home. My parents
— you know." He took a step toward the door and then
turned back. "Oh, the other thing. May I ask the other?"

"What is it?"

"The other thing is — I've got relatives in St. Louis, and
they say they'll give me a whole Passover dinner if I can
get down there. God, Sergeant, that'd mean an awful lot
to me."

I stood up. "No passes during basic, Grossbart."

"But we're off from now till Monday morning, Sergeant.
I could leave the post and no one would even know."

"I'd know. You'd know."

"But that's all. Just the two of us. Last night, I called my
aunt, and you should have heard her. 'Come — come,' she
said. 'I got gefilte fish, *chrain* — the works!' Just a day, Sergeant. I'd take the blame if anything happened."

"The Captain isn't here to sign a pass."

"You could sign."

"Look, Grossbart — "

"Sergeant, for two months, practically, I've been eating
trafe till I want to die."

"I thought you'd made up your mind to live with it. To
be minus a little bit of heritage."

He pointed a finger at me. "You!" he said. "That wasn't
for you to read."

"I read it. So what?"

"That letter was addressed to a congressman."

"Grossbart, don't feed me any baloney. You *wanted* me
to read it."

"Why are you persecuting me, Sergeant?"

"Are you kidding!"

"I've run into this before," he said, "but never from my own!"

"Get out of here, Grossbart! Get the hell out of my sight!"

He did not move. "Ashamed, that's what you are," he said. "So you take it out on the rest of us. They say Hitler himself was half a Jew. Hearing you, I wouldn't doubt it."

"What are you trying to do with me, Grossbart?" I asked him. "What are you after? You want me to give you special privileges, to change the food, to find out about your orders, to give you weekend passes."

"You even talk like a goy!" Grossbart shook his fist. "Is this just a weekend pass I'm asking for? Is a Seder sacred, or not?"

Seder! It suddenly occurred to me that Passover had been celebrated weeks before. I said so.

"That's right," he replied. "Who says no? A month ago — and I was in the field eating hash! And now all I ask is a simple favor. A Jewish boy I thought would understand. My aunt's willing to go out of her way — to make a Seder a month later. . . ." He turned to go, mumbling.

"Come back here!" I called. He stopped and looked at me. "Grossbart, why can't you be like the rest? Why do you have to stick out like a sore thumb?"

"Because I'm a Jew, Sergeant. I *am* different. Better, maybe not. But different."

"This is a war, Grossbart. For the time being *be* the same."

"I refuse."

"What?"

"I refuse. I can't stop being me, that's all there is to it."

Tears came to his eyes. "It's a hard thing to be a Jew. But now I understand what Mickey says — it's a harder thing to stay one." He raised a hand sadly toward me. "Look at *you.*"

"Stop crying!"

"Stop this, stop that, stop the other thing! *You* stop, Sergeant. Stop closing your heart to your own!" And, wiping his face with his sleeve, he ran out the door. "The least we can do for one another — the least . . ."

An hour later, looking out of the window, I saw Grossbart headed across the field. He wore a pair of starched khakis and carried a little leather ditty bag. I went out into the heat of the day. It was quiet; not a soul was in sight except, over by the mess hall, four K.P.s sitting around a pan, sloped forward from their waists, gabbing and peeling potatoes in the sun.

"Grossbart!" I called.

He looked toward me and continued walking.

"Grossbart, get over here!"

He turned and came across the field. Finally, he stood before me.

"Where are you going?" I asked.

"St. Louis. I don't care."

"You'll get caught without a pass."

"So I'll get caught without a pass."

"You'll go to the stockade."

"I'm *in* the stockade." He made an about-face and headed off.

I let him go only a step or two. "Come back here," I said, and he followed me into the office, where I typed out a pass and signed the Captain's name, and my own initials after it.

He took the pass and then, a moment later, reached out and grabbed my hand. "Sergeant, you don't know how much this means to me."

"O.K.," I said. "Don't get in any trouble."

"I wish I could show you how much this means to me."

"Don't do me any favors. Don't write any more congressmen for citations."

He smiled. "You're right. I won't. But let me do something."

"Bring me a piece of that gefilte fish. Just get out of here."

"I will!" he said. "With a slice of carrot and a little horseradish. I won't forget."

"All right. Just show your pass at the gate. And don't tell *anybody*."

"I won't. It's a month late, but a good Yom Tov to you."

"Good Yom Tov, Grossbart," I said.

"You're a good Jew, Sergeant. You like to think you have a hard heart, but underneath you're a fine, decent man. I mean that."

Those last three words touched me more than any words from Grossbart's mouth had the right to. "All right, Grossbart," I said. "Now call me 'sir,' and get the hell out of here."

He ran out the door and was gone. I felt very pleased with myself; it was a great relief to stop fighting Grossbart, and it had cost me nothing. Barrett would never find out, and if he did, I could manage to invent some excuse. For a while, I sat at my desk, comfortable in my decision. Then the screen door flew back and Grossbart burst in again. "Sergeant!" he said. Behind him I saw Fishbein and Halpern, both in starched khakis, both carrying ditty bags like Grossbart's.

"Sergeant, I caught Mickey and Larry coming out of the movies. I almost missed them."

"Grossbart—did I say tell no one?" I said.

"But my aunt said I could bring friends. That I should, in fact."

"*I'm* the Sergeant, Grossbart — not your aunt!"

Grossbart looked at me in disbelief. He pulled Halpern up by his sleeve. "Mickey, tell the Sergeant what this would mean to you."

Halpern looked at me and, shrugging, said, "A lot."

Fishbein stepped forward without prompting. "This would mean a great deal to me and my parents, Sergeant Marx."

"No!" I shouted.

Grossbart was shaking his head. "Sergeant, I could see you denying me, but how you can deny Mickey, a Yeshiva boy — that's beyond me."

"I'm not denying Mickey anything," I said. "You just pushed a little too hard, Grossbart. *You* denied him."

"I'll give him my pass, then," Grossbart said. "I'll give him my aunt's address and a little note. At least let him go."

In a second, he had crammed the pass into Halpern's pants pocket. Halpern looked at me, and so did Fishbein. Grossbart was at the door, pushing it open. "Mickey, bring me a piece of gelfilte fish, at least," he said, and then he was outside again.

The three of us looked at one another, and then I said, "Halpern, hand that pass over."

He took it from his pocket and gave it to me. Fishbein

had now moved to the doorway, where he lingered. He stood there for a moment with his mouth slightly open, and then he pointed to himself. "And me?" he asked.

His utter ridiculousness exhausted me. I slumped down in my seat and felt pulses knocking at the back of my eyes. "Fishbein," I said, "you understand I'm not trying to deny you anything, don't you? If it was my Army, I'd serve gefilte fish in the mess hall. I'd sell *kugel* in the PX, honest to God."

Halpern smiled.

"You understand, don't you, Halpern?"

"Yes, Sergeant."

"And you, Fishbein? I don't want enemies. I'm just like you — I want to serve my time and go home. I miss the same things you miss."

"Then, Sergeant," Fishbein said, "why don't you come, too?"

"Where?"

"To St. Louis. To Shelly's aunt. We'll have a regular Seder. Play hide-the-matzoh." He gave me a broad, black-toothed smile.

I saw Grossbart again, on the other side of the screen.

"Pst!" He waved a piece of paper. "Mickey, here's the address. Tell her I couldn't get away."

Halpern did not move. He looked at me, and I saw the shrug moving up his arms into his shoulders again. I took the cover off my typewriter and made out passes for him and Fishbein. "Go," I said. "The three of you."

I thought Halpern was going to kiss my hand.

That afternoon, in a bar in Joplin, I drank beer and listened with half an ear to the Cardinal game. I tried to look squarely at what I'd become involved in, and began to wonder if perhaps the struggle with Grossbart wasn't as much my fault as his. What was I that I had to *muster* generous feelings? Who was I to have been feeling so grudging, so tight-hearted? After all, I wasn't being asked to move the world. Had I a right, then, or a reason, to clamp down on Grossbart, when that meant clamping down on Halpern, too? And Fishbein — that ugly, agreeable soul? Out of the many recollections of my childhood that had tumbled over me these past few days I heard my grandmother's voice: "What are you making a *tsimmes?*" It was what she would ask my mother when, say, I had cut myself while doing something I shouldn't have done, and her daughter was busy bawling me out. I needed a hug and a kiss, and my mother would moralize. But my grandmother knew — mercy overrides justice. I should have known it, too. Who was Nathan Marx to be such a penny pincher with kindness? Surely, I thought, the Messiah himself — if He should ever come — won't niggle over nickels and dimes. God willing, he'll hug and kiss.

The next day, while I was playing softball over on the parade ground, I decided to ask Bob Wright, who was noncom in charge of Classification and Assignment, where he thought our trainees would be sent when their cycle ended, in two weeks. I asked casually, between innings, and he said, "They're pushing them all into the Pacific. Shulman cut the orders on your boys the other day."

The news shocked me, as though I were the father of Halpern, Fishbein, and Grossbart.

That night, I was just sliding into sleep when someone tapped on my door. "Who is it?" I asked.

"Sheldon."

He opened the door and came in. For a moment, I felt his presence without being able to see him. "How was it?" I asked.

He popped into sight in the near-darkness before me. "Great, Sergeant." Then he was sitting on the edge of the bed. I sat up.

"How about you?" he asked. "Have a nice weekend?"

"Yes."

"The others went to sleep." He took a deep, paternal breath. We sat silent for a while, and a homey feeling invaded my ugly little cubicle; the door was locked, the cat was out, the children were safely in bed.

"Sergeant, can I tell you something? Personal?"

I did not answer, and he seemed to know why. "Not about me. About Mickey. Sergeant, I never felt for anybody like I feel for him. Last night I heard Mickey in the bed next to me. He was crying so, it could have broken your heart. Real sobs."

"I'm sorry to hear that."

"I had to talk to him to stop him. He held my hand, Sergeant — he wouldn't let it go. He was almost hysterical. He kept saying if he only knew where we were going. Even if he knew it *was* the Pacific, that would be better than nothing. Just to know."

Long ago, someone had taught Grossbart the sad rule that only lies can get the truth. Not that I couldn't believe in the fact of Halpern's crying; his eyes *always* seemed red-rimmed. But, fact or not, it became a lie when Grossbart uttered it. He was entirely strategic. But then — it came with the force of indictment — so was I! There are strategies of aggression, but there are strategies of retreat as well.

And so, recognizing that I myself had not been without craft and guile, I told him what I knew. "It is the Pacific."

He let out a small gasp, which was not a lie. "I'll tell him. I wish it was otherwise."

"So do I."

He jumped on my words. "You mean you think you could do something? A change, maybe?"

"No, I couldn't do a thing."

"Don't you know anybody over at C. and A.?"

"Grossbart, there's nothing I can do," I said. "If your orders are for the Pacific, then it's the Pacific."

"But Mickey — "

"Mickey, you, me — everybody, Grossbart. There's nothing to be done. Maybe the war'll end before you go. Pray for a miracle."

"But — "

"Good night, Grossbart." I settled back, and was relieved to feel the springs unbend as Grossbart rose to leave. I could see him clearly now; his jaw had dropped, and he looked like a dazed prizefighter. I noticed for the first time a little paper bag in his hand.

"Grossbart." I smiled. "My gift?"

"Oh, yes, Sergeant. Here — from all of us." He handed me the bag. "It's egg roll."

"Egg roll?" I accepted the bag and felt a damp grease spot on the bottom. I opened it, sure that Grossbart was joking.

"We thought you'd probably like it. You know — Chinese egg roll. We thought you'd probably have a taste for — "

"Your aunt served egg roll?"

"She wasn't home."

"Grossbart, she invited you. You told me she invited you and your friends."

"I know," he said. "I just reread the letter. *Next* week."

I got out of bed and walked to the window. "Grossbart," I said. But I was not calling to him.

"What?"

"What are you, Grossbart? Honest to God, what are you?"

I think it was the first time I'd asked him a question for which he didn't have an immediate answer.

"How can you do this to people?" I went on.

"Sergeant, the day away did us all a world of good. Fishbein, you should see him, he *loves* Chinese food."

"But the Seder," I said.

"We took second best, Sergeant."

Rage came charging at me. I didn't sidestep. "Grossbart, you're a liar!" I said. "You're a schemer and a crook. You've got no respect for anything. Nothing at all. Not for me, for the truth — not even for poor Halpern! You use us all — "

"Sergeant, Sergeant, I feel for Mickey. Honest to God, I do. I *love* Mickey. I try — "

"You try! You feel!" I lurched toward him and grabbed his shirt front. I shook him furiously. "Grossbart, get out! Get out and stay the hell away from me. Because if I see you, I'll make your life miserable. *You understand that?*"

"Yes."

I let him free, and when he walked from the room, I wanted to spit on the floor where he had stood. I couldn't stop the fury. It engulfed me, owned me, till it seemed I could only rid myself of it with tears or an act of violence. I snatched from the bed the bag Grossbart had given me and, with all my strength, threw it out the window. And the next morning, as the men policed the area around the barracks, I heard a great cry go up from one of the trainees, who had been anticipating only his morning handful of cigarette butts and candy wrappers. "Egg roll!" he shouted. "Holy Christ, Chinese goddam egg roll!"

A week later, when I read the orders that had come down from C. and A., I couldn't believe my eyes. Every single trainee was to be shipped to Camp Stoneman, California, and from there to the Pacific — every trainee but one. Private Sheldon Grossbart. He was to be sent to Fort Monmouth, New Jersey. I read the mimeographed sheet several times. Dee, Farrell, Fishbein, Fuselli, Fylypowycz, Glinicki, Gromke, Gucwa, Halpern, Hardy, Helebrandt, right down to Anton Zygadlo — all were to be headed West before the month was out. All except Grossbart. He had pulled a string, and I wasn't it.

I lifted the phone and called C. and A.

The voice on the other end said smartly, "Corporal Shulman, sir."

"Let me speak to Sergeant Wright."

"Who is this calling, sir?"

"Sergeant Marx."

And, to my surprise, the voice said, "*Oh!*" Then, "Just a minute, Sergeant."

Shulman's "*Oh!*" stayed with me while I waited for Wright to come to the phone. Why "*Oh!*"? Who was Shulman? And then, so simply, I knew I'd discovered the string that Grossbart had pulled. In fact, I could hear Grossbart the day he'd discovered Shulman in the PX, or in the bowling alley, or maybe even at services. "Glad to meet

you. Where you from? Bronx? Me, too. Do you know So-
and-So? And So-and-So? Me, too! You work at C. and A.?
Really? Hey, how's chances of getting East? Could you do
something? Change something? Swindle, cheat, lie? We
gotta help each other, you know. If the Jews in Germany . . ."

Bob Wright answered the phone. "How are you, Nate?
How's the pitching arm?"

"Good. Bob, I wonder if you could do me a favor." I
heard clearly my own words, and they so reminded me of
Grossbart that I dropped more easily than I could have
imagined into what I had planned. "This may sound crazy,
Bob, but I got a kid here on orders to Monmouth who
wants them changed. He had a brother killed in Europe,
and he's hot to go to the Pacific. Says he'd feel like a
coward if he wound up Stateside. I don't know, Bob —
can anything be done? Put somebody else in the Monmouth
slot?"

"Who?" he asked cagily.

"Anybody. First guy in the alphabet. I don't care. The
kid just asked if something could be done."

"What's his name?"

"Grossbart, Sheldon."

Wright didn't answer.

"Yeah," I said. "He's a Jewish kid, so he thought I could
help him out. You know."

"I guess I can do something," he finally said. "The Major
hasn't been around here for weeks. Temporary duty to the
golf course. I'll try, Nate, that's all I can say."

"I'd appreciate it, Bob. See you Sunday." And I hung up,
perspiring.

The following day, the corrected orders appeared: Fishbein, Fuselli, Fylypowycz, Glinicki, Gromke, Grossbart, Gucwa, Halpern, Hardy . . . Lucky Private Harley Alton was to go to Fort Monmouth, New Jersey, where, for some reason or other, they wanted an enlisted man with infantry training.

After chow that night, I stopped back at the orderly room to straighten out the guard-duty roster. Grossbart was waiting for me. He spoke first.

"You son of a bitch!"

I sat down at my desk, and while he glared at me, I began to make the necessary alterations in the duty roster.

"What do you have against me?" he cried. "Against my family? Would it kill you for me to be near my father, God knows how many months he has left to him?"

"Why so?"

"His heart," Grossbart said. "He hasn't had enough troubles in a lifetime, you've got to add to them. I curse the day I ever met you, Marx! Shulman told me what happened over there. There's no limit to your anti-Semitism, is there? The damage you've done here isn't enough. You have to make a special phone call! You really want me dead!"

I made the last few notations in the duty roster and got up to leave. "Good night, Grossbart."

"You owe me an explanation!" He stood in my path.

"Sheldon, you're the one who owes explanations."

He scowled. "To *you*?"

"To me, I think so — yes. Mostly to Fishbein and Halpern."

"That's right, twist things around. I owe nobody nothing, I've done all I could do for them. Now I think I've got the right to watch out for myself."

defending the faith (handwritten margin note)

"For each other we have to learn to watch out, Sheldon. You told me yourself."

"You call this watching out for me — what you did?"

"No. For all of us."

I pushed him aside and started for the door. I heard his furious breathing behind me, and it sounded like steam rushing from an engine of terrible strength.

"*You'll* be all right," I said from the door. And, I thought, so would Fishbein and Halpern be all right, even in the Pacific, if only Grossbart continued to see — in the obsequiousness of the one, the soft spirituality of the other — some profit for himself.

I stood outside the orderly room, and I heard Grossbart weeping behind me. Over in the barracks, in the lighted windows, I could see the boys in their T shirts sitting on their bunks talking about their orders, as they'd been doing for the past two days. With a kind of quiet nervousness, they polished shoes, shined belt buckles, squared away underwear, trying as best they could to accept their fate. Behind me, Grossbart swallowed hard, accepting his. And then, resisting with all my will an impulse to turn and seek pardon for my vindictiveness, I accepted my own.

EPSTEIN

MICHAEL, the weekend guest, was to spend the night in one of the twin beds in Herbie's old room, where the baseball pictures still hung on the wall. Lou Epstein lay with his wife in the room with the bed pushed cater-corner. His daughter Sheila's bedroom was empty; she was at a meeting with her fiancé, the folk singer. In the corner of her room a childhood teddy bear balanced on its bottom, a VOTE SOCIALIST button pinned to its left ear; on her bookshelves, where volumes of Louisa May Alcott once gathered dust, were now collected the works of Howard Fast. The house was quiet. The only light burning was downstairs in the dining room where the *shabus* candles flickered in their tall golden holders and Herbie's *jahrzeit* candle trembled in its glass.

Epstein looked at the dark ceiling of his bedroom and let his head that had been bang-banging all day go blank for a moment. His wife Goldie breathed thickly beside him, as though she suffered from eternal bronchitis. Ten minutes before she had undressed and he had watched as she dropped her white nightdress over her head, over the breasts which had funneled down to her middle, over the

behind like a bellows, the thighs and calves veined blue
like a roadmap. What once could be pinched, what once
was small and tight, now could be poked and pulled. Everything hung. He had shut his eyes while she had dressed
for sleep and had tried to remember the Goldie of 1927,
the Lou Epstein of 1927. Now he rolled his stomach
against her backside, remembering, and reached around
to hold her breasts. The nipples were dragged down like a
cow's, long as his little finger. He rolled back to his own
side.

A key turned in the front door — there was whispering,
then the door gently shut. He tensed and waited for the
noises — it didn't take those Socialists long. At night the
noise from the zipping and the unzipping was enough to
keep a man awake. "What are they doing down there?" he
had screamed at his wife one Friday night, "trying on
clothes?" Now, once again, he waited. It wasn't that he
was against their playing. He was no puritan, he believed
in young people enjoying themselves. Hadn't he been a
young man himself? But in 1927 he and his wife were
handsome people. Lou Epstein had never resembled that
chinless, lazy smart aleck whose living was earned singing
folk songs in a saloon, and who once had asked Epstein if
it hadn't been "thrilling" to have lived through "a period
of great social upheaval" like the thirties.

And his daughter, why couldn't she have grown up to be
like — like the girl across the street whom Michael had
the date with, the one whose father had died. Now there
was a pretty girl. But not his Sheila. What happened, he
wondered, what happened to that little pink-skinned baby?
What year, what month did those skinny ankles grow thick
as logs, the peaches-and-cream turn to pimples? That

lovely child was now a twenty-three-year-old woman with
"a social conscience"! Some conscience, he thought. She
hunts all day for a picket line to march in so that at night
she can come home and eat like a horse . . . For her and
that guitar plucker to touch each other's unmentionables
seemed worse than sinful — it was disgusting. When Epstein tossed in bed and heard their panting and the zipping
it sounded in his ears like thunder.

Zip!

They were at it. He would ignore them, think of his
other problems. The business . . . here he was a year away
from the retirement he had planned but with no heir to
Epstein Paper Bag Company. He had built the business
from the ground, suffered and bled during the Depression
and Roosevelt, only, finally, with the war and Eisenhower
to see it succeed. The thought of a stranger taking it over
made him sick. But what could be done? Herbie, who
would have been twenty-eight, had died of polio, age
eleven. And Sheila, his last hope, had chosen as her intended a lazy man. What could he do? Does a man of
fifty-nine all of a sudden start producing heirs?

Zip! Pant-pant-pant! Ahh!

He shut his ears and mind, tighter. He tried to recollect
things and drown himself in them. For instance, dinner . . .

He had been startled when he arrived home from the
shop to find the soldier sitting at his dinner table. Surprised because the boy, whom he had not seen for ten or
twelve years, had grown up with the Epstein face, as his
son would have, the small bump in the nose, the strong
chin, dark skin, and shock of shiny black hair that, one
day, would turn gray as clouds.

"Look who's here," his wife shouted at him the moment he entered the door, the day's dirt still under his fingernails. "Sol's boy."

The soldier popped up from his chair and extended his hand. "How do you do, Uncle Louis?"

"A Gregory Peck," Epstein's wife said, "a Monty Clift your brother has. He's been here only three hours already he has a date. And a regular gentleman . . ."

Epstein did not answer.

The soldier stood at attention, square, as though he'd learned courtesy long before the Army. "I hope you don't mind my barging in, Uncle Louis. I was shipped to Monmouth last week and Dad said I should stop off to see you people. I've got the weekend off and Aunt Goldie said I should stay — " He waited.

"Look at him," Goldie was saying, "a Prince!"

"Of course," Epstein said at last, "stay. How is your father?" Epstein had not spoken to his brother Sol since 1945 when he had bought Sol's share of the business and his brother had moved to Detroit, with words.

"Dad's fine," Michael said. "He sends his regards."

"Sure, I send mine too. You'll tell him."

Michael sat down, and Epstein knew that the boy must think just as his father did: that Lou Epstein was a coarse man whose heart beat faster only when he was thinking of Epstein Paper Bag.

When Sheila came home they all sat down to eat, four, as in the old days. Goldie Epstein jumped up and down, up and down, slipping each course under their noses the instant they had finished the one before. "Michael," she said historically, "Michael, as a child you were a very poor eater. Your sister Ruthie, God bless her, was a nice eater. Not a good eater, but a nice eater."

For the first time Epstein remembered his little niece Ruthie, a little dark-haired beauty, a Bible Ruth. He looked at his own daughter and heard his wife go on, and on. "No, Ruthie wasn't such a good eater. But she wasn't a picky eater. Our Herbie, he should rest in peace, was a picky eater..." Goldie looked towards her husband as though he would remember precisely what category of eater his beloved son had been; he stared into his pot roast.

"But," Goldie Epstein resumed, "You should live and be well, Michael, you turned out to be a good eater..."

Ahhh! Ahhh!

The noises snapped Epstein's recollection in two.

Aaahhhh!

Enough was enough. He got out of bed, made certain that he was tucked into his pajamas, and started down to the living room. He would give them a piece of his mind. He would tell them that — that 1927 was not 1957! No, that was what they would tell him.

But in the living room it was not Sheila and the folk singer. Epstein felt the cold from the floor rush up the loose legs of his pajamas and chill his crotch, raising goose flesh on his thighs. They did not see him. He retreated a step, back behind the archway to the dining room. His eyes, however, remained fixed on the living room floor, on Sol's boy and the girl from across the street.

The girl had been wearing shorts and a sweater. Now they were thrown over the arm of the sofa. The light from the candles was enough for Epstein to see that she was naked. Michael lay beside her, squirming and potent, wearing only his army shoes and khaki socks. The girl's breasts were like two small white cups. Michael kissed them, and more. Epstein tingled; he did not dare move, he did not want to move, until the two, like cars in a railroad yard, slammed fiercely together, coupled, shook. In their noise Epstein tiptoed, trembling, up the stairs and back to his wife's bed.

He could not force himself to sleep for what seemed like hours, not until the door had opened downstairs and the two young people had left. When, a minute or so later, he heard another key turn in the lock he did not know whether it was Michael returning to go to sleep, or —

Zip!

Now it was Sheila and the folk singer! The whole world, he thought, the whole young world, the ugly ones and the pretty ones, the fat and the skinny ones, zipping and unzipping! He grabbed his great shock of gray hair and pulled it till his scalp hurt. His wife shuffled, mumbled a noise. "Brrr . . . brrrrr . . ." She captured the blankets and pulled them over her. "Brrr . . ."

Butter! She's dreaming about butter. Recipes she dreams while the world zips. He closed his eyes and pounded himself down down into an old man's sleep.

2

How far back must you go to discover the beginning of trouble? Later, when Epstein had more time he would ask himself this question. When did it begin? That night he'd seen those two on the floor? Or the summer night seventeen years before when he had pushed the doctor away from the bed and put his lips to his Herbie's? Or, Epstein wondered, was it that night fifteen years ago when instead of smelling a woman between his sheets he smelled Bab-o? Or the time when his daughter had first called him "capitalist" as though it were a dirty name, as though it were a crime

to be successful? Or was it none of these times? Maybe to
look for a beginning was only to look for an excuse. Hadn't
the trouble, the big trouble, begun simply when it appeared to, the morning he saw Ida Kaufman waiting for the
bus?

And about Ida Kaufman, why in God's name was it a
stranger, nobody he loved or ever could love, who had
finally changed his life? — she, who had lived across the
street for less than a year, and who (it was revealed by
Mrs. Katz, the neighborhood Winchell) would probably
sell her house now that Mr. Kaufman was dead and move
all-year-round into their summer cottage at Barnegat?
Until that morning Epstein had not more than noticed
the woman: dark, good-looking, a big chest. She hardly
spoke to the other housewives, but spent every moment,
until a month ago, caring for her cancer-eaten husband.
Once or twice Epstein had tipped his hat to her, but
even then he had been more absorbed in the fate of Epstein Paper Bag than in the civility he was practicing.
Actually then, on that Monday morning it would not have
been unlikely for him to have driven right past the bus
stop. It was a warm April day, certainly not a bad day to
be waiting for a bus. Birds fussed and sang in the elm
trees, and the sun glinted in the sky like a young ath-
lete's trophy. But the woman at the bus stop wore a thin
dress and no coat, and Epstein saw her waiting, and beneath the dress, the stockings, the imagined underthings
he saw the body of the girl on his living room rug, for Ida
Kaufman was the mother of Linda Kaufman, the girl
Michael had befriended. So Epstein pulled slowly to
the curb and, stopping for the daughter, picked up the
mother.

"Thank you, Mr. Epstein," she said. "This is kind of you."

"It's nothing," Epstein said. "I'm going to Market Street."

"Market Street will be fine."

He pressed down too hard on the accelerator and the big Chrysler leaped away, noisy as a hot-rodder's Ford. Ida Kaufman rolled down her window and let the breeze waft in; she lit a cigarette. After a while she asked, "That was your nephew, wasn't it, that took Linda out Saturday night?"

"Michael? Yes." Epstein flushed, for reasons Ida Kaufman did not know. He felt the red on his neck and coughed to make it appear that some respiratory failure had caused the blood to rush up from his heart.

"He's a very nice boy, extremely polite," she said.

"My brother Sol's," Epstein said, "in Detroit." And he shifted his thoughts to Sol so that the flush might fade: if there had been no words with Sol it would be Michael who would be heir to Epstein Paper Bag. Would he have wanted that? Was it any better than a stranger . . . ?

While Epstein thought, Ida Kaufman smoked, and they drove on without speaking, under the elm trees, the choir of birds, and the new spring sky unfurled like a blue banner.

"He looks like you," she said.

"What? Who?"

"Michael."

"No," Epstein said, "him, he's the image of Sol."

"No, no, don't deny it — " and she exploded with laughter, smoke dragoning out of her mouth; she jerked her head back mightily, "No, no, no, he's got your face!"

Epstein looked at her, wondering: the lips, big and red,

over her teeth, grinning. Why? Of course — your little boy looks like the iceman, she'd made that joke. He grinned, mostly at the thought of going to bed with his sister-in-law, whose everything had dropped even lower than his wife's.

Epstein's grin provoked Ida Kaufman into more extravagant mirth. What the hell, he decided, he would try a joke himself.

"Your Linda, who does *she* look like?"

Ida Kaufman's mouth straightened; her lids narrowed, killing the light in her eyes. Had he said the wrong thing? Stepped too far? Defiled the name of a dead man, a man who'd had cancer yet? But no, for suddenly she raised her arms in front of her, and shrugged her shoulders as though to say, "Who knows, Epstein, who knows?"

Epstein roared. It was so long since he had been with a woman who had a sense of humor; his wife took everything he said seriously. Not Ida Kaufman, though — she laughed so hard her breasts swelled over the top of her tan dress. They were not cups but pitchers. The next thing Epstein knew he was telling her another joke, and another, in the middle of which a cop screamed up alongside him and gave him a ticket for a red light which, in his joy, he had not seen. It was the first of three tickets he received that day; he earned a second racing down to Barnegat later that morning, and a third speeding up the Parkway at dusk, trying not to be too late for dinner. The tickets cost him $32 in all, but, as he told Ida, when you're laughing so hard you have tears in your eyes, how can you tell the green lights from the red ones, fast from slow?

At seven o'clock that evening he returned Ida to the bus stop on the corner and squeezed a bill into her hands.

"Here," he said, "Here — buy something"; which brought
the day's total to fifty-two.

Then he turned up the street, already prepared with a
story for his wife: a man interested in buying Epstein Paper
Bag had kept him away all day, a good prospect. As he
pulled into his driveway he saw his wife's square shape back
of the venetian blinds. She ran one hand across a slat,
checking for dust while she awaited her husband's homecoming.

3

Prickly heat?

He clutched his pajama trousers around his knees and
looked at himself in the bedroom mirror. Downstairs a key
turned in the lock but he was too engaged to hear it.
Prickly heat is what Herbie always had — a child's com-
plaint. Was it possible for a grown man to have it? He
shuffled closer to the mirror, tripping on his half-hoisted
pajamas. Maybe it was a sand rash. Sure, he thought, for
during those three warm, sunny weeks, he and Ida Kaufman, when they were through, would rest on the beach in
front of the cottage. Sand must have gotten into his trousers and irritated him on the drive up the Parkway. He
stepped back now and was squinting at himself in the mirror when Goldie walked into the bedroom. She had just
emerged from a hot tub — her bones ached, she had said
— and her flesh was boiled red. Her entrance startled Epstein, who had been contemplating his blemish with the
intensity of a philosopher. When he turned swiftly from
his reflection, his feet caught in his pants leg, he tripped,
and the pajamas slipped to the floor. So there they were,
naked as Adam and Eve, except that Goldie was red all

over, and Epstein had prickly heat, or a sand rash, or —
and it came to him as a first principle comes to a meta-
physician. Of course! His hands shot down to cover his
crotch.

Goldie looked at him, mystified, while Epstein searched
for words appropriate to his posture.

At last: "You had a nice bath?"

"Nice, shmice, it was a bath," his wife mumbled.

"You'll catch a cold," Epstein said. "Put something
on."

"I'll catch a cold? *You'll* catch a cold!" She looked at
the hands laced across his crotch. "Something hurts?"

"It's a little chilly," he said.

"Where?" She motioned towards his protection.
"There?"

"All over."

"Then cover all over."

He leaned over to pick up his pajama trousers; the instant he dropped the fig leaf of his hands Goldie let out a
short airless gasp. "What is *that?*"

"What?"

"That!"

He could not look into the eyes of her face, so concen-
trated instead on the purple eyes of her droopy breasts.
"A sand rash, I think."

"*Vus far* sand!"

"A rash then," he said.

She stepped up closer and reached out her hand, not
to touch but to point. She drew a little circle of the area
with her index finger. "A rash, there?"

"Why not there?" Epstein said. "It's like a rash on the
hand or the chest. A rash is a rash."

"But how come all of a sudden?" his wife said.

"Look, I'm not a doctor," Epstein said. "It's there to-day, maybe tomorrow it'll be gone. How do I know! I probably got it from the toilet seat at the shop. The *shvartzes* are pigs —"

Goldie made a clicking sound with her tongue.

"You're calling me a liar?"

She looked up. "Who said liar?" And she gave her own form a swift looking-over, checked limbs, stomach, breasts, to see if she had perhaps caught the rash from him. She looked back at her husband, then at her own body again, and suddenly her eyes widened. "You!" she screamed.

"Shah," Epstein said, "you'll wake Michael."

"You pig! Who, who was it!"

"I told you, the *shvartzes* — "

"Liar! Pig!" Wheeling her way back to the bed, she flopped onto it so hard the springs squeaked. "Liar!" And then she was off the bed pulling the sheets from it. "I'll burn them, I'll burn every one!"

Epstein stepped out of the pajamas that roped his ankles and raced to the bed. "What are you doing — it's not catching. Only on the toilet seat. You'll buy a little ammonia —"

"Ammonia!" she yelled, "you should *drink* ammonia!"

"No," Epstein shouted, "no," and he grabbed the sheets from her and threw them back over the bed, tucking them in madly. "Leave it be — " He ran to the back of the bed but as he tucked there Goldie raced around and ripped up what he had tucked in the front; so he raced back to the front while Goldie raced around to the back. "Don't touch me." she screamed, "don't come near me, you filthy pig! Go touch some filthy whore!" Then she yanked the sheets off again in one swoop, held them in a ball before her and spat. Epstein grabbed them back and the tug-of-war began, back and forth, back and forth, until they had torn them to shreds. Then for the first time Goldie cried. With white strips looped over her arms she began to sob. "My sheets, my nice clean sheets —" and she threw herself on the bed.

Two faces appeared in the doorway of the bedroom. Sheila Epstein groaned, "Holy Christ!"; the folk singer peeped in, once, twice, and then bobbed out, his feet scuttling down the stairs. Epstein whipped some white strands about him to cover his privates. He did not say a word as his daughter entered.

"Mamma, what's the matter?"

"Your father," the voice groaned from the bed, "he has — a rash!" And so violently did she begin to sob that the flesh on her white buttocks rippled and jumped.

"That's right," Epstein said, "a rash. That's a crime? Get out of here! Let your mother and father get some sleep."

"Why is she crying?" Sheila demanded. "I want an answer!"

"How do I know! I'm a mind reader? This whole family is crazy, who knows what they think!"

"Don't call my mother crazy!"

"Don't you raise your voice to me! Respect your father!" He pulled the white strips tighter around him. "Now get out of here!"

"No!"

"Then I'll throw you out." He started for the door; his daughter did not move, and he could not bring himself to reach out and push her. Instead he threw back his head and addressed the ceiling. "She's picketing my bedroom! Get out, you lummox!" He took a step towards her and growled, as though to scare away a stray cat or dog. With all her one hundred and sixty pounds she pushed her father back; in his surprise and hurt he dropped the sheet. And the daughter looked on the father. Under her lipstick she turned white.

Epstein looked up at her. He pleaded, "I got it from the toilet seat. The *shvartzes* — "

Before he could finish, a new head had popped into the doorway, hair messed and lips swollen and red; it was Michael, home from Linda Kaufman, his regular weekend date. "I heard the noise, is any — " and he saw his aunt naked on the bed. When he turned his eyes away, there was Uncle Lou.

"All of you," Epstein shouted. "Get out!"

But no one obeyed. Sheila blocked the door, politically committed; Michael's legs were rooted, one with shame, the other curiosity.

"Get out!"

Feet now came pounding up the stairs. "Sheila, should I call somebody — " And then the guitar plucker appeared in the doorway, eager, big-nosed. He surveyed the scene and his gaze, at last, landed on Epstein's crotch; the beak opened.

"What's he got? The syph?"

The words hung for a moment, bringing peace. Goldie Epstein stopped crying and raised herself off the bed. The young men in the doorway lowered their eyes. Goldie arched her back, flopped out her breasts, and began to move her lips. "I want . . ." she said. "I want . . ."

"What, Mamma?" Sheila demanded. "What is it?"

"I want...a divorce!" She looked amazed when she said it, though not as amazed as her husband; he smacked his palm to his head.

"Divorce! Are you crazy?" Epstein looked around; to Michael he said, "She's crazy!"

"I want one," she said, and then her eyes rolled up into her head and she passed out across the sheetless mattress.

After the smelling salts Epstein was ordered to bed in Herbie's room. He tossed and turned in the narrow bed which he was unused to; in the twin bed beside him he heard Michael breathing. Monday, he thought, Monday he would seek help. A lawyer. No, first a doctor. Surely in a minute a doctor could take a look and tell him what he already knew — that Ida Kaufman was a clean woman. Epstein would swear by it — he had smelled her flesh! The doctor would reassure him: his blemish resulted simply from their rubbing together. It was a temporary thing, produced by two, not transmitted by one. He was innocent! Unless what made him guilty had nothing to do with some dirty bug. But either way the doctor would prescribe for him. And then the lawyer would prescribe. And by then everyone would know, including, he suddenly realized, his brother Sol who would take special pleasure in thinking the worst. Epstein rolled over and looked to Michael's bed. Pinpoints of light gleamed in the boy's head; he was awake, and wearing the Epstein nose, chin, and brow.

"Michael?"

"Yes."

"You're awake?"

"Yes."

"Me too," Epstein said, and then apologetically, "all the excitement..."

He looked back to the ceiling. "Michael?"

"Yes?"

"Nothing..." But he was curious as well as concerned. "Michael, you haven't got a rash, have you?"

Michael sat up in bed; firmly he said, "No."

"I just thought," Epstein said quickly. " You know, I have this rash..." He dwindled off and looked away from the boy, who, it occurred to him again, might have been heir to the business if that stupid Sol hadn't... But what difference did the business make now. The business had never been for him, but for them. And there was no more them.

He put his hands over his eyes. "The change, the change," he said. "I don't even know when it began. Me, Lou Epstein, with a rash. I don't even feel any more like Lou Epstein. All of a sudden, pffft! and things are changed." He looked at Michael again, speaking slowly now, stressing every word, as though the boy were more than a nephew, more, in fact, than a single person. "All my life I tried. I swear it, I should drop dead on the spot, if all my life I didn't try to do right, to give my family what I didn't have..."

He stopped; it was not exactly what he wanted to say. He flipped on the bedside light and started again, a new way. "I was seven years old, Michael. I came here I was a boy seven years old, and that day, I can remember it like it was yesterday. Your grandparents and me — your father wasn't born yet, this stuff believe me he doesn't know. With your grandparents I stood on the dock, waiting for

Charlie Goldstein to pick us up. He was your grandfather's partner in the old country, the thief. Anyway, we waited, and finally he came to pick us up, to take us where we would live. And when he came he had a big can in his hand. And you know what was in it? Kerosene. We stood there and Charlie Goldstein poured it on all our heads. He rubbed it in, to delouse us. It tasted awful. For a little boy it was awful . . ."

Michael shrugged his shoulder.

"Eh! How can you understand?" Epstein grumbled. "What do you know? Twenty years old . . ."

Michael shrugged again. "Twenty-two," he said softly.

There were more stories Epstein could tell, but he wondered if any of them would bring him closer to what it was he had on his mind but could not find the words for. He got out of bed and walked to the bedroom door. He opened it and stood there listening. On the downstairs sofa he could hear the folk singer snoring. Some night for guests! He shut the door and came back into the room, scratching his thigh. "Believe me, *she's* not losing any sleep . . . She doesn't deserve me. What, she cooks? That's a big deal? She cleans? That deserves a medal? One day I should come home and the house should be a *mess*. I should be able to write my initials in the dust, somewhere, in the basement at least. Michael, after all these years that would be a pleasure!" He grabbed at his gray hair. "How did this happen? My Goldie, that such a woman should become a cleaning machine. Impossible." He walked to the far wall and stared into Herbie's baseball pictures, the long jaw-muscled faces, faded technicolor now, with signatures at the bottom: Charlie Keller, Lou Gehrig, Red Ruffing . . . A long time. How Herbie had loved his Yankees.

"One night," Epstein started again, "it was before the Depression even . . . you know what we did, Goldie and me?" He was staring at Red Ruffing now, through him. "You didn't know my Goldie, what a beautiful beautiful woman she was. And that night we took pictures, photos. I set up the camera — it was in the old house — and we took pictures, in the bedroom." He stopped, remembered. "I wanted a picture of my wife naked, to carry with me. I admit it. The next morning I woke up and there was Goldie tearing up the negatives. She said God forbid I should get in an accident one day and the police would take out my wallet for identification, and then oy-oy-oy!" He smiled. "You know, a woman, she worries . . . But at least we took the pictures, even if we didn't develop them. How many people even do that?" He wondered, and then turned away from Red Ruffing to Michael, who was, faintly, at at the corners of his mouth, smiling.

"What, the photos?"

Michael started to giggle.

"Huh?" Epstein smiled. "What, you never had that kind of idea? I admit it. Maybe to someone else it would seem wrong, a sin or something, but who's to say — "

Michael stiffened, at last his father's son. "Somebody's got to say. Some things just aren't right."

Epstein was willing to admit a youthful lapse. "Maybe," he said, "maybe she was even right to tear — "

Michael shook his head vehemently. "No! Some things aren't right. They're just not!"

And Epstein saw the finger pointing not at Uncle Lou the Photographer, but at Uncle Lou the Adulterer. Suddenly he was shouting. "Right, wrong! From you and your father that's all I ever hear. Who are you, what are you, King Solomon!" He gripped the bedposts. "Should

I tell you what else happened the night we took pictures? That my Herbie was started that night, I'm sure of it. Over a year we tried and tried till I was *oysgamitched*, and that was the night. After the pictures, because of the pictures. Who knows!"

"But —"

"But what! But *this?*" He was pointing at his crotch. "You're a boy, you don't understand. When they start taking things away from you, you reach out, you *grab* — maybe like a pig even, but you grab. And right, wrong, who knows! With tears in your eyes, who can even see the difference!" His voice dropped now, but in a minor key the scolding grew more fierce. "Don't call *me* names. I didn't see you with Ida's girl, there's not a name for that? For *you* it's right?"

Michael was kneeling in his bed now. "You — saw?"

"I saw!"

"But it's different —"

"Different?" Epstein shouted.

"To be married is different!"

"What's different you don't know about. To have a wife, to be a father, twice a father — and then they start taking things away —" and he fell weak-kneed across Michael's bed. Michael leaned back and looked at his uncle, but he did not know what to do or how to chastise, for he had never seen anybody over fifteen years old cry before.

4

Usually Sunday morning went like this: at nine-thirty Goldie started the coffee and Epstein walked to the corner for the lox and the Sunday *News*. When the lox was on the

table, the bagels in the oven, the rotogravure section of the
News two inches from Goldie's nose, then Sheila would descend the stairs, yawning, in her toe-length housecoat. They
would sit down to eat, Sheila cursing her father for buying
the *News* and "putting money in a Fascist's pocket." Outside, the Gentiles would be walking to church. It had always been the same, except, of course, that over the years
the *News* had come closer to Goldie's nose and further
from Sheila's heart; she had the *Post* delivered.

This Sunday, when he awoke, Epstein smelled coffee
bubbling in the kitchen. When he sneaked down the
stairs, past the kitchen — he had been ordered to use the
basement bathroom until he'd seen a doctor — he could
smell lox. And, at last, when he entered the kitchen,
shaved and dressed, he heard newspapers rattling. It was
as if another Epstein, his ghost, had risen an hour earlier
and performed his Sunday duties. Beneath the clock,
around the table, sat Sheila, the folk singer, and Goldie.
Bagels toasted in the oven, while the folk singer, sitting
backwards in a chair, strummed his guitar and sang —

> *I've been down so long*
> *It look like up to me . . .*

Epstein clapped his hands and rubbed them together, pre-
paratory to eating. "Sheila, you went out for this?" He
gestured towards the paper and the lox. "Thank you."

The folk singer looked up, and in the same tune, impro-
vised —

> *I went out for the lox . . .*

and grinned, a regular clown.

"Shut up!" Sheila told him. ·

He echoed her words, plunk! plunk!

"Thank *you*, then, young man," Epstein said.

"His name is Marvin," Sheila said, "for your informa-tion."

"Thank you, Martin."

"Mar*vin*," the young man said.

"I don't hear so good."

Goldie Epstein looked up from the paper. "Syphilis softens the brain."

"What!"

"Syphilis softens the brain . . ."

Epstein stood up, raging. "Did you tell her that?" he shouted at his daughter. "Who told her that?"

The folk singer stopped plucking his guitar. Nobody answered; a conspiracy. He grabbed his daughter by the shoulders. "You respect your father, you understand!"

She jerked her shoulder away. "You're not *my* father!"

And the words hurled him back — to the joke Ida Kaufman had made in the car, to her tan dress, the spring sky . . . He leaned across the table to his wife. "Goldie, Goldie, look at me! Look at *me*, Lou!"

She stared back into the newspaper, though she held it far enough from her nose for Epstein to know she could not see the print; with everything else, the optometrist said the muscles in her eyes had loosened. "Goldie," he said, "Goldie, I did the worst thing in the world? Look me in the eyes, Goldie. Tell me, since when do Jewish people get a divorce? Since when?"

She looked up at him, and then at Sheila. "Syphilis makes soft brains. I can't live with a pig!"

"We'll work it out. We'll go to the rabbi — "

"He wouldn't recognize you — "

"But the children, what about the children?"

"What children?"

Herbie was dead and Sheila a stranger; she was right.

"A grown-up child can take care of herself," Goldie said. "If she wants, she can come to Florida with me. I'm thinking I'll move to Miami Beach."

"Goldie!"

"Stop shouting," Sheila said, anxious to enter the brawl. "You'll wake Michael."

Painfully polite, Goldie addressed her daughter. "Michael left early this morning. He took his Linda to the beach for the day, to their place in Belmar."

"Barnegat," Epstein grumbled, retreating from the table.

"What did you say?" Sheila demanded.

"Barnegat." And he decided to leave the house before any further questions were asked.

At the corner luncheonette he bought his own paper and sat alone, drinking coffee and looking out the window beyond which the people walked to church. A pretty young *shiksa* walked by, holding her white round hat in her hand; she bent over to remove her shoe and shake a pebble from it. Epstein watched her bend, and he spilled some coffee on his shirt front. The girl's small behind was round as an apple beneath the close-fitting dress. He looked, and then as though he were praying, he struck himself on the chest with his fist, again and again. "What have I done! Oh, God!"

When he finished his coffee, he took his paper and started up the street. To home? What home? Across the street in her backyard he saw Ida Kaufman, who was wearing shorts and a halter, and was hanging her daughter's underwear on the clothesline. Epstein looked around

and saw only the Gentiles walking to church. Ida saw him
and smiled. Growing angry, he stepped off the curb and,
passionately, began to jaywalk.

At noon in the Epstein house those present heard a siren
go off. Sheila looked up from the *Post* and listened; she
looked at her watch. "Noon? I'm fifteen minutes slow.
This lousy watch, my father's present."

Goldie Epstein was leafing through the ads in the travel
section of the *New York Times*, which Marvin had gone
out to buy for her. She looked at her watch. "I'm fourteen
minutes slow. Also," she said to her daughter, "a watch
from him . . ."

The wail grew louder. "God," Sheila said, "it sounds
like the end of the world."

And Marvin, who had been polishing his guitar with
his red handkerchief, immediately broke into song, a high-
pitched, shut-eyed Negro tune about the end of the world.

"Quiet!" Sheila said. She cocked her ear. "But it's
Sunday. The sirens are Saturday —"

Goldie shot off the couch. "It's a real air raid? Oy,
that's all we need!"

"It's the police," Sheila said, and fiery-eyed she raced to
the front door, for she was politically opposed to police.
"It's coming up the street — an ambulance!"

She raced out the door, followed by Marvin, whose guitar
still hung around his neck. Goldie trailed behind, her feet
slapping against her slippers. On the street she suddenly
turned back to the house to make sure the door was shut
against daytime burglars, bugs, and dust. When she turned
again she had not far to run. The ambulance had pulled up
across the street in Kaufman's driveway.

Already a crowd had gathered, neighbors in bathrobes, housecoats, carrying the comic sections with them; and too, churchgoers, *shiksas* in white hats. Goldie could not make her way to the front where her daughter and Marvin stood, but even from the rear of the crowd she could see a young doctor leap from the ambulance and race up to the porch, his stethoscope wiggling in his back pocket as he took two steps at a time.

Mrs. Katz arrived. A squat red-faced woman whose stomach seemed to start at her knees, she tugged at Goldie's arm. "Goldie, more trouble here?"

"I don't know, Pearl. All that racket. It sounded like an atomic bomb."

"When it's that, you'll know," Pearl Katz said. She surveyed the crowd, then looked at the house. "Poor woman," she said, remembering that only three months before, on a windy March morning an ambulance had arrived to take Mrs. Kaufman's husband to the nursing home, from which he never returned.

"Troubles, troubles..." Mrs. Katz was shaking her head, a pot of sympathy. "Everybody has their little bundle, believe me. I'll bet she had a nervous breakdown. That's not a good thing. Gallstones, you have them out and they're out. But a nervous breakdown, it's very bad... You think maybe it's the daughter who's sick?"

"The daughter isn't home," Goldie said. "She's away with my nephew, Michael."

Mrs. Katz saw that no one had emerged from the house yet; she had time to gather a little information. "He's who, Goldie? The son of the brother-in-law that Lou doesn't talk to? That's his father?"

"Yes, Sol in Detroit—"

But she broke off, for the front door had opened, though

still no one could be seen. A voice at the front of the crowd was commanding. "A little room here. Please! A little room, damn it!" It was Sheila. "A little room! Marvin, help me!"

"I can't put down my guitar — I can't find a place — "

"Get them back!" Sheila said.

"But my instrument — "

The doctor and his helper were now wiggling and tilting the stretcher through the front door. Behind them stood Mrs. Kaufman, a man's white shirt tucked into her shorts. Her eyes peered out of two red holes; she wore no make-up, Mrs. Katz noted.

"It must be the girl," said Pearl Katz, up on her toes. "Goldie, can you see, who is it — it's the girl?"

"The girl's *away* — "

"Stay back!" Sheila commanded. "Marvin, for crying out loud, help!"

The young doctor and his attendant held the stretcher steady as they walked sideways down the front steps.

Mrs. Katz jumped up and down. "Who *is* it?"

"I can't see," Goldie said. "I can't — " She pushed up on her toes, out of her slippers. "I — oh God! My God!" And she was racing forward, screaming, "Lou! Lou!"

"Mamma, stay back." Sheila found herself fighting off her mother. The stretcher was sliding into the ambulance now.

"Sheila, let me go, it's your father!" She pointed to the ambulance, whose red eye spun slowly on top. For a moment Goldie looked back to the steps. Ida Kaufman stood there yet, her fingers fidgeting at the buttons of the shirt. Then Goldie broke for the ambulance, her daughter beside her, propelling her by her elbows.

"Who are you?" the doctor said. He took a step to-

wards them to stop their forward motion, for it seemed as
if they intended to dive right into the ambulance on top
of his patient.

"The wife — " Sheila shouted.

The doctor pointed to the porch. "Look, lady — "

"I'm the *wife*," Goldie cried. "Me!"

The doctor looked at her. "Get in."

Goldie wheezed as Sheila and the doctor helped her into
the ambulance, and she let out a gigantic gasp when she
saw the white face sticking up from the gray blanket; his
eyes were closed, his skin grayer than his hair. The doctor
pushed Sheila aside, climbed in, and then the ambulance
was moving, the siren screaming. Sheila ran after the ambulance a moment, hammering on the door, but then she
turned the other way and was headed back through the
crowd and up the stairs to Ida Kaufman's house.

Goldie turned to the doctor. "He's dead?"

"No, he had a heart attack."

She smacked her face.

"He'll be all right," the doctor said.

"But a heart attack. Never in his life."

"A man sixty, sixty-five, it happens." The doctor
snapped the answers back while he held Epstein's wrist.

"He's only fifty-nine."

"Some only," the doctor said.

The ambulance zoomed through a red light and made
a sharp right turn that threw Goldie to the floor. She sat
there and spoke. "But how does a healthy man — "

"Lady, don't ask questions. A grown man can't act like a
boy."

She put her hands over her eyes as Epstein opened
his.

"He's awake now," the doctor said. "Maybe he wants to hold your hand or something."

Goldie crawled to his side and looked at him. "Lou, you're all right? Does anything hurt?"

He did not answer. "He knows it's me?"

The doctor shrugged his shoulders. "Tell him."

"It's me, Lou."

"It's your wife, Lou," the doctor said. Epstein blinked his eyes. "He knows," the doctor said. "He'll be all right. All he's got to do is live a normal life, normal for sixty."

"You hear the doctor, Lou. All you got to do is live a normal life."

Epstein opened his mouth. His tongue hung over his teeth like a dead snake.

"Don't you talk," his wife said. "Don't you worry about anything. Not even the business. That'll work out. Our Sheila will marry Marvin and that'll be that. You won't have to sell, Lou, it'll be in the family. You can retire, rest, and Marvin can take over. He's a smart boy, Marvin, a *mensch*."

Lou rolled his eyes in his head.

"Don't try to talk. I'll take care. You'll be better soon and we can go someplace. We can go to Saratoga, to the mineral baths, if you want. We'll just go, you and me — " Suddenly she gripped his hand. "Lou, you'll live normal, won't you? *Won't you?*" She was crying. " 'Cause what'll happen, Lou, is you'll kill yourself! You'll keep this up and that'll be the end — "

"All right," the young doctor said, "you take it easy now. We don't want two patients on our hands."

The ambulance was pulling down and around into the

side entrance of the hospital and the doctor knelt at the back door.

"I don't know why I'm crying." Goldie wiped her eyes. "He'll be all right? You say so, I believe you, you're a doctor." And as the young man swung open the door with the big red cross painted on the back, she asked, softly, "Doctor, you have something that will cure what else he's got — this rash?" She pointed.

The doctor looked at her. Then he lifted for a moment the blanket that covered Epstein's nakedness.

"Doctor, it's bad?"

Goldie's eyes and nose were running.

"An irritation," the doctor said.

She grabbed his wrist. "You can clean it up?"

"So it'll never come back," the doctor said, and hopped out of the ambulance.

YOU CAN'T
TELL A MAN
BY THE SONG
HE SINGS

It was in a freshman high school class called "Occupations" that, fifteen years ago, I first met the ex-con, Alberto Pelagutti. The first week my new classmates and I were given "a battery of tests" designed to reveal our skills, deficiencies, tendencies, and psyches. At the end of the week, Mr. Russo, the Occupations teacher, would add the skills, subtract the deficiencies, and tell us what jobs best suited our talents; it was all mysterious but scientific. I remember we first took a "Preference Test": "Which would you prefer to do, this, that, or the other thing..." Albie Pelagutti sat one seat behind me and to my left, and while this first day of high school I strolled happily through the test, examining ancient fossils here, defending criminals there, Albie, like the inside of Vesuvius, rose, fell, pitched, tossed, and swelled in his chair. When he finally made a decision, he made it. You could hear his pencil drive the x into the column opposite the activity in which he thought it wisest to prefer to engage. His agony reinforced the legend that had preceded him: he was seventeen; had just left Jamesburg Reformatory; this was his third high school, his third freshman year; but now — I heard

another x driven home — he had decided "to go straight."
Halfway through the hour Mr. Russo left the room.
"I'm going for a drink," he said. Russo was forever at pains
to let us know what a square-shooter he was and that, unlike other teachers we might have had, he would not go out
the front door of the classroom to sneak around to the back
door and observe how responsible we were. And sure
enough, when he returned after going for a drink, his lips
were wet; when he came back from the men's room, you
could smell the soap on his hands. "Take your time, boys,"
he said, and the door swung shut behind him.

His black wingtipped shoes beat down the marble corridor and five thick fingers dug into my shoulder. I turned
around; it was Pelagutti. "What?" I said. "Number
twenty-six," Pelagutti said, "What's the answer?" I gave him
the truth: "Anything." Pelagutti rose halfway over his
desk and glared at me. He was a hippopotamus, big, black,
and smelly; his short sleeves squeezed tight around his
monstrous arms as though they were taking his own blood
pressure — which at that moment was sky-bound: "What's
the answer!" Menaced, I flipped back three pages in my
question booklet and reread number twenty-six. "Which
would you prefer to do: (1) Attend a World Trade Convention. (2) Pick cherries. (3) Stay with and read to a sick
friend. (4) Tinker with automobile engines." I looked
blank-faced back to Albie, and shrugged my shoulders.
"It doesn't matter — there's no right answer. Anything."
He almost rocketed out of his seat. "Don't give me that
crap! What's the answer!" Strange heads popped up all
over the room — thin-eyed glances, hissing lips, shaming
grins — and I realized that any minute Russo, wet-lipped,
might come back and my first day in high school I would

be caught cheating. I looked again at number twenty-six; then back to Albie; and then propelled — as I always was towards him — by anger, pity, fear, love, vengeance, and an instinct for irony that was at the time delicate as a mallet, I whispered, "Stay and read to a sick friend." The volcano subsided, and Albie and I had met.

We became friends. He remained at my elbow throughout the testing, then throughout lunch, then after school. I learned that Albie, as a youth, had done all the things I, under direction, had not: he had eaten hamburgers in strange diners; he had gone out after cold showers, wet-haired, into winter weather; he had been cruel to animals; he had trafficked with whores; he had stolen, he had been caught, and he had paid. But now he told me, as I unwrapped my lunch in the candy store across from school, "Now, I'm through crappin' around. I'm gettin' an education. I'm gonna — " and I think he picked up the figure from a movie musical he had seen the previous afternoon while the rest of us were in English class — "I'm gonna put my best foot forward." The following week when Russo read the results of the testing it appeared that Albie's feet were not only moving forward but finding strange, wonderful paths. Russo sat at his desk, piles of tests stacked before him like ammunition, charts and diagrams mounted huge on either side, and delivered our destinies. Albie and I were going to be lawyers.

Of all that Albie confessed to me that first week, one fact in particular fastened on my brain: I soon forgot the town in Sicily where he was born; the occupation of his father (he either made ice or delivered it); the year and model of the cars he had stolen. I did not forget though that Albie had apparently been the star of the Jamesburg Reformatory baseball team. When I was selected by the gym teacher, Mr. Hopper, to captain one of my gym class's softball teams (we played softball until the World Series was over, then switched to touch football), I knew that I had to get Pelagutti on my side. With those arms he could hit the ball a mile.

The day teams were to be selected Albie shuffled back and forth at my side, while in the lockerroom I changed into my gym uniform — jockstrap, khaki-colored shorts, T-shirt, sweat socks, and sneakers. Albie had already changed: beneath his khaki gym shorts he did not wear a support but retained his lavender undershorts; they hung down three inches below the outer shorts and looked like a long fancy hem. Instead of a T-shirt he wore a sleeveless undershirt; and beneath his high, tar-black sneakers he wore thin black silk socks with slender arrows embroidered up the sides. Naked he might, like some centuries-dead ancestor, have tossed lions to their death in the Colosseum; the outfit, though I didn't tell him, detracted from his dignity.

As we left the lockerroom and padded through the dark basement corridor and up onto the sunny September playing field, he talked continually, "I didn't play sports when I was a kid, but I played at Jamesburg and baseball came to me like nothing." I nodded my head. "What you think of Pete Reiser?" he asked. "He's a pretty good man," I said. "What you think of Tommy Henrich?" "I don't know," I answered, "he's dependable, I guess." As a Dodger fan I preferred Reiser to the Yankees' Henrich; and besides, my tastes have always been a bit baroque, and Reiser, who re-

peatedly bounced off outfield walls to save the day for
Brooklyn, had won a special trophy in the Cooperstown of
my heart. "Yeh," Albie said, "I like all them Yankees."

I didn't have a chance to ask Albie what he meant by
that, for Mr. Hopper, bronzed, smiling, erect, was flipping
a coin; I looked up, saw the glint in the sun, and I was calling "heads." It landed tails and the other captain had first
choice. My heart flopped over when he looked at Albie's
arms, but calmed when he passed on and chose first a tall,
lean, first-baseman type. Immediately I said, "I'll take
Pelagutti." You don't very often see smiles like the one that
crossed Albie Pelagutti's face that moment: you would
think I had paroled him from a life sentence.

The game began. I played shortstop — left-handed —
and batted second; Albie was in center field and, at his
wish, batted fourth. Their first man grounded out, me to
the first baseman. The next batter hit a high, lofty fly ball
to center field. The moment I saw Albie move after it I
knew Tommy Henrich and Pete Reiser were only names
to him; all he knew about baseball he'd boned up on the
night before. While the ball hung in the air, Albie jumped
up and down beneath it, his arms raised upward directly
above his head; his wrists were glued together, and his two
hands flapped open and closed like a butterfly's wings,
begging the ball toward them.

"C'mon," he was screaming to the sky, "c'mon you bastard . . ." And his legs bicycle-pumped up and down, up
and down. I hope the moment of my death does not take
as long as it did for that damn ball to drop. It hung, it
hung, Albie cavorting beneath like a Holy Roller. And then
it landed, smack into Albie's chest. The runner was round-

ing second and heading for third while Albie twirled all around, looking, his arms down now, stretched out, as though he were playing ring-around-a-rosy with two invisible children. "Behind you, Pelagutti!" I screamed. He stopped moving. "What?" he called back to me. I ran halfway out to center field. "Behind you — relay it!" And then, as the runner rounded third, I had to stand there defining "relay" to him.

At the end of the first half of the first inning we came to bat behind, 8–0 — eight home runs, all relayed in too late by Pelagutti.

Out of a masochistic delight I must describe Albie at the plate: first, he *faced* the pitcher; then, when he swung at the ball — and he did, at every one — it was not to the side but down, as though he were driving a peg into the ground. Don't ask if he was right-handed or left-handed. I don't know.

While we changed out of our gym uniforms I was silent. I boiled as I watched Pelagutti from the corner of my eye. He kicked off those crazy black sneakers and pulled his pink gaucho shirt on over his undershirt — there was still a red spot above the U front of the undershirt where the first fly ball had hit him. Without removing his gym shorts he stuck his feet into his gray trousers — I watched as he hoisted the trousers over the red splotches where ground balls had banged off his shins, past the red splotches where pitched balls had smacked his knee caps and thighs.

Finally I spoke. "Damn you, Pelagutti, you wouldn't know Pete Reiser if you fell over him!" He was stuffing his sneakers into his locker; he didn't answer. I was talking to his mountainous pink shirt back. "Where do you come off telling me you played for that prison team?" He mumbled something. "What?" I said. "I did," he grumbled. "Bull-shit!" I said. He turned and, black-eyed, glared at me: "I did!" "That must've been some team!" I said. We did not speak as we left the lockerroom. As we passed the gym office on our way up to Occupations, Mr. Hopper looked up from his desk and winked at me. Then he motioned his head at Pelagutti to indicate that he knew I'd picked a lemon, but how could I have expected a bum like Pelagutti to be an All-American boy in the first place? Then Mr. Hopper turned his sun-lamped head back to his desk.

"Now," I said to Pelagutti as we turned at the second floor landing, "now I'm stuck with you for the rest of the term." He shuffled ahead of me without answering; his oxlike behind should have had a tail on it to flick the flies away — it infuriated me. "You goddamn liar!" I said.

He spun around as fast as an ox can. "You ain't stuck with nobody." We were at the top of the landing headed into the locker-lined corridor; the kids who were piling up the stairs behind stopped, listened. "No you ain't, you snot-ass!" And I saw five hairy knuckles coming right at my mouth. I moved but not in time, and heard a crash inside the bridge of my nose. I felt my hips dip back, my legs and head come forward, and, curved like the letter *c*, I was swept fifteen feet backward before I felt cold marble beneath the palms of my hands. Albie stepped around me and into the Occupations room. Just then I looked up to see Mr. Russo's black wingtipped shoes enter the room. I'm almost sure he had seen Albie blast me but I'll never know. Nobody, including Albie and myself, ever mentioned it again. Perhaps it had been a mistake for me to call Albie a liar, but if he had starred at baseball, it was in some league I did not know.

By way of contrast I want to introduce Duke Scarpa, another ex-con who was with us that year. Neither Albie nor the Duke, incidentally, was a typical member of my high school community. Both lived at the other end of Newark, "down neck," and they had reached us only after the Board of Education had tried Albie at two other schools and the Duke at four. The Board hoped finally, like Marx, that the higher culture would absorb the lower.

Albie and Duke had no particular use for each other; where Albie had made up his mind to go straight, one always felt that the Duke, in his oily quietness, his boneless grace, was planning a job. Yet, though affection never lived between them, Duke wandered after Albie and me, aware, I suspect, that if Albie despised him it was because he was able to read his soul — and that such an associate was easier to abide than one who despises you because he does not know your soul at all. Where Albie was a hippopotamus, an ox, Duke was reptilian. Me? I don't know; it is easy to spot the animal in one's fellows.

During lunch hour, the Duke and I used to spar with each other in the hall outside the cafeteria. He did not know a hook from a jab and disliked having his dark skin roughened or his hair mussed; but he so delighted in moving, bobbing, coiling, and uncoiling, that I think he would have paid for the privilege of playing the serpent with me. He hypnotized me, the Duke; he pulled some slimy string inside me — where Albie Pelagutti sought and stretched a deeper and, I think, a nobler cord.

But I make Albie sound like peaches-and-cream. Let me tell you what he and I did to Mr. Russo.

Russo believed in his battery of tests as his immigrant parents (and Albie's, and maybe Albie himself) believed in papal infallibility. If the tests said Albie was going to be a lawyer then he was going to be a lawyer. As for Albie's past, it seemed only to increase Russo's devotion to the prophecy: he approached Albie with salvation in his eyes. In September, then, he gave Albie a biography to read, the life of Oliver Wendell Holmes; during October, once a week, he had the poor fellow speak impromptu before the class; in November he had him write a report on the Constitution, which I wrote; and then in December, the final indignity, he sent Albie and me (and two others who displayed a legal bent) to the Essex County Court House where we could see "real lawyers in action."

It was a cold, windy morning and as we flicked our cigarettes at the Lincoln statue on the courtyard plaza, and started up the long flight of white cement steps, Albie suddenly did an about-face and headed back across the plaza and out to Market Street. I called to him but he shouted back that he had seen it all before, and then he was not walking, but running towards the crowded downtown streets, pursued not by police, but by other days. It wasn't that he considered Russo an ass for having sent him to visit the Court House — Albie respected teachers too much for that; rather I think he felt Russo had tried to rub his nose in it.

No surprise, then, when the next day after gym Albie announced his assault on the Occupations teacher; it was the first crime he had planned since his decision to go straight back in September. He outlined the action to me and indicated that I should pass the details on to the other members of the class. As liaison between Albie and the well-behaved, healthy nonconvicts like myself who made up the rest of the class, I was stationed at the classroom door and as each member passed in I unfolded the plot into his ear: "As soon after ten-fifteen as Russo turns to the blackboard, you bend over to tie your shoelace." If a classmate looked back at me puzzled, I would motion to Pelagutti hulking over his desk; the puzzled expression would vanish and another accomplice would enter the room. The only one who gave me any trouble was the Duke. He listened to the plan and then scowled back at me with the look of a man who's got his own syndicate, and, in fact, has never even heard of yours.

Finally the bell rang; I closed the door behind me and moved noiselessly to my desk. I waited for the clock to move to a quarter after; it did; and then Russo turned to the board to write upon it the salary range of aluminum workers. I bent to tie my shoelaces —beneath all the desks I saw other upside-down grinning faces. To my left behind me I heard Albie hissing; his hands fumbled about his black silk socks, and the hiss grew and grew until it was a rush of Sicilian, muttered, spewed, vicious. The exchange was strictly between Russo and himself. I looked to the front of the classroom, my fingers knotting and unknotting my shoelaces, the blood pumping now to my face. I saw Russo's legs turn. What a sight he must have seen — where there had been twenty-five faces, now there was nothing. Just desks. "Okay," I heard Russo say, "okay." And then he gave a little clap with his hands. "That's enough now, fellas. The joke is over. Sit up." And then Albie's hiss traveled to all the blood-pinked ears below the desks; it rushed about us like a subterranean stream — "Stay down!"

While Russo asked us to get up we stayed down. And we did not sit up until Albie told us to; and then under his direction we were singing —

> Don't sit under the apple tree
> With anyone else but me,
> Anyone else but me,
> Anyone else but me,
> Oh, no, no, don't sit under the apple tree . . .

And then in time to the music we clapped. What a noise!

Mr. Russo stood motionless at the front of the class, listening, astonished. He wore a neatly pressed dark blue pin-striped suit, a tan tie with a collie's head in the center, and a tieclasp with the initials R.R. engraved upon it; he had on the black wingtipped shoes; they glittered. Russo, who believed in neatness, honesty, punctuality, planned destinies — who believed in the future, in Occupations! And next to me, behind me, inside me, all over me — Albie! We looked at each other, Albie and I, and my lungs split with joy: *"Don't sit under the apple tree —"* Albie's monotone boomed out, and then a thick liquid crooner's voice behind Albie bathed me in sound: it was the Duke's; he clapped to a tango beat.

Russo leaned for a moment against a visual aids chart — "Skilled Laborers: Salaries and Requirements" — and then scraped back his chair and plunged down into it, so far down it looked to have no bottom. He lowered his big head to the desk and his shoulders curled forward like the ends of wet paper; and that was when Albie pulled his coup. He stopped singing "Don't Sit Under the Apple Tree"; we all stopped. Russo looked up at the silence; his eyes black and baggy, he stared at our leader, Alberto Pelagutti. Slowly

Russo began to shake his head from side to side: this was no Capone, this was a Garibaldi! Russo waited, I waited, we all waited. Albie slowly rose, and began to sing *"Oh, say can you see, by the dawn's early light, what so proudly we hailed —"* And we all stood and joined him. Tears sparkling on his long black lashes, Mr. Robert Russo dragged himself wearily up from his desk, beaten, and as the Pelagutti basso boomed disastrously behind me, I saw Russo's lips begin to move, *"the bombs bursting in air, gave proof —"* God, did we sing!

Albie left school in June of that year — he had passed only Occupations — but our comradeship, that strange vessel, was smashed to bits at noon one day a few months earlier. It was a lunch hour in March, the Duke and I were sparring in the hall outside the cafeteria, and Albie, who had been more hospitable to the Duke since the day his warm, liquid voice had joined the others — Albie had decided to act as our referee, jumping between us, separating our clinches, warning us about low blows, grabbing out for the Duke's droopy crotch, in general having a good time. I remember that the Duke and I were in a clinch; as I showered soft little punches to his kidneys he squirmed in my embrace. The sun shone through the window behind him, lighting up his hair like a nest of snakes. I fluttered his sides, he twisted, I breathed hard through my nose, my eyes registered on his snaky hair, and suddenly Albie wedged between and knocked us apart — the Duke plunged sideways, I plunged forward, and my fist crashed through the window that Scarpa had been using as his corner. Feet pounded; in a second a wisecracking, guiltless, chewing crowd was gathered around me, just me. Albie and the Duke were gone. I cursed them both, the honorless bastards! The crowd did not drift back to lunch until the head dietitian, a huge, varicose-veined matron in a laundry-stiff white uniform had written down my name and led me to the nurse's office to have the glass picked out of my knuckles. Later in the afternoon I was called for the first and only time to the office of Mr. Wendell, the Principal.

Fifteen years have passed since then and I do not know what has happened to Albie Pelagutti. If he is a gangster he was not one with notoriety or money enough for the Kefauver Committee to interest itself in several years ago. When the Crime Committee reached New Jersey I followed their investigations carefully but never did I read in the papers the name Alberto Pelagutti or even Duke Scarpa — though who can tell what name the Duke is known by now. I do know, however, what happened to the Occupations teacher, for when another Senate Committee swooped through the state a while back it was discovered that Robert Russo — among others — had been a Marxist while attending Montclair State Teachers' College circa 1935. Russo refused to answer some of the Committee's questions, and the Newark Board of Education met, chastised, and dismissed him. I read now and then in the Newark *News* that Civil Liberties Union attorneys are still trying to appeal his case, and I have even written a letter to the Board of Education swearing that if anything subversive was ever done to my character, it wasn't done by my ex-high school teacher, Russo; if he was a Communist I never knew it. I could not decide whether or not to include in the letter a report of the "Star-Spangled Banner" incident: who knows what is and is not proof to the crotchety ladies and chainstore owners who sit and die on Boards of Education?

And if (to alter an Ancient's text) a man's history is his fate, who knows whether the Newark Board of Education will ever attend to a letter written to them by me. I mean, have fifteen years buried that afternoon I was called to see the Principal?

. . . He was a tall, distinguished gentleman and as I entered his office he rose and extended his hand. The same sun that an hour earlier had lit up snakes in the Duke's hair now slanted through Mr. Wendell's blinds and warmed his deep green carpet. "How do you do?" he said. "Yes," I answered, non sequiturly, and ducked my bandaged hand under my unbandaged hand. Graciously he said, "Sit down, won't you?" Frightened, unpracticed, I performed an aborted curtsy and sat. I watched Mr. Wendell go to his metal filing cabinet, slide one drawer open, and take from it a large white index card. He set the card on his desk and motioned me over so I might read what was typed on the card. At the top, in caps, was my whole name — last, first, and middle; below the name was a Roman numeral one, and beside it, "Fighting in corridor; broke window (3/19/42)." Already documented. And on a big card with plenty of space.

I returned to my chair and sat back as Mr. Wendell told me that the card would follow me through life. At first I listened, but as he talked on and on the drama went out of what he said, and my attention wandered to his filing cabinet. I began to imagine the cards inside, Albie's card and the Duke's, and then I understood — just short of forgiveness — why the two of them had zoomed off and left me to pay penance for the window by myself. Albie, you see, had always known about the filing cabinet and these index cards; I hadn't; and Russo, poor Russo, has only recently found out.

ELI,

THE

FANATIC

Leo Tzuref stepped out from back of a white column to welcome Eli Peck. Eli jumped back, surprised; then they shook hands and Tzuref gestured him into the sagging old mansion. At the door Eli turned, and down the slope of lawn, past the jungle of hedges, beyond the dark, untrampled horse path, he saw the street lights blink on in Woodenton. The stores along Coach House Road tossed up a burst of yellow — it came to Eli as a secret signal from his townsmen: "Tell this Tzuref where we stand, Eli. This is a modern community, Eli, we have our families, we pay taxes . . ." Eli, burdened by the message, gave Tzuref a dumb, weary stare.

"You must work a full day," Tzuref said, steering the attorney and his briefcase into the chilly hall.

Eli's heels made a racket on the cracked marble floor, and he spoke above it. "It's the commuting that's killing," he said, and entered the dim room Tzuref waved open for him. "Three hours a day . . . I came right from the train." He dwindled down into a harp-backed chair. He expected it would be deeper than it was and consequently jarred himself on the sharp bones of his seat. It woke him, this shiver of the behind, to his business. Tzuref, a bald shaggy-browed man who looked as if he'd once been very fat, sat back of an empty desk, halfway hidden, as though he were settled on the floor. Everything around him was empty. There were no books in the bookshelves, no rugs on the floor, no draperies in the big casement windows. As Eli began to speak Tzuref got up and swung a window back on one noisy hinge. "May and it's like August," he said, and with his back to Eli, he revealed the black circle on the back of his head. The crown of his head was missing! He returned through the dimness — the lamps had no bulbs — and Eli realized all he'd seen was a skullcap. Tzuref struck a match and lit a candle, just as the half-dying shouts of children at play rolled in through the open window. It was as though Tzuref had opened it so Eli could hear them.

"Aah, now," he said. "I received your letter."

Eli poised, waiting for Tzuref to swish open a drawer and remove the letter from his file. Instead the old man leaned forward onto his stomach, worked his hand into his pants pocket, and withdrew what appeared to be a week-old handkerchief. He uncrumpled it; he unfolded it; he ironed it on the desk with the side of his hand. "So," he said.

Eli pointed to the grimy sheet which he'd gone over word-by-word with his partners, Lewis and McDonnell. "I expected an answer," Eli said. "It's a week."

"It was so important, Mr. Peck, I knew you would come."

Some children ran under the open window and their mysterious babble — not mysterious to Tzuref, who smiled — entered the room like a third person. Their noise caught up against Eli's flesh and he was unable to restrain a shud-

der. He wished he had gone home, showered and eaten
dinner, before calling on Tzuref. He was not feeling as
professional as usual — the place was too dim, it was too
late. But down in Woodenton they would be waiting, his
clients and neighbors. He spoke for the Jews of Woodenton, not just himself and his wife.

"You understood?" Eli said.

"It's not hard."

"It's a matter of zoning..." and when Tzuref did not
answer, but only drummed his fingers on his lips, Eli said,
"We didn't make the laws..."

"You respect them."

"They protect us...the community."

"The law is the law," Tzuref said.

"Exactly!" Eli had the urge to rise and walk about the
room.

"And then of course" — Tzuref made a pair of scales
in the air with his hands —"The law is not the law. When
is the law that is the law not the law?" He jiggled the
scales. "And vice versa."

"Simply," Eli said sharply. "You can't have a boarding
school in a residential area." He would not allow Tzuref to
cloud the issue with issues. "We thought it better to tell
you before any action is undertaken."

"But a house in a residential area?"

"Yes. That's what residential means." The DP's English was perhaps not as good as it seemed at first. Tzuref
spoke slowly, but till then Eli had mistaken it for craft —
or even wisdom. "Residence means home," he added.

"So this is my residence."

"But the children?"

"It is their residence."

"*Seventeen* children?"

"Eighteen," Tzuref said.

"But you *teach* them here."

"The Talmud. That's illegal?"

"That makes it school."

Tzuref hung the scales again, tipping slowly the balance.

"Look, Mr. Tzuref, in America we call such a place a boarding school."

"Where they teach the Talmud?"

"Where they teach period. You are the headmaster, they are the students."

Tzuref placed his scales on the desk. "Mr. Peck," he said, "I don't believe it..." but he did not seem to be referring to anything Eli had said.

"Mr. Tzuref, that is the law. I came to ask what you intend to do."

"What I *must* do?"

"I hope they are the same."

"They are." Tzuref brought his stomach into the desk. "We stay." He smiled. "We are tired. The headmaster is tired. The students are tired."

Eli rose and lifted his briefcase. It felt so heavy packed with the grievances, vengeances, and schemes of his clients. There were days when he carried it like a feather — in Tzuref's office it weighed a ton.

"Goodbye, Mr. Tzuref."

"Sholom," Tzuref said.

Eli opened the door to the office and walked carefully down the dark tomb of a corridor to the door. He stepped out on the porch and, leaning against a pillar, looked down across the lawn to the children at play. Their voices whooped and rose and dropped as they chased each other

round the old house. The dusk made the children's game
look like a tribal dance. Eli straightened up, started off the
porch, and suddenly the dance was ended. A long piercing
scream trailed after. It was the first time in his life anyone
had run at the sight of him. Keeping his eyes on the lights
of Woodenton, he headed down the path.

And then, seated on a bench beneath a tree, Eli saw
him. At first it seemed only a deep hollow of blackness —
then the figure emerged. Eli recognized him from the
description. There he was, wearing the hat, that hat
which was the very cause of Eli's mission, the source of
Woodenton's upset. The town's lights flashed their message once again: "Get the one with the hat. What a nerve,
what a nerve . . ."

Eli started towards the man. Perhaps he was less stubborn than Tzuref, more reasonable. After all, it was the
law. But when he was close enough to call out, he didn't.
He was stopped by the sight of the black coat that fell down
below the man's knees, and the hands which held each
other in his lap. By the round-topped, wide-brimmed Talmudic hat, pushed onto the back of his head. And by the
beard, which hid his neck and was so soft and thin it fluttered away and back again with each heavy breath he took.
He was asleep, his sidelocks curled loose on his cheeks.
His face was no older than Eli's.

Eli hurried towards the lights.

The note on the kitchen table unsettled him. Scrib-
blings on bits of paper had made history this past week.
This one, however, was unsigned. "Sweetie," it said, "I
went to sleep. I had a sort of Oedipal experience with the
baby today. Call Ted Heller."

She had left him a cold soggy dinner in the refrigerator. He hated cold soggy dinners, but would take one gladly in place of Miriam's presence. He was ruffled, and she never helped that, not with her infernal analytic powers. He loved her when life was proceeding smoothly — and that was when she loved him. But sometimes Eli found being a lawyer surrounded him like quicksand — he couldn't get his breath. Too often he wished he were pleading for the other side; though if he were on the other side, then he'd wish he were on the side he was. The trouble was that sometimes the law didn't seem to be the answer, *law* didn't seem to have anything to do with what was aggravating everybody. And that, of course, made him feel foolish and unnecessary . . . Though that was not the situation here — the townsmen had a case. But not *exactly*, and if Miriam were awake to see Eli's upset, she would set about explaining his distress to him, understanding him, forgiving him, so as to get things back to Normal, for Normal was where they loved one another. The difficulty with Miriam's efforts was they only upset him more; not only did they explain little to him about himself or his predicament, but they convinced him of *her* weakness. Neither Eli nor Miriam, it turned out, was terribly strong. Twice before he'd faced this fact, and on both occasions had found solace in what his neighbors forgivingly referred to as "a nervous breakdown."

Eli ate his dinner with his briefcase beside him. Halfway through, he gave in to himself, removed Tzuref's notes, and put them on the table, beside Miriam's. From time to time he flipped through the notes, which had been carried into town by the one in the black hat. The first note, the incendiary:

To whom it may concern:

Please give this gentleman the following: Boys shoes with rubber heels and soles.

5 prs size 6c

3 prs size 5c

3 prs size 5b

2 prs size 4a

3 prs size 4c

1 pr size 7b

1 pr size 7c

Total 18 prs. boys shoes. This gentleman has a check already signed. Please fill in correct amount.

L. Tzuref
Director, Yeshivah of
Woodenton, N.Y.
(5/8/48)

"Eli, a regular greenhorn," Ted Heller had said. "He didn't say a word. Just handed me the note and stood there, like in the Bronx the old guys who used to come around selling Hebrew trinkets."

"A Yeshivah!" Artie Berg had said. "Eli, in Woodenton, a Yeshivah! If I want to live in Brownsville, Eli, I'll live in Brownsville."

"Eli," Harry Shaw speaking now, "the old Puddington place. Old man Puddington'll roll over in his grave. Eli, when I left the city, Eli, I didn't plan the city should come to me."

Note number two:

Dear Grocer:

Please give this gentleman ten pounds of sugar. Charge it to our account, Yeshivah of Woodenton, NY — which we will now open with you and expect a bill each month. The gentleman will be in to see you once or twice a week.

L. Tzuref, Director
(5/10/48)

P.S. Do you carry kosher meat?

"He walked right by my window, the greenie," Ted had said, "and he nodded, Eli. He's my *friend* now."

"Eli," Artie Berg had said, "he handed the damn thing to a *clerk* at Stop N' Shop — and in that hat yet!"

"Eli," Harry Shaw again, "it's not funny. Someday, Eli, it's going to be a hundred little kids with little *yamalkahs* chanting their Hebrew lessons on Coach House Road, and then it's not going to strike you funny."

"Eli, what goes on up there — my kids hear strange sounds."

"Eli, this is a modern community."

"Eli, we pay taxes."

"Eli."

"Eli!"

"*Eli!*"

At first it was only another townsman crying in his ear; but when he turned he saw Miriam, standing in the doorway, behind her belly.

"Eli, sweetheart, how was it?"

"He said no."

"Did you see the other one?" she asked.

"Sleeping, under a tree."

"Did you let him know how people feel?"

"He was sleeping."

"Why didn't you wake him up? Eli, this isn't an everyday thing."

"He was tired!"

"Don't shout, please," Miriam said.

" 'Don't shout. I'm pregnant. The baby is heavy.' " Eli found he was getting angry at nothing she'd said yet; it was what she was going to say.

"He's a very heavy baby the doctor says," Miriam told him.

"Then sit *down* and make my dinner." Now he found himself angry about her not being present at the dinner which he'd just been relieved that she wasn't present at. It was as though he had a raw nerve for a tail, that he kept stepping on. At last Miriam herself stepped on it.

"Eli, you're upset. I understand."

"You *don't* understand."

She left the room. From the stairs she called, "I do, sweetheart."

It was a trap! He would grow angry knowing she would be "understanding." She would in turn grow more understanding seeing his anger. He would in turn grow angrier ... The phone rang.

"Hello," Eli said.

"Eli, Ted. So?"

"So nothing."

"Who is Tzuref? He's an American guy?"

"No. A DP. German."

"And the kids?"

"DP's too. He teaches them."

"What? What subjects?" Ted asked.

"I don't know."

"And the guy with the hat, you saw the guy with the hat?"

"Yes. He was sleeping."

"Eli, he sleeps with the *hat*?"

"He sleeps with the hat."

"Goddam fanatics," Ted said. "This is the twentieth century, Eli. Now it's the guy with the hat. Pretty soon all the little Yeshivah boys'll be spilling down into town."

"Next thing they'll be after our daughters."

"Michele and Debbie wouldn't look at them."

"Then," Eli mumbled, "you've got nothing to worry about, Teddie," and he hung up.

In a moment the phone rang. "Eli? We got cut off. We've got nothing to worry about? You worked it out?"

"I have to see him again tomorrow. We can work something out."

"That's fine, Eli. I'll call Artie and Harry."

Eli hung up.

"I thought you said *nothing* worked out." It was Miriam.

"I did."

"Then why did you tell Ted *something* worked out?"

"It did."

"Eli, maybe you should get a little more therapy."

"That's enough of that, Miriam."

"You can't function as a lawyer by being neurotic. That's no answer."

"You're ingenious, Miriam."

She turned, frowning, and took her heavy baby to bed.

The phone rang.

"Eli, Artie. Ted called. You worked it out? No trouble?"

"Yes."

"When are they going?"

"Leave it to me, will you, Artie? I'm tired. I'm going to sleep."

In bed Eli kissed his wife's belly and laid his head upon it to think. He laid it lightly, for she was that day entering the second week of her ninth month. Still, when she slept, it was a good place to rest, to rise and fall with her breathing and figure things out. "If that guy would take off that crazy hat. I know it, what eats them. If he'd take off that crazy hat everything would be all right."

"What?" Miriam said.

"I'm talking to the baby."

Miriam pushed herself up in bed. "Eli, please, baby, shouldn't you maybe stop in to see Dr. Eckman, just for a little conversation?"

"I'm fine."

"Oh, sweetie!" she said, and put her head back on the pillow.

"You know what your mother brought to this marriage — a sling chair and a goddam New School enthusiasm for Sigmund Freud."

Miriam feigned sleep, he could tell by the breathing.

"I'm telling the kid the truth, aren't I, Miriam? A sling chair, three months to go on a *New Yorker* subscription, and *An Introduction to Psychoanalysis*. Isn't that right?"

"Eli, must you be aggressive?"

"That's all you worry about, is your insides. You stand in front of the mirror all day and look at yourself being pregnant."

"Pregnant mothers have a relationship with the fetus that fathers can't understand."

"Relationship my ass. What is my liver doing now? What is my small intestine doing now? Is my island of Langerhans on the blink?"

"Don't be jealous of a little fetus, Eli."

"I'm jealous of your island of Lagerhans!"

"Eli, I can't argue with you when I know it's not me you're really angry with. Don't you see, sweetie, you're angry with yourself."

"You and Eckman."

"Maybe he could help, Eli."

"Maybe he could help you. You're practically lovers as it is."

"You're being hostile again," Miriam said.

"What do you care — it's only *me* I'm being hostile towards."

"Eli, we're going to have a beautiful baby, and I'm going to have a perfectly simple delivery, and you're going to make a fine father, and there's absolutely no reason to be obsessed with whatever is on your mind. All we have to worry about — " she smiled at him " — is a name."

Eli got out of bed and slid into his slippers. "We'll name the kid Eckman if it's a boy and Eckman if it's a girl."

"Eckman Peck sounds terrible."

"He'll have to live with it," Eli said, and he went down to his study where the latch on his briefcase glinted in the moonlight that came through the window.

He removed the Tzuref notes and read through them all again. It unnerved him to think of all the flashy reasons his wife could come up with for his reading and rereading the notes. "Eli, why are you so *preoccupied* with Tzuref?" "Eli, stop getting *involved*. Why do you think you're getting *involved*, Eli?" Sooner or later, everybody's wife finds their weak spot. His goddam luck he had to be neurotic! Why couldn't he have been born with a short leg.

He removed the cover from his typewriter, hating Miriam for the edge she had. All the time he wrote the letter, he could hear what she would be saying about his not being *able* to let the matter drop. Well, her trouble was that she wasn't *able* to face the matter. But he could hear her answer already: clearly, he was guilty of "a reaction formation." Still, all the fancy phrases didn't fool Eli: all she wanted really was for Eli to send Tzuref and family on their way, so that the community's temper would quiet, and the calm circumstances of their domestic happiness return. All she wanted were order and love in her private world. Was she so wrong? Let the world bat its brains out —in Woodenton there should be peace. He wrote the letter anyway:

Dear Mr. Tzuref:
Our meeting this evening seems to me inconclusive. I don't think there's any reason for us not to be able to come up with some sort of compromise that will satisfy the Jewish community of Woodenton and the Yeshivah and yourself. It seems to me that what most disturbs my neighbors are the visits to town by the gentleman in the black hat, suit, etc. Woodenton is a progressive suburban community whose members, both Jewish and Gentile, are anxious that their families live in comfort and beauty and serenity. This is, after all, the twentieth century, and we do not think it too much to ask that the members of our

community dress in a manner appropriate to the time and place.

Woodenton, as you may not know, has long been the home of well-to-do Protestants. It is only since the war that Jews have been able to buy property here, and for Jews and Gentiles to live beside each other in amity. For this adjustment to be made, both Jews and Gentiles alike have had to give up some of their more extreme practices in order not to threaten or offend the other. Certainly such amity is to be desired. Perhaps if such conditions had existed in prewar Europe, the persecution of the Jewish people, of which you and those 18 children have been victims, could not have been carried out with such success — in fact, might not have been carried out at all.

Therefore, Mr. Tzuref, will you accept the following conditions? If you can, we will see fit not to carry out legal action against the Yeshivah for failure to comply with township Zoning ordinances No. 18 and No. 23. The conditions are simply:

1. The religious, educational, and social activities of the Yeshivah of Woodenton will be confined to the Yeshivah grounds.

2. Yeshivah personnel are welcomed in the streets and stores of Woodenton provided they are attired in clothing usually associated with American life in the 20th century.

If these conditions are met, we see no reason why the Yeshivah of Woodenton cannot live peacefully and satisfactorily with the Jews of Woodenton — as the Jews of Woodenton have come to live with the Gentiles of Woodenton. I would appreciate an immediate reply.

Sincerely,

ELI PECK, Attorney

Two days later Eli received his immediate reply:

Mr. Peck:
   The suit the gentleman wears is all he's got.
                         Sincerely,
                            LEO TZUREF, Headmaster

Once again, as Eli swung around the dark trees and onto
the lawn, the children fled. He reached out with his briefcase as if to stop them, but they were gone so fast all he saw
moving was a flock of skullcaps.
   "Come, come..." a voice called from the porch. Tzuref
appeared from behind a pillar. Did he *live* behind those
pillars? Was he just watching the children at play? Either
way, when Eli appeared, Tzuref was ready, with no fore-
warning.
   "Hello," Eli said.
   "Sholom."
   "I didn't mean to frighten them."
   "They're scared, so they run."
   "I didn't do anything."
   Tzuref shrugged. The little movement seemed to Eli
strong as an accusation. What he didn't get at home, he
got here.
   Inside the house they took their seats. Though it was
lighter than a few evenings before, a bulb or two would
have helped. Eli had to hold his briefcase towards the window for the last gleamings. He removed Tzuref's letter
from a manila folder. Tzuref removed Eli's letter from his
pants pocket. Eli removed the carbon of his own letter
from another manila folder. Tzuref removed Eli's first letter from his back pocket. Eli removed the carbon from his

briefcase. Tzuref raised his palms. "...It's all I've got..."

Those upraised palms, the mocking tone — another accusation. It was a crime to keep carbons! Everybody had an edge on him — Eli could do no right.

"I offered a compromise, Mr. Tzuref. You refused."

"Refused, Mr. Peck? What is, is."

"The man could get a new suit."

"That's all he's got."

"So you told me," Eli said.

"So I told you, so you know."

"It's not an insurmountable obstacle, Mr. Tzuref. We have stores."

"For that too?"

"On Route 12, a Robert Hall —"

"To take away the one thing a man's got?"

"Not take away, *replace*."

"But I tell you he has nothing. *Nothing*. You have that word in English? *Nicht? Gornisht?*"

"Yes, Mr. Tzuref, we have the word."

"A mother and a father?" Tzuref said. "No. A wife? No. A baby? A little ten-month-old baby? No! A village full of friends? A synagogue where you knew the feel of every seat under your pants? Where with your eyes closed you could smell the cloth of the Torah?" Tzuref pushed out of his chair, stirring a breeze that swept Eli's letter to the floor. At the window he leaned out, and looked, beyond Woodenton. When he turned he was shaking a finger at Eli. "And a medical experiment they performed on him yet! That leaves nothing, Mr. Peck. Absolutely nothing!"

"I misunderstood."

"No news reached Woodenton?"

"About the suit, Mr. Tzuref. I thought he couldn't afford another."

"He can't."

They were right where they'd begun. "Mr. Tzuref!" Eli demanded. "*Here?*" He smacked his hand to his billfold.

"Exactly!" Tzuref said, smacking his own breast.

"Then we'll buy him one!" Eli crossed to the window and taking Tzuref by the shoulders, pronounced each word slowly. "We-will-pay-for-it. All right?"

"Pay? What, diamonds!"

Eli raised a hand to his inside pocket, then let it drop. Oh stupid! Tzuref, father to eighteen, had smacked not what lay under his coat, but deeper, under the ribs.

"Oh . . ." Eli said. He moved away along the wall. "The suit is all he's got then."

"You got my letter," Tzuref said.

Eli stayed back in the shadow, and Tzuref turned to his chair. He swished Eli's letter from the floor, and held it up. "You say too much . . . all this reasoning . . . all these conditions . . ."

"What can I do?"

"You have the word 'suffer' in English?"

"We have the word suffer. We have the word law too."

"Stop with the law! You have the word suffer. Then try it. It's a little thing."

"They won't," Eli said.

"But you, Mr. Peck, how about you?"

"I am them, they are me, Mr. Tzuref."

"Aach! You are us, we are you!"

Eli shook and shook his head. In the dark he suddenly felt that Tzuref might put him under a spell. "Mr. Tzuref, a little light?"

Tzuref lit what tallow was left in the holders. Eli was

afraid to ask if they couldn't afford electricity. Maybe candles were all they had left.

"Mr. Peck, who made the law, may I ask you that?"

"The people."

"No."

"Yes."

"Before the people."

"No one. Before the people there was no law." Eli didn't care for the conversation, but with only candle-light, he was being lulled into it.

"Wrong," Tzuref said.

"We make the law, Mr. Tzuref. It is our community. These are my neighbors. I am their attorney. They pay me. Without law there is chaos."

"What you call law, I call shame. The heart, Mr. Peck, the heart is law! God!" he announced.

"Look, Mr. Tzuref, I didn't come here to talk meta-physics. People use the law, it's a flexible thing. They protect what they value, their property, their well-being, their happiness —"

"Happiness? They hide their shame. And you, Mr. Peck, you are shameless?"

"We do it," Eli said, wearily, "for our children. This is the twentieth century . . ."

"For the goyim maybe. For me the Fifty-eighth." He pointed at Eli. "That is too old for shame."

Eli felt squashed. Everybody in the world had evil reasons for his actions. Everybody! With reasons so cheap, who buys bulbs. "Enough wisdom, Mr. Tzuref. Please. I'm exhausted."

"Who isn't?" Tzuref said.

He picked Eli's papers from his desk and reached up with them. "What do you intend for us to do?"

"What you must," Eli said. "I made the offer."

"So he must give up his suit?"

"Tzuref, Tzuref, leave me be with that suit! I'm not the only lawyer in the world. I'll drop the case, and you'll get somebody who won't talk compromise. Then you'll have no home, no children, nothing. Only a lousy black suit! Sacrifice what you want. I know what I would do."

To that Tzuref made no answer, but only handed Eli his letters.

"It's not me, Mr. Tzuref, it's them."

"They are you."

"No," Eli intoned, "I am me. They are them. You are you."

"You talk about leaves and branches. I'm dealing with under the dirt."

"Mr. Tzuref, you're driving me crazy with Talmudic wisdom. This is that, that is the other thing. Give me a straight answer."

"Only for straight questions."

"Oh, God!"

Eli returned to his chair and plunged his belongings into his case. "Then, that's all," he said angrily.

Tzuref gave him the shrug.

"Remember, Tzuref, you called this down on yourself."

"I did?"

Eli refused to be his victim again. Double-talk proved nothing.

"Goodbye," he said.

But as he opened the door leading to the hall, he heard Tzuref.

"And your wife, how is she?"

"Fine, just fine." Eli kept going.

"And the baby is due when, any day?"

Eli turned. "That's right."

"Well," Tzuref said, rising. "Good luck."

"You know?"

Tzuref pointed out the window — then, with his hands, he drew upon himself a beard, a hat, a long, long coat. When his fingers formed the hem they touched the floor. "He shops two, three times a week, he gets to know them."

"He *talks* to them?"

"He sees them."

"And he can tell which is my wife?"

"They shop at the same stores. He says she is beautiful. She has a kind face. A woman capable of love . . . though who can be sure."

"*He* talks about *us*, to *you?*" demanded Eli.

"You talk about us, to her?"

"Goodbye, Mr. Tzuref."

Tzuref said, "Sholom. And good luck — I know what it is to have children. Sholom," Tzuref whispered, and with the whisper the candles went out. But the instant before, the flames leaped into Tzuref's eyes, and Eli saw it was not luck Tzuref wished him at all.

Outside the door, Eli waited. Down the lawn the children were holding hands and whirling around in a circle. At first he did not move. But he could not hide in the shadows all night. Slowly he began to slip along the front of the house. Under his hands he felt where bricks were out. He moved in the shadows until he reached the side. And then, clutching his briefcase to his chest, he broke across the darkest spots of the lawn. He aimed for a distant glade of woods, and when he reached it he did not stop, but ran through until he was so dizzied that the trees seemed to be running beside him, fleeing not towards Woodenton

but away. His lungs were nearly ripping their seams as he
burst into the yellow glow of the Gulf station at the edge
of town.

"Eli, I had pains today. Where were you?"

"I went to Tzuref."

"Why didn't you call? I was worried."

He tossed his hat past the sofa and onto the floor.
"Where are my winter suits?"

"In the hall closet. Eli, it's May."

"I need a strong suit." He left the room, Miriam behind
him.

"Eli, talk to me. Sit down. Have dinner. Eli, what are
you doing? You're going to get moth balls all over the
carpet."

He peered out from the hall closet. Then he peered in
again — there was a zipping noise, and suddenly he swept
a greenish tweed suit before his wife's eyes.

"Eli, I love you in that suit. But not now. Have something to eat. I made dinner tonight — I'll warm it."

"You've got a box big enough for this suit?"

"I got a Bonwit's box, the other day. Eli, *why?*"

"Miriam, you see me doing something, let me do it."

"You haven't eaten."

"I'm *doing* something." He started up the stairs to the
bedroom.

"Eli, would you please tell me what it is you want, and
why?"

He turned and looked down at her. "Suppose this time
you give me the reasons *before* I tell you what I'm doing.
It'll probably work out the same anyway."

"Eli, I want to help."

"It doesn't concern you."

"But I want to help *you*," Miriam said.

"Just be quiet, then."

"But you're upset," she said, and she followed him up the stairs, heavily, breathing for two.

"Eli, what now?"

"A shirt." He yanked open all the drawers of their new teak dresser. He extracted a shirt.

"Eli, batiste? With a tweed suit?" she inquired.

He was at the closet now, on his knees. "Where are my cordovans?"

"Eli, why are you doing this so compulsively? You look like you *have* to do something."

"Oh, Miriam, you're supersubtle."

"Eli, stop this and talk to me. Stop it or I'll call Dr. Eckman."

Eli was kicking off the shoes he was wearing. "Where's the Bonwit box?"

"Eli, do you want me to have the baby right *here!*"

Eli walked over and sat down on the bed. He was draped not only with his own clothing, but also with the greenish tweed suit, the batiste shirt, and under each arm a shoe. He raised his arms and let the shoes drop onto the bed. Then he undid his necktie with one hand and his teeth and added that to the booty.

"Underwear," he said. "He'll need underwear."

"Who!"

He was slipping out of his socks.

Miriam kneeled down and helped him ease his left foot out of the sock. She sat with it on the floor. "Eli, just lie back. Please."

"Plaza 9-3103."

"What?"

"Eckman's number," he said. "It'll save you the trouble."

"Eli —"

"You've got that goddam tender 'You need help' look in your eyes, Miriam, don't tell me you don't."

"I don't."

"I'm not flipping," Eli said.

"I know, Eli."

"Last time I sat in the bottom of the closet and chewed on my bedroom slippers. That's what I did."

"I know."

"And I'm not doing that. This is not a nervous breakdown, Miriam, let's get that straight."

"Okay," Miriam said. She kissed the foot she held. Then, softly, she asked, "What *are* you doing?"

"Getting clothes for the guy in the hat. Don't tell me why, Miriam. Just let me do it."

"That's all?" she asked.

"That's all."

"You're not leaving?"

"No."

"Sometimes I think it gets too much for you, and you'll just leave."

"What gets too much?"

"I don't *know*, Eli. Something gets too much. Whenever everything's peaceful for a long time, and things are nice and pleasant, and we're expecting to be even happier. Like now. It's as if you don't think we *deserve* to be happy."

"Damn it, Miriam! I'm giving this guy a new suit, is that all right? From now on he comes into Woodenton like everybody else, is that all right with you?"

"And Tzuref moves?"

"I don't even know if he'll take the suit, Miriam! What do you have to bring up moving!"

"Eli, I didn't bring up moving. Everybody did. That's what everybody wants. Why make everybody un*happy*. It's even a law, Eli."

"Don't tell me what's the law."

"All right, sweetie. I'll get the box."

"*I'll* get the box. Where is it?"

"In the basement."

When he came up from the basement, he found all the clothes neatly folded and squared away on the sofa: shirt, tie, shoes, socks, underwear, belt, and an old gray flannel suit. His wife sat on the end of the sofa, looking like an anchored balloon.

"Where's the green suit?" he said.

"Eli, it's your loveliest suit. It's my favorite suit. Whenever I think of you, Eli, it's in that suit."

"Get it out."

"Eli, it's a Brooks Brothers suit. You say yourself how much you love it."

"Get it out."

"But the gray flannel's more practical. For shopping."

"Get it out."

"You go overboard, Eli. That's your trouble. You won't do anything in moderation. That's how people destroy themselves."

"I do *everything* in moderation. That's my trouble. The suit's in the closet again?"

She nodded, and began to fill up with tears. "Why does it have to be *your* suit? Who are you even to decide to give a suit? What about the others?" She was crying openly, and holding her belly. "Eli, I'm going to have a

baby. Do we need all *this?*" and she swept the clothes off
the sofa to the floor.

At the closet Eli removed the green suit. "It's a J.
Press," he said, looking at the lining.

"I hope to hell he's happy with it!" Miriam said, sob-
bing.

A half hour later the box was packed. The cord he'd
found in the kitchen cabinet couldn't keep the outfit from
popping through. The trouble was there was too much: the
gray suit *and* the green suit, an oxford shirt as well as the
batiste. But let him have two suits! Let him have three,
four, if only this damn silliness would stop! And a hat
— of course! God, he'd almost forgotten the hat. He took
the stairs two at a time and in Miriam's closet yanked a
hatbox from the top shelf. Scattering hat and tissue paper
to the floor, he returned downstairs, where he packed away
the hat he'd worn that day. Then he looked at his wife, who
lay outstretched on the floor before the fireplace. For the
third time in as many minutes she was saying, "Eli, this
is the real thing."

"Where?"

"Right under the baby's head, like somebody's squeez-
ing oranges."

Now that he'd stopped to listen he was stupefied. He
said, "But you have two more weeks..." Somehow he'd
really been expecting it was to go on not just another two
weeks, but another nine months. This led him to suspect,
suddenly, that his wife was feigning pain so as to get his
mind off delivering the suit. And just as suddenly he resented himself for having such a thought. God, what had
he become! He'd been an unending bastard towards her

since this Tzuref business had come up — just when her pregnancy must have been most burdensome. He'd allowed her no access to him, but still, he was sure, for good reasons: she might tempt him out of his confusion with her easy answers. He could be tempted all right, it was why he fought so hard. But now a sweep of love came over him at the thought of her contracting womb, and his child. And yet he would not indicate it to her. Under such splendid marital conditions, who knows but she might extract some promise from him about his concern with the school on the hill.

Having packed his second bag of the evening, Eli sped his wife to Woodenton Memorial. There she proceeded not to have her baby, but to lie hour after hour through the night having at first oranges, then bowling balls, then basketballs, squeezed back of her pelvis. Eli sat in the waiting room, under the shattering African glare of a dozen rows of fluorescent bulbs, composing a letter to Tzuref.

Dear Mr. Tzuref:
The clothes in this box are for the gentleman in the hat. In a life of sacrifice what is one more? But in a life of no sacrifices even one is impossible. Do you see what I'm saying, Mr. Tzuref? I am not a Nazi who would drive eighteen children, who are probably frightened at the sight of a firefly, into homelessness. But if you want a home here, you must accept what we have to offer. The world is the world, Mr. Tzuref. As you would say, what is, is. All we say to this man is change your clothes. Enclosed are two suits and two shirts, and everything else he'll need, including a new hat. When he needs new clothes let me know.

We await his appearance in Woodenton, as we await friendly relations with the Yeshivah of Woodenton.

He signed his name and slid the note under a bursting flap and into the box. Then he went to the phone at the end of the room and dialed Ted Heller's number.

"Hello."

"Shirley, it's Eli."

"Eli, we've been calling all night. The lights are on in your place, but nobody answers. We thought it was burglars."

"Miriam's having the baby."

"At home?" Shirley said. "Oh, Eli, what a fun-idea!"

"Shirley, let me speak to Ted."

After the ear-shaking clatter of the phone whacking the floor, Eli heard footsteps, breathing, throat-clearing, then Ted. "A boy or a girl?"

"Nothing yet."

"You've given Shirley the bug, Eli. Now she's going to have *our* next one at home."

"Good."

"That's a terrific way to bring the family together, Eli."

"Look, Ted, I've settled with Tzuref."

"When are they going?"

"They're not exactly going, Teddie. I settled it — you won't even know they're there."

"A guy dressed like 1000 B.C. and I won't know it? What are you thinking about, pal?"

"He's changing his clothes."

"Yeah, to what? Another funeral suit?"

"Tzuref promised me, Ted. Next time he comes to town, he comes dressed like you and me."

"What! Somebody's kidding somebody, Eli."

Eli's voice shot up. "If he says he'll do it, he'll do it!"

"And, Eli," Ted asked, "he said it?"

"He said it." It cost him a sudden headache, this invention.

"And suppose he doesn't change, Eli. Just suppose. I mean that *might* happen, Eli. This might just be some kind of stall or something."

"No," Eli assured him.

The other end was quiet a moment. "Look, Eli," Ted said, finally, "he changes. Okay? All right? But they're still up there, aren't they? *That* doesn't change."

"The point is you won't know it."

Patiently Ted said, "Is this what we asked of you, Eli? When we put our faith and trust in you, is that what we were asking? We weren't concerned that this guy should become a Beau Brummel, Eli, believe me. We just don't think this is the community for them. And, Eli, we isn't me. The Jewish members of the community appointed me, Artie, and Harry to see what could be done. And we appointed you. And what's happened?"

Eli heard himself say, "What happened, happened."

"Eli, you're talking in crossword puzzles."

"My wife's having a baby," Eli explained, defensively.

"I realize that, Eli. But this is a matter of zoning, isn't it? Isn't that what we discovered? You don't abide by the ordinance, you go. I mean I can't raise mountain goats, say, in my backyard —"

"This isn't so simple, Ted. People are involved—"

"People? Eli, we've been through this and through this. We're not just dealing with people — these are religious fanatics is what they are. Dressing like that. What I'd really like to find out is what goes on up there. I'm getting

more and more skeptical, Eli, and I'm not afraid to admit it.
It smells like a lot of hocus-pocus abracadabra stuff to me.
Guys like Harry, you know, they think and they think and
they're afraid to admit what they're thinking. I'll tell you.
Look, I don't even know about this Sunday school business.
Sundays I drive my oldest kid all the way to Scarsdale to
learn Bible stories . . . and you know what she comes up
with? This Abraham in the Bible was going to kill his own
kid for a sacrifice. She gets nightmares from it, for God's
sake! You call that religion? Today a guy like that they'd
lock him up. This is an age of science, Eli. I size people's
feet with an X-ray machine, for God's sake. They've dis-
proved all that stuff, Eli, and I refuse to sit by and watch it
happening on my own front lawn."

"Nothing's happening on your front lawn, Teddie.
You're exaggerating, nobody's sacrificing their kid."

"You're damn right, Eli — I'm not sacrificing mine.
You'll see when you have your own what it's like. All the
place is, is a hideaway for people who can't face life. It's a
matter of *needs*. They have all these superstitions, and why
do you think? Because they can't face the world, because
they can't take their place in society. That's no environ-
ment to bring kids up in, Eli."

"Look, Ted, see it from another angle. We can convert
them," Eli said, with half a heart.

"What, make a bunch of Catholics out of them? Look,
Eli — pal, there's a good healthy relationship in this town
because it's modern Jews and Protestants. That's the point,
isn't it, Eli? Let's not kid each other, I'm not Harry. The
way things are now are fine — like human beings. There's
going to be no pogroms in Woodenton. Right? 'Cause
there's no fanatics, no crazy people —" Eli winced, and
closed his eyes a second — "just people who respect each

other, and leave each other be. Common sense is the ruling
thing, Eli. I'm for common sense. Moderation."

"Exactly, exactly, Ted. I agree, but common sense,
maybe, says make this guy change his clothes. Then
maybe —"

"Common sense says that? Common sense says to me
they go and find a nice place somewhere else, Eli. New
York is the biggest city in the world, it's only 30 miles away
— why don't they go there?"

"Ted, give them a chance. Introduce them to common
sense."

"Eli, you're dealing with *fanatics*. Do they display common sense? Talking a dead language, that makes sense?
Making a big thing out of suffering, so you're going oy-oy-oy
all your life, that's common sense? Look, Eli, we've been
through all this. I don't know if you know — but there's
talk that *Life* magazine is sending a guy out to the Yeshivah
for a story. With pictures."

"Look, Teddie, you're letting your imagination get in-
flamed. I don't think *Life's* interested."

"But I'm interested, Eli. And we thought you were supposed to be."

"I am," Eli said, "I am. Let him just change the clothes,
Ted. Let's see what happens."

"They live in the medieval ages, Eli — it's some supersti-
tion, some *rule*."

"Let's just *see*," Eli pleaded.

"Eli, every day —"

"One more day," Eli said. "If he doesn't change in one
more day. . . ."

"What?"

"Then I get an injunction first thing Monday. That's
that."

"Look, Eli — it's not up to me. Let me call Harry —"

"You're the spokesman, Teddie. I'm all wrapped up here with Miriam having a baby. Just give me the day — them the day."

"All right, Eli. I want to be fair. But tomorrow, that's all. Tomorrow's the judgment day, Eli, I'm telling you."

"I hear trumpets," Eli said, and hung up. He was shaking inside — Teddie's voice seemed to have separated his bones at the joints. He was still in the phone booth when the nurse came to tell him that Mrs. Peck would positively not be delivered of a child until the morning. He was to go home and get some rest, he looked like *he* was having the baby. The nurse winked and left.

But Eli did not go home. He carried the Bonwit box out into the street with him and put it in the car. The night was soft and starry, and he began to drive the streets of Woodenton. Square cool windows, apricot-colored, were all one could see beyond the long lawns that fronted the homes of the townsmen. The stars polished the permanent baggage carriers atop the station wagons in the driveways. He drove slowly, up, down, around. Only his tires could be heard taking the gentle curves in the road.

What peace. What incredible peace. Have children ever been so safe in their beds? Parents — Eli wondered — so full in their stomachs? Water so warm in its boilers? Never. Never in Rome, never in Greece. Never even did walled cities have it so good! No wonder then they would keep things just as they were. Here, after all, were peace and safety — what civilization had been working toward for centuries. For all his jerkiness, that was all Ted Heller was asking for, peace and safety. It was what his parents had asked for in the Bronx, and his grandparents in Poland, and theirs in Russia or Austria, or wherever else they'd fled to or from. It was what Miriam was asking for. And now they had it — the world was at last a place for families, even Jewish families. After all these centuries, maybe there just had to be this communal toughness — or numbness — to protect such a blessing. Maybe that was the trouble with the Jews all along — too soft. Sure, to live takes guts . . . Eli was thinking as he drove on beyond the train station, and parked his car at the darkened Gulf station. He stepped out, carrying the box.

At the top of the hill one window trembled with light. What *was* Tzuref doing up there in that office? Killing babies — probably not. But studying a language no one understood? Practicing customs with origins long forgotten? Suffering sufferings already suffered once too often? Teddie was right — why keep it up! However, if a man chose to be stubborn, then he couldn't expect to survive. The world is give-and-take. What sense to sit and brood over a suit. Eli would give him one last chance.

He stopped at the top. No one was around. He walked slowly up the lawn, setting each foot into the grass, listening to the shh shhh shhhh his shoes made as they bent the wetness into the sod. He looked around. Here there was nothing. Nothing! An old decaying house — and a suit.

On the porch he slid behind a pillar. He felt someone was watching him. But only the stars gleamed down. And at his feet, off and away, Woodenton glowed up. He set his package on the step of the great front door. Inside the cover of the box he felt to see if his letter was still there. When he touched it, he pushed it deeper into the green suit, which his fingers still remembered from winter. He should have included some light bulbs. Then he slid back by the pillar again, and this time there was something on the lawn. It was the second sight he had of him. He was facing Woodenton and barely moving across the open space towards the trees. His right fist was beating his chest. And then Eli heard a sound rising with each knock on the chest. What a moan! It could raise hair, stop hearts, water eyes. And it did all three to Eli, plus more. Some feeling crept into him for whose deepness he could find no word. It was strange. He listened — it did not hurt to hear this moan. But he wondered if it hurt to make it. And so, with only stars to hear, he tried. And it did hurt. Not the bumble-bee of noise that turned at the back of his throat and winged out his nostrils. What hurt buzzed down. It stung and stung inside him, and in turn the moan sharpened. It became a scream, louder, a song, a crazy song that whined through the pillars and blew out to the grass, until the strange hatted creature on the lawn turned and threw his arms wide, and looked in the night like a scarecrow.

Eli ran, and when he reached the car the pain was only a bloody scratch across his neck where a branch had whipped back as he fled the greenie's arms.

The following day his son was born. But not till one in the afternoon, and by then a great deal had happened.

First, at nine-thirty the phone rang. Eli leaped from the sofa — where he'd dropped the night before — and picked it screaming from the cradle. He could practically smell the hospital as he shouted into the phone, "Hello, yes!"

"Eli, it's Ted. Eli, he *did* it. He just walked by the store. I was opening the door, Eli, and I turned around and I swear I thought it was you. But it was him. He still walks like he did, but the clothes, Eli, the clothes."

"Who?"

"The greenie. He has on man's regular clothes. And the suit, it's a beauty."

The suit barreled back into Eli's consciousness, pushing all else aside. "What color suit?"

"Green. He's just strolling in the green suit like it's a holiday. Eli . . . is it a Jewish holiday?"

"Where is he now?"

"He's walking straight up Coach House Road, in this damn tweed job. Eli, it worked. You were right."

"We'll see."

"What next?"

"We'll see."

He took off the underwear in which he'd slept and went into the kitchen where he turned the light under the coffee. When it began to perk he held his head over the pot so it would steam loose the knot back of his eyes. It still hadn't when the phone rang.

"Eli, Ted again. Eli, the guy's walking up and down every street in town. Really, he's on a tour or something. Artie called me, Herb called me. Now Shirley calls that he just walked by our house. Eli, go out on the porch you'll see."

Eli went to the window and peered out. He couldn't see past the bend in the road, and there was no one in sight.

"Eli?" He heard Ted from where he dangled over the telephone table. He dropped the phone into the hook, as a few last words floated up to him — "Eliyousawhim . . . ?" He threw on the pants and shirt he'd worn the night before and walked barefoot on to his front lawn. And sure enough, his apparition appeared around the bend: in a brown hat a little too far down on his head, a green suit too far back on the shoulders, an unbuttoned-down button-down shirt, a tie knotted so as to leave a two-inch tail, trousers that cascaded onto his shoes — he was shorter than that black hat had made him seem. And moving the clothes was that walk that was not a walk, the tiny-stepped shlumpy gait. He came round the bend, and for all his strangeness — it clung to his whiskers, signaled itself in his locomotion — he looked as if he belonged. Eccentric, maybe, but he belonged. He made no moan, nor did he invite Eli with wide-flung arms. But he did stop when he saw him. He stopped and put a hand to his hat. When he felt for its top, his hand went up too high. Then it found the level and fiddled with the brim. The fingers fiddled, fumbled, and when they'd finally made their greeting, they traveled down the fellow's face and in an instant seemed to have touched each one of his features. They dabbed the eyes, ran the length of the nose, swept over the hairy lip, until they found their home in the hair that hid a little of his collar. To Eli the fingers said, *I have a face, I have a face at least.* Then his hand came through the beard and when it stopped at his chest it was like a pointer — and the eyes asked a question as tides of water shifted over them. *The face is all right, I can keep it?* Such a look was in those eyes that Eli was still seeing them when he turned his head away. They were the hearts of his jonquils, that only last week had appeared — they were the leaves on his birch, the bulbs in his coach lamp, the droppings on his lawn: those eyes were the eyes in his head. They were his, he had made them. He turned and went into his house and when he peeked out the side of the window, between shade and molding, the green suit was gone.

The phone.

"Eli, Shirley."

"I saw him, Shirley," and he hung up.

He sat frozen for a long time. The sun moved around the windows. The coffee steam smelled up the house. The phone began to ring, stopped, began again. The mailman came, the cleaner, the bakery man, the gardener, the ice cream man, the League of Women Voters lady. A Negro woman spreading some strange gospel calling for the revision of the Food and Drug Act knocked at the front, rapped the windows, and finally scraped a half-dozen pamphlets under the back door. But Eli only sat, without underwear, in last night's suit. He answered no one.

Given his condition, it was strange that the trip and crash at the back door reached his inner ear. But in an instant he seemed to melt down into the crevices of the chair, then to splash up and out to where the clatter had been. At the door he waited. It was silent, but for a fluttering of damp little leaves on the trees. When he finally opened the door, there was no one there. He'd expected to see green, green, green, big as the doorway, topped by his hat, waiting for him with those eyes. But there was no one out there, except for the Bonwit's box which lay bulging at his feet. No string tied it and the top rode high on the bottom.

The coward! He couldn't do it! He couldn't!

The very glee of that idea pumped fuel to his legs. He tore out across his back lawn, past his new spray of forsythia, to catch a glimpse of the bearded one fleeing naked through yards, over hedges and fences, to the safety of his hermitage. In the distance a pile of pink and white stones — which Harriet Knudson had painted the previous day — tricked him. "Run," he shouted to the rocks, "Run, you ..." but he caught his error before anyone else did, and though he peered and craned there was no hint anywhere of a man about his own size, with white, white, ter-

ribly white skin (how white must be the skin of his body!)
in cowardly retreat. He came slowly, curiously, back to the
door. And while the trees shimmered in the light wind,
he removed the top from the box. The shock at first was
the shock of having daylight turned off all at once. Inside
the box was an eclipse. But black soon sorted from black,
and shortly there was the glassy black of lining, the coarse
black of trousers, the dead black of fraying threads, and in
the center the mountain of black: the hat. He picked the
box from the doorstep and carried it inside. For the first
time in his life he *smelled* the color of blackness: a little
stale, a little sour, a little old, but nothing that could over-
whelm you. Still, he held the package at arm's length and
deposited it on the dining room table.

Twenty rooms on a hill and they store their old clothes
with me! What am I supposed to do with them? Give
them to charity? That's where they came from. He picked
up the hat by the edges and looked inside. The crown was
smooth as an egg, the brim practically threadbare. There
is nothing else to do with a hat in one's hands but put it
on, so Eli dropped the thing on his head. He opened the
door to the hall closet and looked at himself in the full-
length mirror. The hat gave him bags under the eyes. Or
perhaps he had not slept well. He pushed the brim lower
till a shadow touched his lips. Now the bags under his
eyes had inflated to become his face. Before the mirror
he unbuttoned his shirt, unzipped his trousers, and then,
shedding his clothes, he studied what he was. What a
silly disappointment to see yourself naked in a hat. Especially in that hat. He sighed, but could not rid himself
of the great weakness that suddenly set on his muscles and
joints, beneath the terrible weight of the stranger's strange
hat.

He returned to the dining room table and emptied the box of its contents: jacket, trousers, and vest (*it* smelled deeper than blackness). And under it all, sticking between the shoes that looked chopped and bitten, came the first gleam of white. A little fringed serape, a gray piece of semi-underwear, was crumpled at the bottom, its thready border twisted into itself. Eli removed it and let it hang free. What is it? For warmth? To wear beneath underwear in the event of a chest cold? He held it to his nose but it did not smell from Vick's or mustard plaster. It was something special, some Jewish thing. Special food, special language, special prayers, why not special BVD's? So fearful was he that he would be tempted back into wearing his traditional clothes — reasoned Eli — that he had carried and buried in Woodenton everything, including the special underwear. For that was how Eli now understood the box of clothes. The greenie was saying, Here, I give up. I refuse even to be tempted. We surrender. And that was how Eli continued to understand it until he found he'd slipped the white fringy surrender flag over his hat and felt it clinging to his chest. And now, looking at himself in the mirror, he was momentarily uncertain as to who was tempting who into what. Why *did* the greenie leave his clothes? Was it even the greenie? Then who was it? And why? But, Eli, for Christ's sake, in an age of science things don't happen like that. Even the goddam pigs take drugs ...

Regardless of who was the source of the temptation, what was its end, not to mention its beginning, Eli, some moments later, stood draped in black, with a little white underneath, before the full-length mirror. He had to pull down on the trousers so they would not show the hollow

of his ankle. The greenie, didn't he wear socks? Or had
he forgotten them? The mystery was solved when Eli mus-
tered enough courage to investigate the trouser pockets.
He had expected some damp awful thing to happen to his
fingers should he slip them down and out of sight — but
when at last he jammed bravely down he came up with a
khaki army sock in each hand. As he slipped them over
his toes, he invented a genesis: a G.I.'s present in 1945.
Plus everything else lost between 1938 and 1945, he had
also lost his socks. Not that he had lost the socks, but that
he'd had to stoop to accepting these, made Eli almost cry.
To calm himself he walked out the back door and stood
looking at his lawn.

On the Knudson back lawn, Harriet Knudson was giving
her stones a second coat of pink. She looked up just as Eli
stepped out. Eli shot back in again and pressed himself
against the back door. When he peeked between the curtain all he saw were paint bucket, brush, and rocks scat-
tered on the Knudsons' pink-spattered grass. The phone
rang. Who was it — Harriet Knudson? Eli, there's a Jew
at your door. *That's me.* Nonsense, Eli, I saw him with my
own eyes. *That's me, I saw you too, painting your rocks
pink.* Eli, you're having a nervous breakdown again. Jimmy,
Eli's having a nervous breakdown again. Eli, this is Jimmy,
hear you're having a little breakdown, anything I can do,
boy? Eli, this is Ted, Shirley says you need help. Eli, this
is Artie, you need help. Eli, Harry, you need help you need
help . . . The phone rattled its last and died.

"God helps them who help themselves," intoned Eli,
and once again he stepped out the door. This time he
walked to the center of his lawn and in full sight of the
trees, the grass, the birds, and the sun, revealed that it
was he, Eli, in the costume. But nature had nothing to

say to him, and so stealthily he made his way to the hedge
separating his property from the field beyond and he cut
his way through, losing his hat twice in the underbrush.
Then, clamping the hat to his head, he began to run, the
threaded tassels jumping across his heart. He ran through
the weeds and wild flowers, until on the old road that
skirted the town he slowed up. He was walking when he
approached the Gulf station from the back. He supported
himself on a huge tireless truck rim, and among tubes,
rusted engines, dozens of topless oil cans, he rested. With
a kind of brainless cunning, he readied himself for the last
mile of his journey.

"How are you, Pop?" It was the garage attendant, rub-
ing his greasy hands on his overalls, and hunting among
the cans.

Eli's stomach lurched and he pulled the big black coat
round his neck.

"Nice day," the attendant said and started around to the
front.

"Sholom," Eli whispered and zoomed off towards the
hill.

The sun was directly overhead when Eli reached the
top. He had come by way of the woods, where it was
cooler, but still he was perspiring beneath his new suit.
The hat had no sweatband and the cloth clutched his
head. The children were playing. The children were always playing, as if it was that alone that Tzuref had to
teach them. In their shorts, they revealed such thin legs
that beneath one could see the joints swiveling as they ran.
Eli waited for them to disappear around a corner before
he came into the open. But something would not let him

wait — his green suit. It was on the porch, wrapped around the bearded fellow, who was painting the base of a pillar. His arm went up and down, up and down, and the pillar glowed like white fire. The very sight of him popped Eli out of the woods onto the lawn. He did not turn back, though his insides did. He walked up the lawn, but the children played on; tipping the black hat, he mumbled, "Shhh . . . shhhh," and they hardly seemed to notice.

At last he smelled paint.

He waited for the man to turn to him. He only painted. Eli felt suddenly that if he could pull the black hat down over his eyes, over his chest and belly and legs, if he could shut out all light, then a moment later he would be home in bed. But the hat wouldn't go past his forehead. He couldn't kid himself — he was there. No one he could think of had forced him to do this.

The greenie's arm flailed up and down on the pillar. Eli breathed loudly, cleared his throat, but the greenie wouldn't make life easier for him. At last, Eli had to say "Hello."

The arm swished up and down; it stopped — two fingers went out after a brush hair stuck to the pillar.

"Good day," Eli said.

The hair came away; the swishing resumed.

"Sholom," Eli whispered and the fellow turned.

The recognition took some time. He looked at what Eli wore. Up close, Eli looked at what he wore. And then Eli had the strange notion that he was two people. Or that he was one person wearing two suits. The greenie looked to be suffering from a similar confusion. They stared long at one another. Eli's heart shivered, and his brain was momentarily in such a mixed-up condition that his hands went out to button down the collar of his shirt that somebody else was wearing. What a mess! The greenie flung his arms over his face.

"What's the matter..." Eli said. The fellow had picked up his bucket and brush and was running away. Eli ran after him.

"I wasn't going to hit..." Eli called. "Stop..." Eli caught up and grabbed his sleeve. Once again, the greenie's hands flew up to his face. This time, in the violence, white paint spattered both of them.

"I only want to..." But in that outfit Eli didn't really know what he wanted. "To talk..." he said finally. "For you to look at me. Please, just *look* at me..."

The hands stayed put, as paint rolled off the brush onto the cuff of Eli's green suit.

"Please... please," Eli said, but he did not know what to do. "Say something, speak *English*," he pleaded.

The fellow pulled back against the wall, back, back, as though some arm would finally reach out and yank him to safety. He refused to uncover his face.

"Look," Eli said, pointing to himself. "It's your suit. I'll take care of it."

No answer — only a little shaking under the hands, which led Eli to speak as gently as he knew how.

"We'll ... we'll moth-proof it. There's a button missing" — Eli pointed — "I'll have it fixed. I'll have a zipper put in ... Please, please — just look at me..." He was talking to himself, and yet how could he stop? Nothing he said made any sense — that alone made his heart swell. Yet somehow babbling on, he might babble something that would make things easier between them. "Look..." He reached inside his shirt to pull the frills of underwear into the light. "I'm wearing the special underwear, even

... Please," he said, "*please, please, please*" he sang, as as if it were some sacred word. "Oh, *please* ..."

Nothing twitched under the tweed suit — and if the eyes watered, or twinkled, or hated, he couldn't tell. It was driving him crazy. He had dressed like a fool, and for what? For this? He reached up and yanked the hands away.

"There!" he said — and in that first instant all he saw of the greenie's face were two white droplets stuck to each cheek.

"Tell me — " Eli clutched his hands down to his sides — "Tell me, what can I do for you, I'll do it ..."

Stiffly, the greenie stood there, sporting his two white tears.

"Whatever I can do ... Look, look, what I've done *already*." He grabbed his black hat and shook it in the man's face.

And in exchange, the greenie gave him an answer. He raised one hand to his chest, and then jammed it, finger first, towards the horizon. And with what a pained look! As though the air were full of razors! Eli followed the finger and saw beyond the knuckle, out past the nail, Woodenton.

"What do you want?" Eli said. "I'll bring it!"

Suddenly the greenie made a run for it. But then he stopped, wheeled, and jabbed that finger at the air again. It pointed the same way. Then he was gone.

And then, all alone, Eli had the revelation. He did not question his understanding, the substance or the source. But with a strange, dreamy elation, he started away.

On Coach House Road, they were double-parked. The

Mayor's wife pushed a grocery cart full of dog food from
Stop N' Shop to her station wagon. The President of the
Lions Club, a napkin around his neck, was jamming pennies into the meter in front of the Bit-in-Teeth Restaurant.
Ted Heller caught the sun as it glazed off the new Byzan-
tine mosaic entrance to his shoe shop. In pinkened jeans,
Mrs. Jimmy Knudson was leaving Halloway's Hardware, a
paint bucket in each hand. Roger's Beauty Shoppe had
its doors open — women's heads in silver bullets far as the
eye could see. Over by the barbershop the pole spun, and
Artie Berg's youngest sat on a red horse, having his hair
cut; his mother flipped through *Look*, smiling: the greenie
had changed his clothes.

And into this street, which seemed paved with chro-
mium, came Eli Peck. It was not enough, he knew, to walk
up one side of the street. That was not enough. Instead
he walked ten paces up one side, then on an angle,
crossed to the other side, where he walked ten more paces,
and crossed back. Horns blew, traffic jerked, as Eli made
his way up Coach House Road. He spun a moan high up
in his nose as he walked. Outside no one could hear him,
but he felt it vibrate the cartilage at the bridge of his
nose.

Things slowed around him. The sun stopped rippling on
spokes and hubcaps. It glowed steadily as everyone put on
brakes to look at the man in black. They always paused
and gaped, whenever he entered the town. Then in a minute, or two, or three, a light would change, a baby squawk,
and the flow continue. Now, though lights changed, no
one moved.

"He shaved his beard," Eric the barber said.

"Who?" asked Linda Berg.

"The . . . the guy in the suit. From the place there."

Linda looked out the window.

"It's Uncle Eli," little Kevin Berg said, spitting hair.

"Oh, God," Linda said, "Eli's having a nervous breakdown."

"A nervous breakdown!" Ted Heller said, but not immediately. Immediately he had said "Hoooly ..."

Shortly, everybody in Coach House Road was aware that Eli Peck, the nervous young attorney with the pretty wife, was having a breakdown. Everybody except Eli Peck. He knew what he did was not insane, though he felt every inch of its strangeness. He felt those black clothes as if they were the skin of his skin — the give and pull as they got used to where he bulged and buckled. And he felt eyes, every eye on Coach House Road. He saw headlights screech to within an inch of him, and stop. He saw mouths: first the bottom jaw slides forward, then the tongue hits the teeth, the lips explode, a little thunder in the throat, and they've said it: Eli Peck Eli Peck Eli Peck Eli Peck. He began to walk slowly, shifting his weight down and forward with each syllable: E–li–Peck–E–li–Peck–E–li–Peck. Heavily he trod, and as his neighbors uttered each syllable of his name, he felt each syllable shaking all his bones. He knew who he was down to his marrow — they were telling him. Eli Peck. He wanted them to say it a thousand times, a million times, he would walk forever in that black suit, as adults whispered of his strangeness and children made "Shame ... shame" with their fingers.

"It's going to be all right, pal ..." Ted Heller was motioning to Eli from his doorway. "C'mon, pal, it's going to be all right ..."

Eli saw him, past the brim of his hat. Ted did not move from his doorway, but leaned forward and spoke with his hand over his mouth. Behind him, three customers peered through the doorway. "Eli, it's Ted, remember Ted . . ."

Eli crossed the street and found he was heading directly towards Harriet Knudson. He lifted his neck so she could see his whole face.

He saw her forehead melt down to her lashes. "Good morning, Mr. Peck."

"Sholom," Eli said, and crossed the street where he saw the President of the Lions.

"Twice before . . ." he heard someone say, and then he crossed again, mounted the curb, and was before the bakery, where a delivery man charged past with a tray of powdered cakes twirling above him. "Pardon me, Father," he said, and scooted into his truck. But he could not move it. Eli Peck had stopped traffic.

He passed the Rivoli Theater, Beekman Cleaners, Harris' Westinghouse, the Unitarian Church, and soon he was passing only trees. At Ireland Road he turned right and started through Woodenton's winding streets. Baby carriages stopped whizzing and creaked — "Isn't that . . ." Gardeners held their clipping. Children stepped from the sidewalk and tried the curb. And Eli greeted no one, but raised his face to all. He wished passionately that he had white tears to show them . . . And not till he reached his own front lawn, saw his house, his shutters, his new jonquils, did he remember his wife. And the child that must have been born to him. And it was then and there he had the awful moment. He could go inside and put on his clothes and go to his wife in the hospital. It was not irrevocable, even the walk wasn't. In Woodenton memories are long but fury short. Apathy works like forgiveness. Besides, when you've flipped, you've flipped — it's Mother Nature.

What gave Eli the awful moment was that he turned

away. He knew exactly what he could do but he chose not
to. To go inside would be to go halfway. There was
more ... So he turned and walked towards the hospital and
all the time he quaked an eighth of an inch beneath his
skin to think that perhaps he'd chosen the crazy way. To
think that he'd *chosen* to be crazy! But if you chose to be
crazy, then you weren't crazy. It's when you didn't choose.
No, he wasn't flipping. He had a child to see.

"Name?"

"Peck."

"Fourth floor." He was given a little blue card.

In the elevator everybody stared. Eli watched his black
shoes rise four floors.

"Four."

He tipped his hat, but knew he couldn't take it off.

"Peck," he said. He showed the card.

"Congratulations," the nurse said. "... the grandfather?"

"The father. Which room?"

She led him to 412. "A joke on the Mrs?" she said, but
he slipped in the door without her.

"Miriam?"

"Yes?"

"Eli."

She rolled her white face towards her husband. "Oh,
Eli ... Oh, Eli."

He raised his arms. "What could I do?"

"You have a son. They called all morning."

"I came to see him."

"Like *that!*" she whispered harshly. "Eli, you can't go
around like that."

"I have a son. I want to see him."

"Eli, why are you doing this to me!" Red seeped back

into her lips. "*He's* not your fault," she explained. "Oh,
Eli, sweetheart, why do you feel guilty about everything.
Eli, change your clothes. I forgive you."

"Stop forgiving me. Stop understanding me."

"But I love you."

"That's something else."

"But, sweetie, you *don't* have to dress like that. You
didn't do anything. You don't have to feel guilty because
... because everything's all right. Eli, can't you see that?"

"Miriam, enough reasons. Where's my son?"

"Oh, please, Eli, don't flip now. I need you now. Is that
why you're flipping — because I need you?"

"In your selfish way, Miriam, you're very generous. I
want my son."

"Don't flip now. I'm afraid, now that he's out." She
was beginning to whimper. "I don't know if I love him,
now that he's out. When I look in the mirror, Eli, he
won't be there ... Eli, Eli, you look like you're going to
your own funeral. Please, can't you leave well enough
alone? Can't we just have a family?"

"No."

In the corridor he asked the nurse to lead him to his son.
The nurse walked on one side of him, Ted Heller on the
other.

"Eli, do you want some help? I thought you might want
some help."

"No."

Ted whispered something to the nurse; then to Eli he
whispered, "Should you be walking around like this?"

"Yes."

In his ear Ted said, "You'll ... you'll frighten the
kid ..."

"There," the nurse said. She pointed to a bassinet in the second row and looked, puzzled, to Ted. "Do I go in?" Eli said.

"No," the nurse said. "She'll roll him over." She rapped on the enclosure full of babies. "Peck," she mouthed to the nurse on the inside.

Ted tapped Eli's arm. "You're not thinking of doing something you'll be sorry for . . . are you, Eli? Eli — I mean you know you're still Eli, don't you?"

In the enclosure, Eli saw a bassinet had been wheeled before the square window.

"Oh, Christ. . . ." Ted said. "You don't have this Bible stuff on the brain — " And suddenly he said, "You wait, pal." He started down the corridor, his heels tapping rapidly.

Eli felt relieved — he leaned forward. In the basket was what he'd come to see. Well, now that he was here, what did he think he was going to say to it? I'm your father, Eli, the Flipper? I am wearing a black hat, suit, and fancy underwear, all borrowed from a friend? How could he admit to this reddened ball — *his* reddened ball — the worst of all: that Eckman would shortly convince him he wanted to take off the whole business. He couldn't admit it! He wouldn't do it!

Past his hat brim, from the corner of his eye, he saw Ted had stopped in a doorway at the end of the corridor. Two interns stood there smoking, listening to Ted. Eli ignored it.

No, even Eckman wouldn't make him take it off! No! He'd wear it, if he chose to. He'd make the kid wear it! Sure! Cut it down when the time came. A smelly hand-me-down, whether the kid liked it or not!

Only Teddie's heels clacked; the interns wore rubber soles — for they were there, beside him, unexpectedly. Their white suits smelled, but not like Eli's.

"Eli," Ted said, softly, "visiting time's up, pal."

"How are you feeling, Mr. Peck? First child upsets everyone. . . ."

He'd just pay no attention; nevertheless, he began to perspire, thickly, and his hat crown clutched his hair.

"Excuse me — Mr. Peck. . . ." It was a new rich bass voice. "Excuse me, rabbi, but you're wanted . . . in the temple." A hand took his elbow, firmly; then another hand, the other elbow. Where they grabbed, his tendons went taut.

"Okay, rabbi. Okay okay okay okay okay okay. . . ." He listened; it was a very soothing word, that okay. "Okay okay everything's going to be okay." His feet seemed to have left the ground some, as he glided away from the window, the bassinet, the babies. "Okay easy does it everything's all right all right — "

But he rose, suddenly, as though up out of a dream, and flailing his arms, screamed: *I'm the father!*

But the window disappeared. In a moment they tore off his jacket — it gave so easily, in one yank. Then a needle slid under his skin. The drug calmed his soul, but did not touch it down where the blackness had reached.